Text Classics

MARK HENSHAW was born in Canberra in 1951. He studied at the Australian National University and the University of Heidelberg in Germany.

His first published work, *Out of the Line of Fire* (1988), was one of the best selling literary novels of the decade in Australia and has been widely translated. It won the FAW Barbara Ramsden Award and the NBC New Writers Award, and was shortlisted for the Miles Franklin Literary Award and the *Age* Book of the Year Award.

In 1989 Henshaw was awarded a Commonwealth Literary Fellowship, and in 1990 he held the Nancy Keesing Studio residency at the Cité Internationale des Arts in Paris. He received the ACT Literary Award in 1994.

Under the pseudonym J. M. Calder, he has written two crime novels in collaboration with the Canberra writer John Clanchy: *If God Sleeps* (1996) and *And Hope to Die* (2007). Both were published in Germany and in France, where they were subsequently republished in Gallimard's Classic Crime Novels series.

From 1986 Henshaw was a Curator of International Art at the National Gallery of Australia. In 2011 he returned to writing full time. His second novel, *The Snow Kimono*, was published by Text in late 2014. It will be published in the United Kingdom and France in 2015.

At various times Mark Henshaw has lived in France, Germany, Yugoslavia and the United States. He lives in Canberra and, when not writing, enjoys spending time on the Australian coast. He is married with two children.

STEPHEN ROMEI is a journalist, writer and critic. He is literary editor of the *Australian* newspaper and a former editor of the *Australian Literary Review*.

ALSO BY MARK HENSHAW

The Snow Kimono

With John Clanchy, as J. M. Calder
If God Sleeps
And Hope to Die

Out of the Line of Fire
Mark Henshaw

Text Publishing Melbourne Australia

textclassics.com.au
textpublishing.com.au

The Text Publishing Company
Swann House
22 William Street
Melbourne Victoria 3000
Australia

First published by Penguin 1988
This edition published by The Text Publishing Company 2014

Cover design by WH Chong
Page design by Text
Typeset by Midland Typesetters

Printed in Australia by Griffin Press, an Accredited ISO AS/NZS 14001:2004 Environmental Management System printer

Primary print ISBN: 9781922182555
Ebook ISBN: 9781925095463
Author: Henshaw, Mark, 1951-
Title: Out of the line of fire / by Mark Henshaw ; introduced by Stephen Romei.
Series: Text classics.
Dewey Number: A823.3

CONTENTS

Where Truth Lies
by Stephen Romei

MARK Henshaw's enigmatic and intriguing novel *Out of the Line of Fire*, published in 1988, the nation's bicentenary year, sparked a debate about Australian writers' place in the world and the relationship of their work to exciting developments elsewhere. It was the same year that *Love in the Time of Cholera* was first published in English—Gabriel García Márquez being the novelist who Peter Carey says 'threw open the door I had been so feebly scratching on'. Eminent Australian critics such as Don Anderson, Peter Pierce and Helen Daniel lauded this debut novel by a thirty-seven-year-old Canberra-born writer, both for its European sensibility and postmodern inclinations, making comparisons with authors such as Italo Calvino and Peter Handke (who are among those with cameos in the book). Others complained on the same grounds, with David Parker arguing that Henshaw's sophisticated European setting and high-literary references, and readers' appreciation of same, were merely a new manifestation of the old cultural cringe. ('Burying the hick, speaking as the chic' was a clever line.)

It's not every novel that arouses such passions, not by a long shot. *Out of the Line of Fire* was shortlisted for the 1989 Miles Franklin Literary Award, though the laurel went to Carey for *Oscar and Lucinda* which, due to a shift in the Miles Franklin timetable, had already won the Booker. As an aside, it is to the credit of the judges that Henshaw's novel, with its ambiguous connection to 'Australian life', was recognised, when in more recent times important works such as David Malouf's *Ransom* and J. M. Coetzee's *The Childhood of Jesus* have not been.

So what is *Out of the Line of Fire* about? Well, that's a good question, one I suspect the author—most authors?—would prefer go unanswered. As there will be readers who are encountering the book for the first time, I will not give away too much of the plot—the novel is on one level a thriller, after all—and I most certainly will not reveal the radical ending, which readers tend to take as a slap in the face or a pat on the back, depending on what they believe a novel is supposed to do. But here is a synopsis, just so you know the book you hold in your hands is not about, say, a child befriending a pelican.

Out of the Line of Fire is in three parts. In the opening section we meet a narrator, an unnamed Australian writer living in an apartment building in 'romantic Heidelberg, Germany's oldest university town' at the start of the 1980s. He is befriended by Wolfi Schönborn, a brilliant Austrian student of philosophy. He becomes fascinated with Wolfi's early life and fractured family. But this narrator is an outsider. We are reminded, via Kafka, that Australia was a penal colony. In Europe in the early 1980s, Australia signifies only distance, physical and cultural. 'For a long time now,' the narrator tells us, 'I have had the impression that I observe life but don't participate in it, that somehow life flows straight through me as if I were transparent.'

He makes a study trip to Rome and when he returns Wolfi is gone, to Berlin it is said. 'It was as though he had never existed, and a couple of weeks later I returned to Australia without having seen or heard from him again.' So, in the space of twenty-odd pages, we have cause to wonder about the very existence of our narrator and our protagonist.

At the end of part one, the narrator, back home in Australia in September 1982, receives in the post a 'carefully wrapped cardboard carton' which contains Wolfi's writings, along with photographs, news clippings, letters, postcards and other miscellany. This is accompanied by an 'infuriatingly brief' note: 'Perhaps *you* can make something of this.'

In part two of the novel, the narrator retreats behind a curtain, becoming the unseen editor parsing Wolfi's papers to try to reconstruct his life: his intense relationship with his mother and sister, Elena; his deflowering by Andrea, a prostitute hired by his grandmother; his involvement, in Berlin, with the members of an experimental theatre group, most importantly the charismatic, criminal Karl. This long section contains the explicit sex and violence that confronted some readers when the novel was published.

The scene with the prostitute is pivotal. It also has one of the funniest lines I've read in fiction: 'For the first time in my life, with Andrea bent tenderly over me, I became conscious of the *real* implications of the Hegelian dialectic...' The experience is transformative in other ways, too. 'I am a man,' Wolfi announces to his family. Elena is impressed. She kisses him on the mouth, and 'After that night things were never to be the same.'

In the short and powerful final section of the novel the narrator, on an academic trip to Berlin in June 1986, stumbles across information that leads him to find out what happened to Wolfi, the role Karl played in his fate, and the true nature of Wolfi's relationships with his father, mother and sister. Or maybe not. As I have said, the reader has a surprise in store that puts phrases such as 'what happened to' and 'true nature' on shifting ground.

Henshaw makes no secret of his metafictional intention to interrogate the lines between fiction and reality, between writer, character and reader. Four pages in, the narrator muses:

> So there appear to be at least two problems confronting the writer writing about real events. Firstly, the words he or she uses seem to add some sort of fictionalizing distortion to the events they purport to describe and, secondly, even when a writer thinks they have got it right there still appears to be infinite room for ambiguity and imprecision. You begin to wonder where truth actually lies.

'Where truth lies' would be a good alternative title for this novel. The actual title words appear once, when we read of the late-teen Wolfi being awoken one morning by a shaft of sunlight reaching through the shutters of a hotel bedroom he shares with his sister, who is sixteen. He moves his head 'out of the line of fire' and looks at his sleeping sibling. Her left breast has come free of her nightdress. This 'sudden confrontation with Elena's emerging beauty' is overwhelming, agonising, a rending of the soul. 'It was as though, unable to raise my hands quickly enough, I had suddenly been blinded by the glare from some accidentally perceived truth.' Another sort of fire, it suggests the start of something dangerous.

Later, when Wolfi is being persuaded by Karl to mug an older, 'dignified-looking' man cruising for gay sex in a public toilet—a sequence that in its irrational yet unavoidable violence evokes the climactic scene of

Camus's *The Outsider*—he thinks (or so we are told): 'I felt like a character in a novel written by himself who runs into a character in a novel written by himself.' Indeed, Henshaw starts this winking at the reader before the novel even begins. It makes me chuckle, still, to read in my 1988 Penguin edition the standard disclaimer that 'All characters are fictional. Any similarity between persons living or dead is purely coincidental' and then, on the facing page, the dedication 'For Wolfi'. I know some people don't like being winked at, but in this case I think it is a compliment: the author is inviting us to take part in his creation.

When I read *Out of the Line of Fire* a quarter of a century ago I was about the same age as its pointedly unreliable narrator. I was thrilled to find an Australian novelist writing about European authors I was only just getting to know: Calvino and Handke, Kafka and Camus, Robert Musil. Rereading the book I better appreciate the nuances of Henshaw's conversation with these writers.

There is a scene in part three where the narrator, seeking information on Wolfi, is granted an audience with a Berlin policeman. The Inspector (that capital I makes me think of Gogol) listens to Wolfi's story impassively. 'When I finished he remained silent for some minutes. "You like Handke?" he said finally.' These are the same words Wolfi puts to the narrator early in part one, at the start of their friendship, yet in the intervening pages the question has evolved from something innocent and happy to something uncertain and unnerving.

So why, in the years after his exhilarating debut, didn't we hear more from Mark Henshaw, who is now sixty-three? The simple answer is that he stopped speaking, in a literary sense. Aside from a couple of crime novels (written, as J. M. Calder, in collaboration with his fellow Canberran John Clanchy), Henshaw did not publish, excepting the catalogues and other pieces produced in the course of his day job as a curator at the National Gallery of Australia.

That long silence was broken in late 2014 with the publication of a new novel, *The Snow Kimono*. Its existence resolves a question its author might appreciate: is Mark Henshaw, author of the remarkable Australian novel *Out of the Line of Fire*, real? Yes, he is.

Out of the Line of Fire

FOR WOLFI

Acknowledgements

Ludwig Wittgenstein's letters to Bertrand Russell are taken from *The Autobiography of Bertrand Russell* [Unwin Books, 1975].

Ramon Fernandez, extended quotes from *Internal Exile and other stories* [Kreuzer Verlag, 1982].

Klaus Brambach, 'W.C.W. meets H.H. in Central Park' from *Neue Gedichte* [Suhrkamp, 1981].

I am grateful to Dr T. Hatzenbühler for allowing me to use five lines from an article by him that appeared in *Schrift*, vol. 9, no. 1, which was originally given as a paper to the Verein Deutscher Schriftsteller in June 1986.

W.H. Walsh's essay on Kant in *The Encyclopedia of Philosophy* [Crowell Collier and Macmillan, Inc, 1967] was of considerable use to me in the transcription of some sections of Part Two.

Note: Wolfi's name is pronounced 'Volfi'. The initial syllable rhymes with 'golf'. Andrea is pronounced 'Un-dray-a'.

ONE

...and since your outer and your inner world are soldered together like the two halves of a shell and enclose you, the mollusk...,

Jean Paul

Even mechanistic views of man which see him as a complex of complex chemical reactions still lead to the most astonishing situation. Here is an arrangement of matter which takes other matter, re-shapes it, and then refers to it as 'art'!

Swen Rhahkma

You are about to begin reading Italo Calvino's new novel, *If on a winter's night a traveler.* These are the words Italo Calvino selected to open his novel *If on a winter's night a traveller.* Astonishingly he sets them out in the same order. Had Walter Abish chosen the same words he might have begun, after, of course, placing them in alphabetical order: You, Italo Calvino, are a winter's night traveler about to begin reading a new novel *If.* But as yet he has not, and until he does we will have to wait.

In fact Calvino begins his novel: 'Stai per cominciare a leggere il nuovo romanzo *Se una notte d'inverno un viaggiatore* di Italo Calvino.' Thus the original avoids a peculiar problem which arises only in the translation—'viagiatore' with a single 'g' would simply be wrong.

The cover of the 1982 English Picador edition of the novel shows the title, 'If on a winter's night a traveller', set into a transcription of the first page. It too begins: 'You are about to begin reading Italo Calvino's new novel *If on a winter's night a traveller.*' There is already then a difference, admittedly a minor difference, between the first line of the text on the cover of the novel and the first line of the text in the body of the novel itself—the difference between 'traveler' and 'traveller.' But is this difference as minor, as insignificant or innocuous, as it first appears? Isn't 'traveller', with its double 'll', English, whereas 'traveler', with its single 'll', is American? And doesn't this alert us to the fact that, as a translation, it has been filtered through a particular linguistic, cultural and conceptual sieve, that an English translation is likely to be substantially different from an American one, and that if we were to compare the cumulative effect of the differences which might arise in these two hypothetical translations against the original, might we not end up reading three entirely different novels? And, in fact, isn't this part of what *If on a winter's night a traveller* is about; not the problems of translation (at least, not exclusively), but the nature of the problem of the perception of the original in the first place.

Beginning a novel then is a difficult thing. Books have been written on the subject, from Tolstoy's *Anna Karenina*: 'Vse schastlivye sem'i pokhozhi drug na druga, kazhdaya neschastlivaya sem'ya neschastliva po-svoemu' [All happy families resemble one another, but each unhappy family is unhappy in its own way] to Camus' *The Outsider*: 'Aujourd'hui Maman est morte' [Mother died today]. And what about Kafka's problematical opening to *The Trial*: 'Jemand musste Josef K. verleumdet haben' [Someone must have slandered Josef K]?

Whatever the case, this first sharp barb designed to ensnare the reader, to capture his or her attention, is likely to cost the writer more time and effort than any other sentence in the entire novel.

But what does one do if the novel is based on fact?

Through the half open door I can see the complementary arcs of an arm and a leg. The gap in the doorway is narrow and I cannot see the person's back, although I can tell that they are facing away from me. Held in the outstretched arm is a wooden-handled mirror and because the arm is raised the shirt sleeve has fallen back to the bend in the elbow leaving most of the forearm bare. It is difficult to tell what the person, who is male, is doing. He could be practising fencing and even while I watch he appears to execute strange little lunging movements. He is muttering to himself as he does so but I am unable to make out just what it is he is saying.

The upstairs toilet flushes and I assume that once again it has been fixed. This is the second time in the week I have been here that it has been blocked. As I move back down the corridor towards the stairs I can hear what sounds like an argument break out in the courtyard below. Then the ground-floor door crashes violently to and someone begins heavily ascending the stairs. I lean over the balustrade and my landlady's large floral buttocks appear briefly on the landing below. I know this is going to be unpleasant. She has already made it clear that we are barely tolerated. Most of us are foreigners, we use too much hot water, our German is bad and worst of all, we compromise her social standing.

She is very overweight and stops two steps short of the second landing. She stands there with one bloated hand on the rail. She has not yet seen me and is wheezing audibly. The noise is quite disgusting. I realize I am witnessing one of those rare and intensely private moments of another human being who, had they realized they were being observed, would have concealed their quite distressing vulnerability. Despite this, I must confess I have difficulty feeling sympathy for her.

Finally she raises her head. When she sees me she gives a tiny involuntary start which sends a tremor coursing up through her body. Then she bellows: Vardashdoo?

I stare uncomprehendingly back at two tiny black eyes set in the fat of her pink face. We are so close that I can see the beads of perspiration that have begun to form on her forehead beneath her hairline and amongst the dark stubble of her upper lip.

Vardashdoo? she repeats even more angrily.

Bitte?

She turns away from me and, with an exasperated wave of her hand, continues up the stairs. Not wanting to get involved in another confrontation with her I make my way down to the ground floor.

Outside it is obvious what has happened. A section of downpipe lies disconnected in the courtyard. Two men in overalls are washing their hands in a bucket of water a few metres away. They glare at me as I pass. One of the other 'guests', the one I had been watching through the open door, is looking down on the scene from his upstairs window. He gives a friendly wave and I wave back. I unlatch the gate and as I head off to town I can hear my landlady's irate voice again coming from one of the open windows above me.

If Italo Calvino had written these lines he would probably stop here and ask: How adequate is this as an introduction? Not very? Why not? After all, this is the way it happened. Perhaps the tone is not quite right. Perhaps the description 'two tiny black eyes set in the fat of her pink face' doesn't sit well with the neutrality of 'two men in overalls are washing their hands in a bucket of water'. But aren't they the same thing? Two little imagist poems, one no different from the other?

I'm sure every writer ponders over such questions. Is this what I want to say? Does this work, is it adequate, does it introduce the themes, the characters, the locations I wish to develop? If not why not, and how do I change it so that it does?

But if a writer is dealing with real events doesn't he or she have a moral obligation not to change them, not to embellish them, not to pollute their ordinariness by poeticizing the banal? Does it really matter that we know nothing about what sort of shirt the person I stood watching through the open door was wearing? If I had said that it was a blue-checked shirt, which it was, whose sleeves were open at the cuff, is this additional information significant? And significant by what criterion? And if I had written that her tiny black eyes were like 'raisins dropped into the soft custard of her face', is the description of her any the better for this? No, of course it isn't. This is dreadful, dreadful stuff.

And then there's the problem of those complementary arcs. Initially one doesn't even know whether they're clothed or unclothed, male or female. Perhaps, at first, we think they are the smooth, naked, sun-tanned limbs of a beautiful young ballerina practising a pas de deux. It is only retrospectively that they become clothed and male, and later wave down to us in the courtyard below.

So there appear to be at least two problems confronting the writer writing about real events. Firstly, the words he or she uses seem to add some sort of fictionalizing distortion to the events they purport to describe and, secondly, even when a writer thinks they have got it right there still appears to be infinite room for ambiguity and imprecision. You begin to wonder where truth actually lies.

Heidelberg	Population: 130,000.
Vehicle registration: HD	Post code: D6900
Altitude: 110 m	Dialling code: 0 6221.

Romantic Heidelberg, Germany's oldest university town. Former capital of the Palatinate, Heidelberg is situated on the banks of the Neckar river where it spills out onto the broad plain of the Rhine. Hölderlin, who went mad, wrote poetry about it. So did Goethe. Famous philosophers (Kant, Hegel, Heidegger) walked its famous Philosophenweg. And if they were alive today they too could walk to the summit of the Heiligenberg and visit the cold grey stone arena where the Party faithful were harangued by the Führer.

Yes, Heidelberg—it's old, it's beautiful, it's romantic and if you've never seen a place like it before it's an enchanting fairy-tale-like town with its famous ruined castle hovering over the city, its narrow streets, its confusion of red-tiled roofs, its sombre churches, its towers and its graceful arched

14

bridges, its undisclosed skeletons in its historical closet and off in the distance the tiny, yet unmistakable, shapes of its nuclear silos. Yes, even the charm of Heidelberg has had to make way for progress.

In December 1795, Hölderlin (1770–1843), óne of Germany's greatest poets, took a post as a tutor in the house of a Frankfurt banker, J. F. Gontard. At the time he was twenty-five years old. Here he soon fell in love with his employer's young wife Suzette who, euphemistically, returned his affection. In 1798, however, he left the household after a scene with Gontard, the exact nature of which remains undisclosed, and after 1799 did not see Suzette again. In 1802 he returned home to Nurtingen in a seriously disturbed mental state. After a period at an institution he was entrusted to the care of a local master carpenter, named Zimmer, with whom he spent the next thirty-seven years of his life, without writing another single line.

Suzette Gontard died, significantly, in 1802, aged thirty-three. There seems, then, to be more to this than meets the eye.

The house itself is an unimpressive three-storeyed L-shaped structure, the walls of which are covered in white stucco. The gables are quite steep and the patterned eaves are painted black. Part of the house is occupied by my landlady's family—three faceless children and a husband who appears not to work—while the rest has been converted into single rooms for visiting students. There is a bathroom and a small kitchen on each floor. The kitchens are ill-equipped,

15

effectively discouraging any unnecessary consumption of electricity. Despite the fact that the house was probably built quite recently, more than likely during the fifties, it still has something characteristically German about it. It is solid. It will last.

3

There is a knock at my door. It is so soft that at first I think I am mistaken. It could so easily have been part of the music which is coming from the radio on the shelf above me. The music too is soft. It is Berg's *Lyric Suite*. I know the piece well and yet it now seems somehow quite strange. This strangeness has something to do with the smooth reassuring voice that introduced it: 'Jetzt hören wir etwas von Alban Berg. Geboren 1885 in Wien, Berg lebte...' At the end I know I will hear the same soft authority announce: 'Und das war Bergs Lyrische Suite. Es ist viertel vor zwölf und...' But until now I have never heard Berg's music enclosed within such a German framework. Somehow this has made the experience quite different.

What is even more disconcerting is that whenever I'm in my room listening to the radio I have the unsettling impression that at any moment the announcer is going to break into English, that this is all part of an enormous deception and all I need to do is get up and go outside and I'll be back amongst the sights, sounds and streets that are familiar to me. When the odd English phrase does occur,

16

in a news item or an advertisement for example, it's like the still surface of a lake being suddenly broken by some small fish leaping out of the water to catch its prey. It happens so quickly, so unexpectedly that it's over before you have time to focus on it. All you have, in effect, is an after-impression which replays itself again and again in your mind, as if to reassure you that you did actually hear what you think you heard.

Again there is a knock. There is no mistaking it this time since it comes in the silence between the second and third movements of Berg's piece. I think of Hanna Fuchs momentarily and glance at my watch. Nearly midnight.

I go to the door and open it. I recognize the blue-checked shirt immediately. His eyes too are blue and his dark curly hair makes him look younger than he really is. He stands there smiling nervously, as though he is stage-struck. He still does not say anything.

Can I help you? I say.

I heard your radio, he says in English.

You speak English, I say superfluously.

Yes, he says shrugging his shoulders. At least, a little.

I can see that for some reason he is still nervous.

Won't you come in, I say. Would you like some coffee?

I don't disturb you?

No, no, not at all. Please, come in.

Actually I came to invite you to take a coffee with me.

He speaks carefully, as though the words are nettles through which he is trying to pick his way.

Well, now that you're here we might as well have it here. What do you think?

17

Yes. This is logical. You're sure I don't disturb you?

Positive. Make yourself at home and I'll just get some water for the jug.

When I come back from the kitchen he is standing by the bookshelf. He has taken one of the books down and is leafing through it. It is Peter Handke's *Ich bin ein Bewohner des Elfenbeinturms (I am an ivory-tower dweller)*.

Peter Handke, he says. You like Peter Handke? I wrote this years ago myself.

You **wrote** it yourself?

I mean, I **read** it myself. Entschuldigung. He laughs. Yes, I read it years ago. I liked it very much. Perhaps my English is really not so good after all. What is your opinion?

I think you speak it very well. You're probably just not used to it, that's all.

No, no. I mean the book. What is your opinion of the book?

Oh, I see—the book! Well yes, I liked it very much too.

I am aware that already, for some reason, I have begun to talk like him.

He lived as a child in my home town, you know.

So you're not German then?

No, Austrian.

From Klagenfurt.

He smiles, surprised. He seems happy that I know something of his home town.

When the water has boiled I pour it into two mugs while he sits there nodding to himself, as though confirming some inner monologue. I hand him his cup.

Danke.

Bitte.

Again, apart from the music playing softly in the background, we sit in silence. I suddenly realize that neither of us knows the other's name. I introduce myself. He jumps up, shakes my hand.

Yes, of course, he says rapidly. I completely forgot. I was standing there, you know, outside, wondering what to say. I had it all prepared: 'Hello, my name is Wolfi Schönborn. Would you care to take a coffee with me?' With me it's always like this. I even get nervous when I open a book, you know, for the first time. It's the same thing, isn't it. You never know what you'll find, do you. Each person, each book, is like a new world...verstehst du?

Yes, I think so, Wolfi.

Yes, that's right. But how did you know?

What?

My name, that my name is Wolfi.

You just told me!

When?

Just then. You said you were standing outside my door and that you had prepared what you were going to say: 'Hello, my name is Wolfi Schönbaum...'

Schön**born**.

Yes, Schönborn and that you were going to ask me to take...to have some coffee with you.

Yes, of course. Now I remember. I wasn't sure whether I had actually said it or not. I'm sorry. You must think I am an idiot. Yes, Wolfi Schönborn. My name is Wolfi Schönborn.

He falls silent again, sits looking around the room holding his mug in his hands.

That was very funny the other day, he says, with the toilette. Frau Bartsch was steaming.

Yes, I know. I had a good laugh myself.

It was Eva, you know, the new Iranian girl. Have you met her yet?

No, not yet.

She seems very nice, but her German is not so good.

Talking of which, how did you know that I spoke English?

Frau Bartsch. I was talking to Frau Bartsch. She told me you come from Australia. He shakes his head. Such a long distance. Australia was previously a ah…Strafkolonie?

Penal colony.

Yes, penal colony. In der Strafkolonie…you know the Kafka?

I nod.

…of the English.

Yes, that's right.

She says you are preparing a book.

I can see Frau Bartsch has a big mouth.

You think so. I must look next time.

I turn towards the wall and try unsuccessfully to stifle a laugh.

Did I say something funny?

No…well, it's just a misunderstanding. It doesn't matter. I'll explain it to you some other time.

He seems confused, offended.

What about you? I say to cover my own embarrassment. What are you doing?

20

My ah...Doktorarbeit.

Your Ph.D., you mean.

Yes, your Ph.D....My Ph.D., I mean.

I am a little stunned by this piece of information. Wolfi doesn't look more than about twenty.

What on?

Bitte?

What on? What's your topic?

Mann o Mann. How should you say it in English. In German it's called 'Metonymische Realitätswahrnehmung'. At first it was called 'Jenseits der Realitätswahrnehmungs-grenze'.

You're kidding?

Yes. How would you call it in English?

God, I don't know. Let me think. 'Metonymische Realitätswahrnehmung', was that it?

He nods.

That would be something like 'The metonymic percep-tion of reality'. Yes, that's right—the metonymic perception of reality. What was the other one?

Jenseits der Realitätswahrnehmungsgrenze.

You Germans are amazing. Why not something complicated? Let's see, that would be...'Beyond the limits of the perception of reality' or 'Reality: Beyond the limits of perception'. How does that sound?

In English it sounds very complicated.

And in German it's not?

Well, yes, when I think about it, in German also it is complicated.

I sit looking at him for a moment, trying to reconcile what he has just told me with the apparent innocence of his fresh young face.

If you don't mind me saying so, Wolfi, you look a bit young to be doing a Ph.D. How old **are** you?

He blushed noticeably.

Twenty-three. I am twenty-three. I would be finished with twenty-two but I left because of the home situation. I was a Wunderkind at the university.

A Wunderkind!

Yes, a Wunderkind. How is this translated in English?

A child prodigy, a genius.

Yes, that's right, a child genius.

Modest too.

Bitte?

Nothing. It's not important.

Oh, I see—bescheiden, modest. You mean this ironically, of course. Sarkastisch.

No, not really. It's just a little unusual to hear someone describe themselves as a Wunderkind.

Yes, but unfortunately it's true. My father is Professor in Philosophy at the university I was studying at in Austria, studying at in Austria, at in...Sounds funny, doesn't it. His ah...Fachgebiet?

Specialist field.

Yes, his special field is logical positivismus. Do you know Wittgenstein?

I don't **know** him but I know who you mean. I thought he was dead?

He is. So what?

I shrugged my shoulders.

Yes, well Wittgenstein was a friend of my father's father [ein Freund meines Vaters Vater!], at least to begin with. He used to visit him when my father was young...

But I didn't think Wittgenstein was a logical positivist.

He's not. Why do you ask?

No particular reason. I just didn't think Wittgenstein was a logical positivist, that's all.

He looked at me weirdly for a moment, then continued.

Yes, but my father is. To him, however, it is more than this. It is his way of life. You know, even as a child I could do nothing without my father wanting to know why I did it or why I said it. 'But how do you know Wolfgang?' he would ask. Even when I was very little he would ask this. I would point to the sky and say the sky was blue and he would ask: 'How do you **know** the sky is blue, Wolfgang?' Can you imagine that? With three years I should answer the question how did I know the sky was blue. Not **why** the sky was blue, but how did I **know** it was.

He was talking quickly now. He had got up out of his chair and was pacing the floor.

My mother would be distressed by this interrogation and they had many arguments over me. For a while he left me alone but in the high school he started it up again. By this time my mother's and father's relationship was no longer existing. So the three of us, my sister and my mother, she was still very young, very beautiful, she married my father with...at seventeen—when she was seventeen years old—and I was born very quickly, you understand.

You mean your mother was pregnant when she got married?

Oh no…God no. That would have been impossible. No, if you knew my father. My father is a Catholic, a very strict Catholic you understand. No, my mother would have to be…would-have-had-to-have-been—English is so complicated—hätte eine Jungfrau gewesen sein müssen… yes, would have had to have been a virgin. My mother is a passionate woman, you can see this from photographs of her and she would have been a passionate young girl. But if you knew my father you would know that it was imperative for my mother to be a virgin. But what was I saying…

You were going to say something about your high school days.

No, no. There was something else I was going to say…

He stood for a moment with his hand to his chin, looking at the floor. He looked around the room and then said distractedly: Now I don't remember. I'm sorry.

He looked embarrassed, as though he had already said too much.

I think perhaps I go now.

He put his cup on the desk, shook my hand rather formally, thanked me for the coffee and left. His departure was so sudden that I stood there for a moment dazed. I went over what he had said, trying to figure out what had made him suddenly decide to leave. The more I thought about it the less real the situation became. Perhaps I had hallucinated the entire conversation. I even opened the door and stepped into the hallway half expecting him to be still standing there. It was empty of course.

24

Wittgenstein (1889–1951) completed his famous *Tractatus* in August 1918. When he was taken prisoner by the Italians in November, he had the manuscript with him. From his prison camp near Monte Cassino he wrote to Bertrand Russell, with whom he had studied in 1912, and a short time later the manuscript was smuggled out of the prison camp and delivered to Russell by diplomatic courier.

On 19 August 1919, Wittgenstein wrote to Russell from Cassino.

Thanks so much for your letter dated 13 August. As to your queries, I cann't answer them <u>now</u>. For firstly I don't know allways what the numbers refer to, having no copy of the MS here. Secondly some of your questions want a lengthy answer and you know how difficult it is for me to write on logic...The main thing is the theory that can be expressed [gesagt] by props—ie by linguage—(and, which comes to the same, what can be <u>thought</u>) and what can not be expressed by props, but only shown [gezeight]; which, I believe, is a cardinal problem of philosophy.

I also sent my MS to Frege. He wrote to me a week ago and I gather he doesn't understand a word of it at all. So my only hope is to see <u>you</u> soon and explain all to you, for it is <u>very</u> hard not to be understood by a single sole!

The age of surrealism began, coincidentally, in 1919 and it is interesting to compare Wittgenstein's letters to Russell in English with those he sent to him in German. In the former he stumbles forward like a blind man, barking his shins on a strange and unfamiliar linguistic landscape, while in the latter he soars like a bird, delighting in his own freedom.

Lieber Russell!   20.9.20

Dank' Dir für. Deinen lieben Brief! Ich habe jetzt eine Anstellung bekommen; und zwar als Volksschullehrer in einem der kleinsten Dörfer; es heisst Trattenbach und liegt vier Stunden stüdlich von Wien im Gebirge. Es dürfte wohl das erste Mal sein, dass der Volksschullehrer von Trattenbach mit einem Universitätsprofessor in Peking korrespondiert. Wie geht es Dir und was trägst Du vor? Philosophie? Dann wollte ich, ich könnte zuhören und dann mit Dir streiten. Ich war bis kurzem <u>schrecklich bedrückt</u> und lebensmüde...

[Dear Russell!   20.9.20

Thank you for your kind letter. I have now got a job— as a teacher at an elementary school in a tiny village called Trattenbach which is situated in the mountains four hours south of Vienna. It must certainly be the first time that a school teacher from Trattenbach has ever corresponded with a university professor in Peking. How are things with you and what are you up to? Philosophy? Then I wish I could be there to listen and to argue with you. Up until a short while ago I was <u>dreadfully depressed</u> and tired of life...]

Wittgenstein's father was one of Austria's wealthiest industrialists and when he died in 1913 Wittgenstein inherited a large fortune. He then proceeded to give most of it away. To his friends, however, he was a difficult companion. He was irritable, nervously sensitive and often depressed. For a long time he contemplated suicide, fearing that he shared the prominent strain of insanity that ran in his family (two of his brothers killed themselves). Before the war, to remove himself from all distraction and to enable him to carry on his philosophical work, he spent a number of years on a farm at Skjolden in Norway. Here he later built a hut in which he lived in complete isolation.

In 1926, having returned to Austria, he inquired at a monastery on the outskirts of Vienna about the possibility of entering upon monastic life, but was discouraged by the Father Superior. It is not difficult to imagine this scenario unfolding.

4

Wolfi's room is no different from mine except that it looks out over the courtyard formed by the rest of the house and the wall of the building opposite. The furniture is rudimentary. It reflects Frau Bartsch's meanness. Against the left wall is a narrow bed and in the remaining space there is a large old-fashioned wardrobe. Housed in the upper panels of each of the wardrobe doors are two badly tarnished mirrors, one of which is cracked along its upper edge. On the wall opposite the door, to the left of the window, is a wash basin. Under the window and extending to the other wall is a wide wooden shelf which serves as a desk. To the right of the window is a notice board. Pinned to it are a number of photographs and some postcards. Against the right-hand wall is a bookshelf. There are surprisingly few books on it. Instead, arranged in neat piles are a number of thick folders. There is a chair at the desk and an old couch behind the door. Apart from a coat that has been thrown onto the bed and an odd boot that lies on its side at the base of the wardrobe, the room is quite uninteresting, quite anonymous. It is as though Wolfi doesn't really live here, or hasn't yet fully moved in. Except for the notice-board, there is nothing in the room that reveals anything about him. On the other hand, perhaps it reveals things about him that don't seem to fit what one might have expected from talking to him or just from looking at him.

I stand looking at the photograph Wolfi has handed me from the shoe-box on his bed. It has been cut down the middle. At least, I assume it has, since the left-hand part of it is missing. Along the top, bottom and right-hand edge the original, decoratively scalloped white border is still visible. The cropping has spoilt the balance of the picture so that now the young woman who stands smiling back at the camera seems unnaturally close to the left-hand edge. Originally her right arm must have been linked through the arm of the person standing beside her. Part of a dark coat-sleeve is outlined against the white of her blouse. She has remarkably penetrating eyes and because her chin is slightly raised there is something challenging about the way she looks back at you. If it weren't for her smile she would appear almost arrogant. But instead, the impression she gives is one of unselfconscious confidence about her own appearance. Wolfi had not exaggerated: she is extraordinarily beautiful.

He tells me that the photograph was taken shortly before his mother's wedding. On the back is written: 'Heidelberg, 1957'. The picture seems older, or rather, not like a fifties' photograph at all. Instead of showing the influence of American fashion on clothes and hairstyles that swept through Germany during the period of the Economic Miracle, his mother is dressed as a young peasant girl. Her blouse does little to conceal the fullness of her figure and its whiteness against the sombre background and the darker tones of her skirt emphasizes the slimness of her waist. Despite this palpability, there is still something old-fashioned about it, something that distances and subverts the immediacy of the impression of sensuality which surrounds her.

I ask Wolfi why she is dressed the way she is. He explains that before his mother's family moved to Heidelberg they had lived on the land. They were wine-growers, but eventually her father had decided to sell his vineyards in order to establish a business in the town. While he had been more than successful he had never lost his love for the land and from time to time liked to have his daughters dress as though they were still living in the country [er war sentimental, weisst du].

I ran my finger down the cut edge of the photograph. After what Wolfi had told me about his relationship with his father and the relationship that existed, or rather had ceased to exist, between his parents, I guessed what the fate of the other part of the picture had been. As though reading my mind, Wolfi stood up and took the photograph from me.

The photograph belongs to the time when my father was courting my mother, he said. They were standing together under the trees but just as it was taken my father sneezed.

He says this matter-of-factly, without smiling.

I have the other half here somewhere.

He handed the photograph back to me and began searching through the box again.

Here's one of them together. This was taken on the same day.

Nothing in the image of his father, who is tall and quite handsome, suggests the tyrant who ruled over Wolfi's life as a boy. He appears to be in his mid thirties, is smartly dressed and is smiling broadly. Because of his slightly receding hairline and his oval-shaped, wire-rimmed glasses he looks like the young Mahler might have looked just after someone had told him a joke. The expression on his mother's face in this photograph, however, is more serious. Her confident serenity has disappeared and the aura of sensuality which surrounded her in the earlier photograph seems more subdued.

No, I can't find it. It doesn't matter anyway. You can see what my father looked like from that one. But this one of my mother, he said getting up off the bed again, this one captures something that is really wonderful about her, something beyond words, don't you think? [etwas das über Wörter hinausgeht].

Yes, I said, she really is very beautiful.

On Wolfi's notice-board are a number of other photographs including one of a young woman in tights who looks remarkably like the photo of his mother.

Who's this then? I ask.

Elena, my sister. That was taken a couple of years ago when she was auditioning for one of the local dance companies.

So there's just the two of you then, besides your mother and father that is?

No, there's also Anya...But she's just a baby really. I have photographs of her here too somewhere.

I step closer to the notice-board to get a better look at the photograph of Elena.

They could be sisters, I say.

Yes. At sixteen my sister was a beautiful woman and at thirty-five my mother was, paradoxically, an equally beautiful young girl. People often mistook them for sisters. The three of us used to go out walking together and my mother's friends would always tease me about having two such attractive girlfriends. I never really knew how to react. My mother used to say that they were just jealous, that they were actually flirting with me. Now that I look back on it, perhaps she was right. These slim, elegantly dressed women with nothing better to do with their time were probably bored with husbands who no longer paid attention to them. But at the time it must have also been obvious to them from the way I behaved when we ran into them that I was still totally inexperienced with women. I'm sure that it was this that made them tease me. I used to hate the way they would look at me, half mocking, half serious. It used to drive me crazy.

31

5

Wolfi has obsessions. He is obsessed about going bald. [Ich werde kahl, davon bin ich überzeugt.] He asks me to check the back of his head. He refuses to kneel down for some reason and suggests I stand on a chair to get a better look. Reluctantly I agree. He pulls the hair at the back of his head apart to try to reveal his scalp. His hair is very thick and I can barely see the strange white skin beneath. I tell him this but he remains unconvinced. He is not only worried about going bald, he is worried about his obsession about going bald. I ask him if his father is bald. He tells me he is not, nor is his mother. I'm glad to hear this, I say.

When I was fourteen I decided I would defeat my father. The school vacations were like an inquisition [wie eine Verfolgung]. He was not interested in what I did but only that I should be able to justify everything I said. He no longer asked how I knew that the sky was blue. Now it was: 'How do you know that your senses aren't deceiving you, Wolfgang? How do you know that anything outside you exists?' This from a logical positivist, can you imagine that? Always, how do you know? how do you know? By this time, my father had become a caricature—an impeccably dressed, cold and pedantic parrot [ein makellos bekleideter, zurückhaltender, sich wiederholender Pedant].

So I began to read like a madman. I read everything—all the classics: Klopstock, Lessing, Goethe, Schiller...

Hölderlin! I read entire histories of philosophy from Hippias to Heidegger, Aristotle to Aquinas. I devoured everything I could get my hands on, and not just philosophy. I mean, I read about music, art, history...everything! I lived my life through books. I had no friends. My friends were Kleist, Kafka, Dostoyevsky, God knows who else. In winter, to keep myself awake at night so that I could study, I used to put my bare feet in a bowl of water with ice in it or stick pins into my hands.

At seventeen, I had a nervous breakdown.

Robert Musil (1880–1940), author of *Der Mann ohne Eigenschaften* [*The man without qualities*], describes in his book *Die Verwirrungen des Zöglings Törless* [*The confusions of young Törless*] the school he actually went to himself as a young boy. It is, in fact, the Militär-Unterrealschule in Eisenstadt. Photographs of it show a long narrow four-storeyed building: cold, formidable, prison-like, with rows of small, mean windows and bare, untreed grounds. It is a military school. Discipline is strict, life is regimented. Musil gives a moving account of his misery there—the bullying, the victimization, the sadism, the futility and the loneliness. Wolfi went to the same school. In the interim, nothing much had changed.

I think that at this time I got so far into my own head that I became lost. The gap between fiction, between abstract speculation and so-called reality became blurred for me. I felt myself lose contact with the outside world. It was as though my self had become concentrated into a tiny

33

nucleus inside my head, except that I was still fully myself, if you know what I mean. Instead of walking around outside I was walking around inside. My eyes seemed like windows away from which I had turned. I watched them become mere specks of light as I moved further back into this inner gloom. At first it was totally dark, but as my eyes became accustomed to their new surroundings I gradually began to perceive vague shapes and contours, until eventually this imaginary world became as real and tangible as the world outside. When finally I found my way back to the windows to look out again at the external world, I felt that this was exactly what I was doing—looking out a window at a world from which I was in fact permanently disconnected, as if I were sitting in a darkened picture theatre and the world was being projected onto the screen, the only difference being that at any given moment I was free to get up and leave the picture theatre for an alternative world outside, that is, the world inside my head, but I was never free to join the action of the real world on the screen. For a long time now I have had the impression that I observe life but don't participate in it, that somehow life flows straight through me as if I were transparent [als ob ich transparent sei].

I stand looking out my window. Although the rain has cleared, it is still cold and windy. A blackbird is sitting unsteadily on the television antenna of the house opposite, buffeted by the wind. At the end of the street, I watch as a man in a dark overcoat stops to light a cigarette. He is having difficulty and turns his back to the wind. He cups his hands to his face. Then—success. Two puffs of white smoke

34

instantly disappear above his head. Needlessly he shakes his hand, as though he has something stuck to his fingers, before flicking the extinguished match into the gutter.

I am about to turn away from the window when I see Wolfi emerge through the gate below. He is wearing his usual lumber jacket and a scarf around his neck. As he passes beneath my window I yell down to him: Hey Du, Du Glatze. Wie geht's? [Hey baldy, how are things?]. He gestures obscenely back at me and then continues on his way.

6

I am sitting in the university dining room with a friend. Her name is Andrea Staiger. She is turning the pages of a book while she is eating. I am feeling uncomfortable but she is unaware of this. The dining room is very crowded and noisy. I have known Andrea for only a week but already we have slept together.

This is not quite correct. I have met her twice. The first time, a week ago, was in the market place. I was introduced to her. I told her she looked like Lauren Bacall, and in fact the resemblance is quite marked. She didn't know who Lauren Bacall was.

You know, Humphrey Bogart...Noch einmal, Sam!

She shrugged her shoulders. She didn't even know who Humphrey Bogart was. Incredible!

35

Across the room I see Wolfi join the queue. He seems unable to decide what to get. The plumpish girl serving food behind the counter is wearing a tight blue uniform and a white cap. She seems prepared to wait. I see Wolfi's mouth move and then return to its characteristic half-smile. Some food is dished onto the plate on his tray and he moves along to another decision.

Andrea's invitation to stay was so entirely unexpected it took me completely by surprise: Why go when you could spend the night with me? she says. She is the first German girl I have slept with.

She is very calm, as though making love with someone she hardly knows is quite normal. When she lifts her jumper over her head I am surprised by how lightly framed she is, although her breasts are quite prominent and she has unusually dark nipples. She has a small pale scar just above her pubic hair.

When she slips into bed we start making love almost immediately. She obviously enjoys making love because she is very energetic and quite vocal. But when she begins to come she falls silent. I feel her body grow tense. She stretches out under me as I imagine she does when she stretches out for the first time in the morning, her skin tight against the thin fingers of her ribs. She remains suspended for a moment, catches her breath, then surrenders to the short percussive rebuttals of her body.

After we have rested for a few minutes she turns to me and says: Noch einmal, Sam.

Wolfi is at the till. I watch him hand his meal ticket to the cashier. He picks up his tray of food and I see him

36

looking around the room for an empty seat. I catch his eye and point to the seat beside me. He comes and sits down and I introduce him to Andrea. There is a slight pause as Andrea looks at him and then at me. Wolfi, who hasn't begun to eat his food, is smiling idiotically.

Hey Du, last night I nearly got arrested, he says. I glance at Andrea. Fortunately she has gone back to her book. I remain silent but despite this Wolfi continues.

You know, it was on the bus. There's something desperate about waiting for a bus, don't you think? This is addressed less to me than to Andrea who has looked up and is now staring at Wolfi impassively. He explains to her how he hates catching empty buses, especially late at night.

I'd rather walk, he says. But last night I got on the bus, you know, to come home. I sat next to an old woman who was sitting towards the back. There were only the two of us, her and me. I had been **glad** she was there, wisst Ihr. Suddenly, for no reason, she starts yelling, screaming that I'm trying to rape her. I stood up to get away from her but she got up too and began following me down the aisle, hitting me with her umbrella. For no reason at all, she just starts hitting me. Then the driver sees what's happening in the rear-vision mirror and stops the bus so suddenly that we both nearly topple over into one of the seats in front of us while a car travelling close behind runs into the back of the bus. The bus driver gets up out of his seat and hurries down to find out what is going on and this mad woman, you know, is still hitting me. Well he tries to intervene, but whether accidentally or not I don't know, she ends up striking him on the forehead. Immediately blood starts issuing from the wound [die Wunde fängt an zu bluten] and this, thank God, brings her to her senses. A few minutes later, with their sirens sounding and their lights flashing, the police arrive. And you know, they end up taking **me** in for questioning. Me, who had nothing to do with it!

As Wolfi is telling his story I become more and more uneasy. When he finishes Andrea gets up without comment. She puts her book in her bag and slips the strap over her shoulder. She picks up the tray with her now empty plates. Before she leaves she turns to me and says: Thank you for last night.

Nothing in the tone of what she says allows me to gauge whether this is meant positively or negatively. It is, in fact, goodbye.

I fail to see the connection between these two incidents.

Forster's exhortation to the novelist was that he must 'connect'. 'Only connect' he said. Forster did not say 'he or she'. This is significant. It tells us a lot about Forster, the fact that he used the word 'he'.

'Only connect'.

In my effort to find the connection between Wolfi's retelling of the incident on the bus and Andrea's enigmatic farewell, I missed, at least initially, the connection between Andrea's **presence** and the conversation with Wolfi that followed.

Retrospectively then, it is not Andrea's disappearance which is significant but the fact that she was there in the first place. And yet I'm sure the two events, Andrea's presence and Wolfi's subsequent conversation are, in reality, totally **disconnected**. Their connection is only illusory, due to something Wolfi calls 'die Elision proximatischer Zufälligkeit' [the elision of proximate coincidence].

But I resent the fact that for apparent reasons of narrative logic a real person seems to have been dropped out of my life, has, as it were, been dispensed with now that she has fulfilled the fictional role assigned to her. The thing is, I still miss her. I try to imagine her at some stage walking into a bookstore, browsing through the books on the shelves, selecting one, this one. She buys it, takes it home. As she reads it she comes to the section which begins: 'I am sitting in the university dining room with a friend. Her name is Andrea Staiger.'

Komisch, she says, ich heisse Andrea Staiger. That's my name.

At first she is prepared to accept it as pure coincidence. But what if she had read 'Unterestrasse', what then?

[Ich glaub' das nicht.] I don't believe it, she says. That was my address. I see her racking her brains, trying to remember what may have been one of many chance encounters in her past. She rereads the passage describing our love-making. Perhaps she really can't remember. And yet there is a vague memory, a memory of a conversation one sunny morning in the market place, sitting on the window sill of the Town Hall. A photograph.

Yes, now I remember...How strange to come across oneself in a work of fiction!

Is she your girlfriend? Wolfi asks.

I'm not sure, I say.

But you sleep with her?

No. Yes, once.

How many women have you slept with?

God, Wolfi, what sort of question is that?

How do you mean?

It's a little blunt, isn't it?

Blunt?

Grob, direkt, was weiss ich.

Oh—unverblümt.

Yes, unverblümt—blunt. How many times do I have to ask you? Talk to me in German, not English.

He is offended.

I didn't mean to pry, he says in German [Ich wollte meine Nase nicht in deine Angelegenheiten stecken]. I was just curious about whether you had slept with many women.

What's many? I say. More than ten, more than a hundred?

I am still annoyed by Andrea's sudden departure.

Georges Simenon, you know, the French author, claims to have slept with over five thousand.

I don't believe it. And besides, he's Belgian.

But it's true. Admittedly most of them were prostitutes. What's more, he didn't care what they looked like, whether they were fat or thin, tall or short. Sometimes he had several a day. He said somewhere that if he couldn't have a woman he felt he had lost something, that you only really know a woman when you have slept with her. He paused for a moment, then said: Have **you** ever slept with a prostitute?

No, I said irritably. Have you?

Yes, once. In fact it was my first time. I was eighteen. She was twenty-two and you know, she was very attractive, very sensual [sehr sinnlich], not what I had expected at all. My grandmother gave me the money for her.

I looked at him incredulously.

Your grandmother gave you the money? Did she know what it was for?

Yes. In fact, she arranged everything. Later I found out she was my grandmother's lover's mistress [die Mätresse des Liebhabers meiner Omi].

Your grandmother's lover's mistress!

Yes, my grandmother's lover's mistress. Her name also was Andrea.

Oh for God's sake, Wolfi. Did you have to tell me that?

7

As an adolescent Wolfi wanted to be tall. He admits that he is above average height and even then was tall for his age.

But I wanted to be really tall, over two metres. I wanted to took like someone you wouldn't want to mess with. So I bought myself a pair of knee-length motor-cycle boots, stuffed them with newspaper and then strapped my feet into them. Then I used to go to one of the cafés in the nearby shopping centre before the lunch-time crowd arrived. I would sit there slouched, wearing my dark glasses, sipping a cup of coffee. You know, sullen—like Marlon Brando in *The Wild One* (He pronounces it 'Der Vild Vun'.) I would wait until the place was full and people were busy eating. Then I would get noisily up, all two metres of me. It always created a sensation. Kids stopped eating, babies started to cry and people would say: 'Jesus, will you take a look at that guy.'

I don't think this was very normal, he says.

Wolfi frequently disappears. Sometimes he is gone for periods of up to a week or more. One minute he is there, the next he is gone. When this happens I find myself knocking on his door to no response. Then, a couple of days later, he'll turn up with some bizarre tale about where he's been. Once he claimed to have gone to Agrigento in Sicily to visit Pirandello's grave just because Pirandello had studied in Heidelberg when he was a student. (Wolfi is mistaken. In reality, Pirandello studied at Bonn.)

It was here, Wolfi said, in Heidelberg, that Pirandello met and fell in love with Jenny Schulz-Lander. But in the end he married his home-town sweetheart Antonietta Portulano. She later went insane because she thought he was having an affair with their daughter Lietta.

So I was hardly surprised one morning to find Wolfi waiting outside in the corridor for me after one of my regular seminars. He suggested we go to Waldheims for coffee. I looked at him dubiously. It had been an unusually cold morning and he was wearing his now familiar lumber jacket, a brightly coloured scarf and sandshoes. His jeans were tucked into his socks and on his head he was wearing a truly ridiculous cap. He looked like a Turkish Gastarbeiter and Turks were not very popular in this part of Germany.

Normally this wouldn't have mattered, but Waldheims is one of Heidelberg's supposedly sophisticated but very pretentious little coffee houses situated in the ritzy part of Hauptstrasse. Here they serve enormous slabs of those rich cakes the Schwarzwald is famous for.

They won't let us in, I said.

Sure they will. You look fine. Don't worry.

From Heugasse we turned into Hauptstrasse and made our way towards Waldheims. Wolfi was being particularly evasive about what he had been up to for the last couple of days. He insisted I wait until we were having coffee. When we arrived a rather stiff and condescending young waitress dressed in black showed us reluctantly to the empty table Wolfi had pointed to by the spotlessly clean (French) windows.

Would we be having the Weintraubenschnitten, the Sachertorte or the Schwarzwälder Kirschtorte, the waitress asked.

What? You have Schwarzwälder Kirschtorte? Wolfi cried in mock surprise.

Yes, of course, the waitress replied haughtily but then, almost instantly, she broke into a grin. She looked around quickly.

Please Wolfi, not again. You'll get me fired.

Okay, okay. Schwarzwälder Kirschtorte for two it is then.

She hurried away. Two datedly elegant women, one in a waist-length fur coat, were sitting at the next table. They were observing us with obvious disdain.

Have you been reading the papers the last couple of days? Wolfi asked.

No, I haven't had time, I said.

He looked disappointed.

So you haven't been following the trial then?

What trial?

The Bessermann trial. It's been in all the papers. I went there, to Munich. I've been in the actual courtroom for the last three days. It's been sensational. All of Germany's talking about it. In Munich, nobody's been talking about anything else.

He stopped for a moment while the waitress placed our coffee and cakes on the table.

And you haven't heard about it?

No Wolfi, I haven't. Now stop playing games and tell me about it.

Well first of all I'll have to fill you in on some of the details. In 1965 a young woman from Daemling, a small town outside Munich, disappeared without trace. I was pretty young at the time and don't remember much about it, and in any case, in itself such disappearances are by no means unusual. But I can remember my mother talking about it years later.

The parents of the young woman, who was an only child, were obviously and naturally distressed. They were well-to-do [wohlhabend] and according to all indications their relationship with their daughter was a source of as much happiness to her as it was to them. There was no reason then for her suddenly to desert the parents who loved her or for her not to contact them had she been able to do so. Nor was it likely that she had run off with someone since she was engaged to be married to a young man with whom she was, apparently, very much in love and who was well liked by her parents. From all reports, she was quite striking to look at and for this reason was well known in the town.

At first the police thought that in fact she **had** run away for reasons unknown to her parents. Even the most idyllic family appearances sometimes conceal hidden passions [Sogar Familien die ganz idyllisch scheinen, haben manchmal ihre eigenen heimlichen Leidenschaften]. But as the weeks went by even they began to assume that something dreadful had happened to her. For months the whole town mourned her disappearance.

Then one day, over a year later, she was found wandering the streets of Munich, totally disoriented and in a state of extreme agitation. She was taken to hospital and heavily sedated. In her bag they found a large sum of money.

Her parents were overjoyed to hear that she had been found. They had begun to think that they would never see their daughter again. In the hospital the doctor who examined her discovered that she had recently given birth. Both her parents and her fiancé were shocked by this news and waited anxiously for the effect of the sedative to wear off. Even as they waited beside her hospital bed she suddenly sat up wide-eyed and cried: 'My baby, my baby'—and then fell back onto the bed in a state of complete unconsciousness.

Finally she awoke. At first she thought she was dreaming, but gradually her parents were able to convince her that they were real, that the nightmare she had been living through for the past year was over. As you can imagine it was a tearful reunion. But despite her obvious happiness at having been delivered into the arms of her loving parents she became distraught when she realized her baby was not with her. She clung to her mother's breast. 'He took my baby, he took my baby,' she sobbed.

Gradually, the full story emerged and much was made of it in the papers at the time. Many of the articles that were written then have been reprinted over the last couple of days. It was like a horrible fairy-tale come true. Some reports remained sceptical about the girl's story, implying that she had made it up, that, in fact, she had fallen pregnant to another lover and to avoid shaming her parents had run away until the child was born. Then she had either killed or abandoned it. Even some of the police refused to accept her account of what had happened and naturally there was a lengthy investigation into all of the circumstances of her disappearance and the disappearance of her child. Despite rigorous questioning and a number of psychiatric examinations, one of which was conducted by Dr Franz Werthold, Munich's most eminent psychiatrist at the time, she stuck to her story. What she maintained happened was this:

She had left the office of the local stationery wholesalers where she worked late because it was the end of the month and there was a backlog of accounts to process. This was not unusual and, moreover, it had not been all that late—it must have been around seven o'clock. What little rush hour traffic there was in the town's business district had cleared. It had rained earlier in the afternoon but despite this the night was warm and she was happy to be out in the clear evening air. She crossed Marienstrasse and began walking towards the laneway which joined it to Humboldtstrasse. From Humboldtstrasse she would catch the bus home to her parents as she always did. It was Thursday and her fiancé, she knew, would be waiting there for her.

She turned into the alley-way. It was well lit and she had no need to feel afraid. She recalled how the overhead lights transformed the polished cobblestones ahead of her into shimmering arcs of light, arcs which seemed to flutter like hundreds of tiny radiant wings as she moved towards them. She had the impression that she was floating, rather than walking, over them. Further along the narrow alley-way she noticed a car parked halfway up on the footpath, directly under one of the street lights. She could see the form of a man wearing a hat standing on the footpath examining what looked like a street map spread out on the car's roof. As she stepped off the footpath to go around the car the man looked up and called her name. His voice sounded warm, familiar. She looked up at him as he stepped out in front of the car, but because of the light overhead and the shadow from the brim of his hat she could not make out his face distinctly. He said her name again in the same friendly tone and stretched out his hand as if to greet her. His gesture had seemed so natural that she had automatically reached out to him in return. It was only as his hand closed over hers that she was gripped by an overwhelming fear. A scream began to rise in her throat but it was already too late. An inexorable chain of events had been set in motion the moment she had turned into the laneway. She smelt the chloroform on the cloth he held to her face and felt herself grow faint.

When she came to she found herself in a lavishly deco-rated room. Her hands and feet had been tied to the arms and legs of an intricately carved chair and she was lightly gagged. The curtains were drawn and the room was lit by a single very elaborate chandelier suspended from the roof by a short piece of gold chain. She could see from the clock on the mantelpiece that it was just after eleven. She tried to free herself but could not. Then a heavy, wooden-panelled door on her left opened and a man walked in. He was well dressed and appeared to be in his early forties. He sat down in a chair opposite her. She began to struggle.

Then he spoke. His voice was clear, firm, reassuring.

In a moment, he said, I will untie you. You must understand that while you are here you will not be harmed by anyone, but there are a few things you should know.

She started to struggle again, then tried to scream, but it was useless. It was clear that, for the moment, she was powerless.

This room and the two adjacent rooms which will be your home for the time being have been completely sound-proofed and isolated from the rest of the house. I have spent a long time preparing for your stay. Everything you need has been provided for, but if there is anything I have overlooked then you have only to ask. You will be here for about twelve months, perhaps a little longer. At the end of this time you will be amply rewarded.

He got up and came over to her.

I hope, in the meantime, you will come to trust me but I can well understand that initially you will be fearful. I assure you that there is absolutely no need for this.

He walked behind her and undid the thin white cloth that had been tied across her mouth. Her immediate reaction was to scream for help. He made no attempt to stop her, as if to convince her of the truth of what he had said to her. She began to sob.

What do you want from me? she cried.

For many years, he said, I have wanted a child. My wife, unfortunately, was unable to have children and when she died I decided for a number of reasons never to remarry. And yet my desire to have a child remained unabated. The few women I considered suitable to be the mother of my child were either already married or would never have been persuaded to enter into a mutually satisfying business arrangement. Three years ago I began my search for the perfect woman or, at least, the woman I considered to be perfect as the mother of my child. Six months ago, I found her. That woman is you.

She looked at him dumbfounded.

Why me?

That's simple, he said. I want a beautiful child. I couldn't live with a child I didn't think was beautiful. I want someone who is enchanting, someone on whom I can lavish everything I have to offer, which is considerable, someone, in short, who is perfect. If you could have been that child I would have had you. But seeing that that is impossible, I have chosen you to bear my child for me.

So for a little over a year he kept her in her luxurious prison. He forced himself upon her and she became pregnant to him. Eventually she gave birth to a baby girl. He had been overjoyed.

She had been allowed to suckle the child for a little over a month. He had been right—the baby was simply the most

49

beautiful creature she had ever seen. Then, one morning after breakfast, she had felt a little drowsy and had lain down to sleep. When she awoke she was sitting in a bus shelter in a narrow street surrounded by high buildings. Her baby was not with her and she was seized with panic.

She had staggered to the end of the street thinking perhaps that she might see a car driving off, but there had been nothing. She was overcome with grief and was discovered not long after wandering through the back streets of Munich not far from the main railway station.

Her story was checked and rechecked. Advertisements were placed in all the regional and national papers pleading for the doctor who delivered the child to come forward. All international departures by train and air were monitored and a description of the man appeared on German television for weeks. All to no avail.

The emotional stress of her harrowing experience, and the agony of the investigation after it, left her a broken woman. Her once beautiful young face quickly vanished in the years that followed. She was haunted by the memory of her terrible ordeal and by the fact that out of it a child had been born, a child who, at the very moment she had begun to love it, had been cruelly taken from her. Unable to accept her story, her fiancé had broken off their engagement and when, eventually, she had returned to work she had been unable to concentrate and her employer had been forced to let her go. For years she lived with her parents in a state of isolation and severe grief.

Eventually, however, she was able to find work again and although she never married the wounds began to heal.

But her face had changed irrevocably and she no longer took the same care over her appearance as she once did. In 1978 both her parents died and she moved to Frankfurt where she got a job as a ticket clerk with one of the airlines. I think you can guess what happened from here.

He took a sip of his now cold coffee and looked around. The two women opposite, both of whom had been listening intently to his story, looked quickly away.

Well?

Well what?

You can't just stop there. What happened?

Well, apparently she had been sitting at her desk checking through the morning's ticket sales when he arrived at the next counter. She had heard him say to her colleague: 'Good morning, my name is Bessermann and I have tickets reserved for my daughter and myself for Buenos Aires'. Even before he had finished his sentence she had recognized his voice. Her hands were trembling as she looked across at the man standing on the other side of the counter. His hair had gone grey and he now wore thick glasses and a short beard. For a moment she thought perhaps her mind was playing tricks on her. She sat there shaking, waiting for him to speak again. Her colleague handed him his two tickets. He thanked her and turned to leave. It was only then that she found herself looking into the face of a young girl who moments before had stood concealed behind him, a girl who was the mirror image of the person she herself had been years before.

After a number of hurried phone calls between airport security and the Frankfurt and Munich police he and his daughter were detained at the baggage check-point before boarding. Initially he had denied everything, but the police were suspicious enough to be able to compel him to postpone his return flight for a day or two.

I listened as Wolfi related the sensational events of what he said had become one of Germany's most notorious trials, how each new piece of evidence had come to light, what a field day the media had had.

They're treating it like a real-life fairy-tale. You wouldn't believe the length that some of these papers will go to to get a story. But being there, actually being there was incredible. And you know, looking at his daughter I can understand in a way why he did it.

He took out a folded newspaper photograph of a young girl.

I had to admit she was **very** striking.

Who's to say that the very existence of this young girl doesn't justify the strange circumstances surrounding her birth. If the same thing happened in some primitive tribe in Africa or Samoa or God's knows where, no one would think twice about it. But the moral righteousness of some of the things that have been written about the trial has to be seen to be believed. I mean, it's all relative, isn't it.

He looked back at the photograph in his hand.

It's all relative, he repeated to himself.

The incredible never happens in fiction, only in reality. The writer has a duty to report what is true, not what he or she would like to be true. How are these two statements to be reconciled?

Wolfi may have been wrong about Pirandello having studied at Heidelberg, but he was right about Antonietta's insane jealousy of her daughter. One day she openly accused Lietta of committing incest with her father. Lietta was so appalled by what her mother had said that she tried to kill herself. She used an old revolver which she found lying about the house. But fortunately the barrel had been blocked by rust and the bullet stuck.

8

When Raymond asks Meursault to visit a prostitute with him in Camus' novel *The Outsider*, he refuses. As readers we ask ourselves: Why? Why is Meursault's refusal important in the definition of his character? That is, we immediately place the character Meursault within a fictional context. We acknowledge then his fictional existence yet, at the same time, demand that his character remain credible. Credible according to what criteria? Against the criterion of reality? Hardly.

Rereading the novel we become aware of how carefully constructed it is. Its construction becomes, literally, the definition of the character Meursault. Camus' initial problem was how to make Meursault's final, perhaps irrational act, the act of killing the Arab on the beach, plausible. Technically then, the process of narrative construction is retrospective and linear. In simple terms: he knew what the end point was, how then was he to go about achieving it?

Does this not, however, involve some dishonesty, what Sartre called 'mauvaise foi' [bad faith], on the part of the novelist? He is obliged to conceal and reveal at the same time, to include, exclude, manipulate and shape his characters with some ulterior purpose in mind. And isn't it exactly this which, in the end, leaves us dissatisfied with Camus' novel as a whole? Isn't it this which separates Camus from a novelist like Kafka before him or Handke after him whose novels develop in a more organic way, in which to a large extent no real end point is ever reached. Or is this to beg the question?

Wovon man nicht sprechen kann, darüber muss man schweigen.
[Whereof one cannot speak, thereof must one be silent]

Wittgenstein's famous statement expresses paradoxically what he saw as the ineffability [Unaussprechlichkeit] of human existence. It cryptically details language's ultimate incapacity to articulate the world. In the end he came to the view that language was essentially powerless.

At first it is difficult to make out what is happening the camera is so close. Slowly it draws back and what appeared at first to have been moving abstract patterns in soft pinks reveal themselves to be the fingers of a hand slowly separating the soft folds of a pair of lips—genital lips. The pubic area which is now visible is completely bare, it has been shaved, and the woman's fingers and her labia glisten under the camera lights. As the camera moves further back it becomes clear that the fingers are those of another woman.

The woman with the shaved pubic hair is lying with her buttocks over the end of a dark, armless leather lounge. The design is conspicuously modern, probably Italian. Her left leg is drawn back so that her foot rests along the back of the lounge, while her right leg rests on the left shoulder of the woman kneeling in front of her. The makers of the film obviously had an eye for aesthetic detail since one of the women, the one lying on the lounge, is blonde, while the other is dark. They are both young.

The girl kneeling wraps her left hand around the other girl's thigh and with her right hand she begins caressing her again. The camera moves closer as the girl's fingers begin to probe her. First one finger, then another, and then three fingers are slowly eased into her. Her thumb flicks over the pale bud of her clitoris. She starts rotating her hand slowly, trying to force the other girl's pubic muscles to relax. The girl's face on the lounge flashes onto the screen. Her head is arched back and her eyes are closed. She is frowning slightly, as though concentrating on what the other woman is doing to her. Her hand reaches down to touch the hand of the girl kneeling between her legs. She draws the three fingers into her as far as they will go. The kneeling girl stops for a moment and withdraws almost entirely. She folds her thumb against the palm of her hand and brings her four fingers together so that her hand forms a conical shape. She places the tip of this cone at the entrance of the prone woman's vagina. She pushes her fingers in gently. At first there is little real resistance. Four fingers disappear up to the second joint of her index finger. The prone girl's hand directs her rhythm. She penetrates a little deeper. The camera has moved in close now. It is only then that I realize that she is going to try to push her entire hand into the other woman.

She withdraws a little, then resumes her relentless pressure. The girl's face flashes momentarily onto the screen again. Her mouth is open and she is breathing heavily. She frowns again as she feels another, deeper thrust. The other girl's hand is now in as far as her knuckles. Despite the fact that this is obviously a performance, I am a little amazed to see that the woman on the lounge is, nevertheless, clearly aroused.

They both seem to relax for a moment. Then, with the blonde girl's hand clasped around her wrist, the dark girl gives one last, long push and her entire hand disappears slowly into her. She moves it tentatively back and forth. With the woman's labia, white at their periphery, encircling her wrist the whole scene suddenly appears wildly surrealistic, as if someone were groping around inside her, trying to find something they had lost. The camera pans up to the prone woman's face again. Her eyes are half-open and her smiling lips suggest the ecstasy she is supposed to be feeling as she is rocked to and fro. Then the rhythm increases and her buttocks seem to respond as though to some reciprocal harmony. She begins writhing, twisting, thrusting at the hand within her. Her movements grow wilder, more violent. Then suddenly her body arches and she appears to shudder. Again and again she shudders, as if she is trying to impale herself on the other woman's arm. Her movements are frenzied, almost frightening. It is as though both of them have suddenly become oblivious to the presence of the camera.

Then, all at once, it is over and they both sink slowly back onto the lounge. The final scene shows the dark-haired woman bending to kiss her companion on the mouth. Her manner is such that her action could easily be mistaken for tenderness.

What, I ask, are we to make of this?

Machiavelli's (1462–1527) political philosophy was scientific and empirical. It was based on his own experience of affairs and was concerned to set forth the means to assigned ends, regardless of the question whether the ends were to be considered good or bad. That is what is so horrifying about it.

Federico Garcia Lorca (1898–1936), one of the outstanding poets and dramatists of this century, was murdered at the age of thirty-nine by Nationalist rebels in his native Granada. The Franco regime sought constantly to suppress the facts surrounding Lorca's death and the death of thousands of other Republican sympathisers executed in the thirties.

This is a familiar story.

What is it about the polarity of human thought which requires the eradication of the agent of its expression? In a dictatorship 'I think, therefore I am' becomes the most fundamentally non-tenable political dictum. Language empowers existence [ermächtigt das Dasein].

How does this square with what Wittgenstein had to say about the **powerlessness** of language?

9

Wolfi bursts into my room. He runs to the radio, turns it on. Nothing happens.

What's the matter with this bloody thing?

It's not plugged in.

Es ist nicht eingesteckt, he repeats.

He fumbles for the cord, plugs it in and switches it on. He searches frantically for the station.

Wait until you hear this.

Also, sensationelle Ereignisse hier in München. Ich bin Dieter Winter, Bayern Drei und Sie hören Nachrichten. Nach einer kurzen Pause—der Papst vergibt seinem Attentäter [After a short break—the Pope forgives his assassin].

Verdammte Scheisse...Idioten!

Forget it, I heard it earlier. They say it's just a flesh wound. He'll live.

No, no, no. Not the Pope. They had a newsflash on the Bessermann trial.

I thought that had finished weeks ago.

No, the commital proceedings had to be held over. His daughter tried to commit suicide. It's just been revealed that she and her father were lovers.

1 0

The Schönborns have been prominent in the cultural life of Klagenfurt since the seventeenth century. Theodore

Schönborn was rector of the nearby university from 1780 to 1791. Kant stayed under his roof during his visit to Klagenfurt in the spring of 1783 and Theodore was his guest at Königsberg a number of times in the years that followed. He wrote a famous introduction to one of Kant's philosophical works (*Die Metaphysik der Sitten in zwei Teilen*). Like his father before him, Wolfi's grandfather was a well-respected intellectual who later became town councillor and, like Wolfi's father, his grandfather married someone considerably younger than himself.

His wife, Wolfi's grandmother, belonged to one of Vienna's most wealthy families, although the rapid decline in the family fortunes through a series of ill-judged business ventures had already set in by the time she married Wolfi's grandfather. She had been great friends with the young and beautiful Manon Gropius until the latter's tragic death in 1935 at the age of twenty. According to Wolfi, his grandmother was a woman of great vitality, quick witted and sharp tongued. At fifteen she scandalized her family by having an affair with the painter Hans Meidner (1884–1939). At twenty she again stunned her family by agreeing to marry Walter Heinrich Schönborn who, at the relatively young age of forty-five, had just been elected vice-chancellor of the university. While everyone agreed that socially it was a good match despite the difference in their ages, it turned out to be a disastrous misalliance of temperaments. He was pompous, bureaucratic and unimaginative. She did not bear the matrimonial yoke well and was always surrounded by scandalous rumour, something she did nothing about and, in fact, seemed positively to encourage. When her husband died eighteen years later, when Wolfi's father was fifteen, his death appeared to be a source of considerable relief to her rather than a cause for any great sorrow.

By contrast, both his mother's parents were open, happy and hospitable people. Her father adored his wife and his three daughters. He was a hard-working, God-fearing man who was not unaware of the good fortune with which he said he had been blessed. His only failure was that when he had had a little too much to drink he was inclined to become red-faced and maudlin. Surprisingly Wolfi's father and he got on well together. They were both keen clay-pigeon shooters and Wolfi's father, as a result of his earlier training as a military cadet, was an impressive horseman, something his mother's father greatly admired.

Wolfi's mother was the eldest of three sisters and from the time she was young she was well known for her remarkable beauty. When she met Wolfi's father she was studying to be a concert pianist. Wolfi had in fact been named after Mozart. His father, who at the time occupied a junior post at Heidelberg university, had first seen her at a performance she gave in the town's Konzertsaal. He had become instantly and completely besotted by her, something that was even more remarkable given the fact that at the time he had a reputation for being, if not exactly a ladies' man [ein Charmeur], then at least someone whose elegant manner would not have gone unnoticed amongst the women with whom he came in contact.

Apparently the first few years of their marriage were idyllic. They were both blissfully happy. His mother had been content to give up her career as a pianist to devote herself to her husband and the child she was now expecting. Even when Elena was born three years later they were still happy. But according to Wolfi, in the years that followed, his father became more and more aloof, more and more involved in his own research and the increasing administrative burden of his university post. It was as though his dead father had cast a shadow over him, a shadow that slowly transformed him into the person his father had been years earlier.

This was very cruel for my mother, Wolfi said. As a girl she had loved life and the early years of her marriage had awakened new demands in her as a woman. Then at the very moment she was discovering her own sensuality my father withdrew her access to it. An affair was something she could not easily contemplate and so for years she remained frustrated and unhappy. Eventually, however, she did discover someone with whom she fell in love and with whom she maintained a passionate and clandestine affair. I think this period was the happiest in my mother's life.

Is such an arrangement so unusual? Wilfried Berghahn, in his short biography of Robert Musil who, coincidentally, was born in Klagenfurt, writes of Musil's mother:

Hermine Bergauer ist, als sie heiratet, zwanzig Jahre alt. Sie scheint auf einen Mann zu hoffen, der ihr Leben fest in seine Hand nimmt und ihre Phantasie beschäftigt. Aber Alfred Musil liegt es offensichtlich nicht, Autorität auszuüben. Er steht dem Temperament und Heftigkeit der Gefühle seiner Frau zeitlebens ein wenig hilflos gegenüber.

Sie indes vermag in seiner beruflichen Karriere keinen Inhalt für ihr eigenes Leben zu finden. Als sie 1881 nach sieben Ehejahren und bald nach der Geburt ihres Sohnes in Komotau einen Bekannten ihres Mannes namens Heinrich Reiter kennenlernt, schliesst sie sich an ihn an. Alfred Musil toleriert dieses Verhältnis. Reiter gehört von stund an zur Familie, begleitet Musils regelmässig in die Sommerferien...Wir finden ihn noch 1924 am Sterbebett Hermine Musils, das zu bewachen und zu besorgen offenbar seine Aufgabe ist, nicht die ihres Mannes.

Wilfried Berghahn, *Robert Musil*. p.22

[When Hermine Bergauer married she was twenty years old. She seemed to be hoping for a man who would take her life in his hands and capture her imagination. But Alfred Musil seemed incapable of exercising any sort of authority. During his entire life he seemed to be a little helpless in the face of his wife's temperament and the passionateness of her feelings. She, on the other hand, could find no satisfaction in her husband's professional career. Then, in 1881, after seven years of marriage and shortly after the birth of her son, she met and formed a liaison with an acquaintance of her husband named Heinrich Reiter. Alfred Musil tolerated this relationship and from that time on Reiter was part of the family, regularly accompanying the Musils on their summer holidays...It was he, and not her husband, who in 1924 attended her on her death-bed.]

What is the real mystery of language? Why do the German sentences above mean nothing to someone who does not read German? Or do they mean nothing? Why is it that as we read the translation in English tiny little scenarios of so much import in the lives of these three people unfold so clearly before our eyes?

Yet how adequate is 'to form a liaison with' as a translation of 'sich anschliessen'? Does it not, in fact, mean 'to join' or 'be connected' to somebody? And if so, connected in what way? And what does 'Heftigkeit der Gefühle' really mean? Doesn't it really mean she liked to fuck her eyes out, or is this putting it too strongly? I would like to put this question to Walter Abish. And, finally, what is the real significance for Wolfi of this quote from Berghahn? Isn't the parallel obvious?

11

Wolfi reads me part of a letter his father sent his mother during their courtship:

I cannot explain what I feel as I write to you. I feel I am dreaming, and I can hardly believe myself, my heart. I think of you, of all the things that could give you pleasure, of the best ways to embellish the life we will lead together. I think of our nest –

Nest!

That's what it says: nest. Ich stelle mir unser Nest vor—I think of or imagine our little nest.

But this doesn't fit the picture I have of your father at all. Not from what you've told me.

I know, incredible isn't it. But you haven't heard anything yet. Just listen to this. Now where was I...ah yes, our little nest. I think of our little nest, of the house that will welcome us; I am building up a whole world of plans for the future...The dawn of my new life has put to flight forever the mists that were clouding my mind. Now the future appears clearly before my eyes. Now my sun is born! You are my sun, my peace, my purpose. I have your image present and living before my eyes. On the journey back I gazed for hours at the star you liked. I am awaiting your portrait impatiently. When will it come? As soon as possible, I beg you...Think of me, love me...You will love me, you must love me because I...

These last few words Wolfi delivers in a melodramatic parody. He clearly knows these lines well. With the piece of paper held in his outstretched hand above his head, he clutches desperately at the lapel of his coat with the other.

And to think that my mother was sucked in by this crap.

On Wolfi's notice-board there is a postcard of a painting of an adolescent girl. The format is unusual. It is shaped like an open doorway or window. The girl in the painting is naked. Closer inspection, however, shows that she is still wearing a slipper on her right foot. She is half sitting on a bed and although her body faces us her head is turned sharply to her right. One leg, her left leg, is stretched out so that her foot rests on the floor, although this is not shown. The other leg lies along the bed and is drawn up under her. Against the darker background the soft flesh tones of

64

her body appear almost orange, as though she is lit by the glow from a late afternoon sun.

She appears to have no pubic hair. Either she is too young, although this is unlikely because there are shadows clearly indicating her developing breasts, or the artist has chosen not to depict it. Her weight falls heavily on her right buttock and her torso is noticeably twisted upright in order for her to maintain her balance. Because of this one can feel the tension in the muscles of her right leg. Her arms are held high, as if she is using her hands to adjust a clip in her hair. Or perhaps she is merely stretching. This accounts for the title of the picture: *Nu aux bras levés*. In front of her is an ill-defined mass of crimson, while in the extreme foreground is the back and part of the seat of a simple chair.

It is only as you come back to view the composition as a whole that you realize that you, as viewer, are standing at the point from which the girl's body would have been lit and that this is intentional. You are the picture's illumination.

Why is it that having made this realization I can no longer look at the painting purely in terms of its pictorial content? What complex chemical reaction has taken place to effect this minute, but irrevocable, change to the overall composition of my self? Does Henriette Gomes, who owns the painting, also view it in this way?

On the back Wolfi had scrawled: 'Was war die eigentliche Beziehung zwischen Rilke und der Mutter des Künstlers?' [What was the real nature of Rilke's relationship with the artist's mother?].

65

It is also curious to note that the anonymous donations upon which Rilke was forced to live from time to time came, in fact, from Ludwig Wittgenstein.

At the bottom of Hauptstrasse is Bismarckplatz, Heidelberg's busiest tram and bus terminus. On one side of Bismarckplatz is Bismarckgarten and on the other side, Hortens, a large department store. Outside Hortens under the plane tree near Sophienstrasse is a lotto-ticket stand. Beside this is a large three-sided billboard. Pedestrians walking down Hauptstrasse wishing to cross Sophienstrasse at the traffic lights are confronted with one facet of this billboard as they step back onto the kerb. It advertises the movies that are on show in the nearby porno theatre. Its displays change regularly but it usually shows some variation on the same theme—a naked woman sits looking (seductively?) back at the viewer. She is half reclined, her legs are spread. One finger is suggestively placed in her mouth. By law her pubes, but not her breasts, are required to be obscured.

When Wolfi asked me if I wanted to see a porno movie with him, I assumed he had some other purpose in mind.

What for? I asked.

I've never seen one.

You mean to say you've been to a prostitute but you've never seen a porno movie?

Yes. But as I've already told you, with Andrea it was different.

Scham (f), no pl. 1) Shame

er wurde rot vor— , he went red with shame

66

die— stieg ihm ins Gesicht (old), he blushed with shame		
Schambein	pubic bone	bone of shame
Schamhügel	pubic arch	hill of shame
Schamhaar	pubic hair	hair of shame
Schamlippen	labia	lips of shame
Schamgegend	pubic region	region of shame
Schamteile	genitals	parts of shame

Metaphor has been described as the yoking together of two fundamentally different experiences. If this is so, what sort of etymological commentary is this on the German people? How much does a language's metaphoric resonance shape the consciousness of a nation? Wie deutsch ist es, eigentlich? [How German is it, really?]. It is no wonder that Freud was a native German speaker. [Es ist kein Wunder.]

'Sex is such a weird business.' Wolfi's only comment after we left the theatre.

12

Elena sent me the most wonderful poster today [ein wunder-schönes Plakat] and a photo of her and Anya. You must come down and have a look at them some time.

The poster, in black and white, is an advertisement for Herzen's new ballet *Die Marquise von O*, based on Heinrich von Kleist's powerful story of the same name. It is to be performed by the Vienna Dance Company and will be Elena's first lead role. The poster shows her as Giulietta in a scene from the first act. She is lying in a swoon in the foreground of a dark, atmospherically lit stage. The lighting emphasizes the deep flowing folds in her gown. Her face is upturned and one hand lies across her breast. Lying there she has the same air of absolute serenity about her that many of Raphael's portraits of the Madonna have.

In the background, to the far left of the stage, a single small floodlight reveals the face and shoulders of a young Russian officer standing in a doorway. He is looking back over his shoulder towards the figure of Giulietta lying on the floor.

The photograph of Elena and Anya is in complete contrast. It has been taken with a Polaroid camera and shows Elena in jeans and a white T-shirt waving back at the camera. On her hip, supported by Elena's other arm, is Anya. She must be about two years old and she too is waving excitedly back at the camera. Unlike Wolfi she is fair haired but she has the same piercing blue eyes. Scrawled along the bottom of the photograph is: 'Viele Grüsse von Deinen zwei Lieblingen' [A big hello from your two little darlings].

On November 20, 1811 Henriette Vogel, Kleist's lover, wrote on the bottom of one of his letters to their friend Sophie Müller:

> Lebt wohl denn! Ihr, meine lieben Freunde, und erinnert Euch in Freud und Leid der zwei wunderlichen Menschen, die bald ihre grosse Entdeckungsreise antreten werden.

[So, my dear friends, live well and in your joy and your sorrow remember the two wonderful people who are about to embark on their great journey of discovery.]

The next morning they went for a walk in the forest near Potsdam. They sat on a bench in the filtered sunlight and talked softly, joyously to one another for a few moments. Then, as arranged, Kleist took the pistol from his pocket and, with Henriette looking towards the lake sparkling through the trees, he shot her through the heart. Then he reloaded the pistol and shot himself.

In 1979, Christa Wolf published a novel entitled *Kein Ort. Nirgends* [No place. Nowhere]. It is a fictional account of a meeting between Kleist and the young poet Karoline von Günderode. Why, we are entitled to ask, did she choose Kleist and von Günderode? What is the real connection? Is it simply that in 1806, when Professor Friedrich Creuzer abandoned his intention to dissolve his marriage in order to marry Karoline, she too took her own life? Surely there is more to it than that?

Creuzer, who was a classical philologist, was professor at Heidelberg from 1807 to 1845. When Karoline died she was only twenty-six.

13

The teleology of memory
Die Teleologie des Erinnerungsvermögens

Are memories only reliable when they serve as an explanation?
Is the powerful integrative function of human consciousness,
whereby difference is recognized, categorized and assimilated,
fundamentally metonymic? Is it also arbitrary?

Do I understand Wolfi correctly?

Sind Erinnerungen nur zuverlässig wenn sie uns als Erkläea-
rungen dienen? Ist die starke integrierende Funktion des
menschlichen Bewusstseins, wodurch Unterschiede erkannt,
klassifiziert und aufgenommen werden, im Grunde metony-
misch? Ist sie auch arbiträr?

I am beginning to realize how sketchy my real knowledge
of Wolfi is. His phrase, 'the teleology of memory', makes
me wonder whether in writing about him I am selecting
what I remember of him to fit my conception of the person I
thought he was. I know now how incomplete my knowledge
of him is and how much what I knew of him then was built
up from intangible things: silences on the bus; laughter over
meals at the university; his peculiar way of squinting, like
a pup unsure whether it was going to be patted or scolded;
his habit of dancing from one foot to the other when he
was excited; watching the changing pattern of moods sweep
across his face as we walked in the cool forest air; or listening
to his voice during hours of conversation about nothing.

Moreover, there were things he remained obstinately
secretive about. I knew he was seeing a girl or a woman
in Heidelberg. I used to catch glimpses of them together
occasionally, but he never mentioned her and was evasive

about her when I did. I used to pick up the mail from time to time so I knew also that he had an old girlfriend in Klagenfurt who wrote to him regularly. And then there was the photograph on his notice-board of a woman named Marta from Berlin with whom he said he was in love.

I am also aware that writing about him has begun to distort my understanding of him. Another Wolfi has been created who exists beside the real one in a relationship of narrational parallax. This shift is even more marked given the volume of material I now have which Wolfi actually wrote himself.

In addition to this, I ask myself how subconsciously easy has it been to suppress information that **appears** to have no connection with him or that is functionless in terms of any narrative momentum. How objective **have** I been? Worse, how much of myself have I inadvertently introduced into my portrait of him? How true, I ask myself, is one able to remain to reality in the first place? Why is it that there is no real sense of place or time in this account of him? How far can one go before the narrative fabric breaks down?

14

So what have you been up to this time?
    I went to see Simenon.
    What for?
    To talk to him about women.
    What did he say?
    Nothing. He wasn't there.

At the end of June, as planned, I went to Rome for a month to look through the papers that formed part of the Ingeborg Bachmann archive at the Biblioteca Nazionale. By this time Wolfi had already decided to leave Heidelberg to continue his studies in Berlin. My return was calculated to precede his departure by a week.

In the event, however, the day before I was due to leave Rome, Italy was paralyzed by yet another rail strike and I ended up being stranded in the capital. I decided to call Wolfi from the pensione I was staying at to let him know what was happening. Frau Bartsch had answered the phone. I told her who I was and asked to speak to Wolfi.

Er ist schon weg, she said gruffly.

Gone! I said. When? When did he go?

Vor zwei Wochen.

There was a malicious tone to her voice, as if to say: See, I told you so. You can't trust a word anybody says these days.

Two weeks ago, I repeated a little stunned. Did he say where he was going?

Berlin.

Berlin. I could hear the resignation in my own voice.

Ja, Berlin.

Then she hung up.

When I got back to Heidelberg, Wolfi had indeed gone. He left no messages, nothing. It was as though he had never existed, and a couple of weeks later I returned to Australia without having seen or heard from him again.

In September 1982, after more than a year had gone by, a carefully wrapped cardboard carton turned up on my doorstep completely unannounced from Germany. Inside were bundles of papers, news-clippings, letters, postcards and God knows what. There was also an infuriatingly brief note which read:

'Vielleicht kannst **Du** etwas damit anfangen.'

[Perhaps **you** can make something of this.]

TWO

I have been cast; to play for no audience and no applause, but solely for the sake of the performance itself which I am and beyond which I am nothing.

Heidegger

16

Und wie steht Kant dazu [Where does Kant stand on this]? He claimed that we cannot know things as they really are through sense perception. If space and time are contributed through the knowing mind then spatial and temporal objects will be altered in the very act of being apprehended. It follows then that the world known through the senses can be no more than a phenomenal world and that above this phenomenal world is another world of real objects, knowable not to the senses but to reason. The ideas of space and time he says are 'intuitive' rather than conceptual; moreover they are 'pure' intuitions insofar as the essential nature of their referents is known in advance of experience and not as a result of it. This is an extraordinary statement; the extraordinariness [Sonderbarkeit] of which seems to have escaped Kant. Elsewhere he says: 'Reason lacks intuitive power, we cannot be acquainted with things as they are.'

If reason lacks intuitive power and we cannot know things as they are through sense perception, where do we go from here?

*

The year before moving into the new house, my father decided we would spend the summer vacation in Yugoslavia.

A few months earlier, against my father's wishes, my mother had come to rescue me one morning from my prison, after the school authorities had informed her that I had collapsed the previous day during one of the 'training' sessions and had had to be taken to the nearby infirmary. That morning the sun had been shining and when my mother was shown into my room she hurried anxiously to my bedside and began covering me with kisses. She had been crying and I was a little overwhelmed by her quite open display of emotion until I realized that it represented not only her concern for my wellbeing but a long-suppressed victory over my father. She had finally dared to go against his will.

After we collected my things we said a relieved goodbye to Colonel Kollwitz, the school's headmaster. He muttered something ambiguous about military schools not being the place for 'dreamers or women', shook my hand and showed us awkwardly to the door. We then took the taxi that had been ordered for us on the short journey to the nearby train station.

It was a perfect day, warm and sunny, and we were virtually the only people at the tiny station. My mother had recovered from her anxiety and now sat composed and smiling on one of the platform's wooden benches. It reminded me of the times when the three of us, Elena, my mother and I, used to go walking in the woods near Klagenfurt or in the beautiful gardens of the university. Instead of feeling nervously exhausted I now felt euphoric. As I paced up and down waiting for the train I watched my mother sitting there, our luggage and one large trunk beside her. I felt like a poet, exhilarated, free and wonderfully alive. All my mother needed was a brightly coloured parasol and we would have been transported back a hundred years. She kept laughing as I ran along the platform kicking my heels in the air. I remember the fat, uniformed station master stepping out from his office at the far end of the platform and standing there for a few moments watching me as he puffed on his cigar. He had pulled a white handkerchief out of his top pocket, took his glasses off and cleaned them. Then he looked down the tracks in the opposite direction, shook his head and went back inside.

I sat down next to my mother and she linked her arm through mine. She lay her head on my shoulder.

It will be so nice to have you home again, she said.

It will be so nice to be home, I said, even if I still have to put up with father's interrogation.

And I remember, when we arrived home that evening, Elena had rushed out to meet us as we opened the gate and made our way up the path to the house. She had kissed me on both cheeks and after cursorily asking me how I felt, started telling me excitedly about the new love of her life— how wonderful he was, how talented, how sophisticated, mature and handsome. When I could I asked who the lucky fellow might be.

Anybody I know?

Yes.

Who?

Guess!

Give me a clue.

His first name is Mikhail.

Mikhail? Mikhail. I don't know any Mikhails.

Yes you do.

I give up.

Baryshnikov! Mikhail Baryshnikov. I'm in love with Mikhail Baryshnikov. He's wonderful.

Isn't he a little old for you?

Not at all. He could have **me** any time.

Elena! my mother exclaimed.

It's true, it's true. I don't care what anyone says.

Even my father seemed happy, if this is not putting it too strongly, to see me. Perhaps he had finally admitted to himself that his school was not the right school for me, that in fact I was different from him. He stood there on the steps, stiff but smiling. He was nervous and didn't know what to say.

Father, I said.

He took my hand and shook it.

Wolfgang.

He looked at my mother and then at Elena. Neither was quite sure how to react. His conciliatory behaviour seemed to set us all on edge. Elena broke the tension by grasping me by the arm and saying: Papa, can I take Wolfi up to my room and show him what I've done to it?

My father fumbled for something to say and Elena, interpreting this to mean yes, pulled me past him through the door and up the stairs to her room.

The next morning the months of misery at school seemed to catch up on me and I awoke feeling dizzy and drained of energy. When I got up to take a shower I must have passed out in the hall. I awoke to find my mother leaning over me asking anxiously if I was alright. She insisted then that I be examined by the family doctor.

When he had finished he told her that I was suffering from severe nervous exhaustion and prescribed bed rest; bed rest and no undue excitement, whatever that was supposed to mean.

80

In the weeks that followed, my father seemed to revert somewhat to his former aloof self although, happily, not to quite the same extent as previously, when mealtimes had been periods of silent torture, each of us forced to flee to some inner sanctuary with only the restrained clatter of cutlery punctuating the silence around us. Except, of course, for the times when Omi came to visit us. She would wreak havoc with my father's pomposity. But now, even without my grandmother, the evenings were less oppressive than they used to be and a workable truce seemed to have been achieved between my two parents. Moreover, Elena's and my behaviour no longer seemed inexplicably to provoke the bitter scenes it once did.

Nevertheless, when my father announced one evening at dinner that we would be taking a holiday in Yugoslavia, it took us all by surprise. We had not been on a holiday as a family for almost ten years. There was a moment's hiatus as my father's words registered in each of our conscious-nesses. We glanced quickly at each other and then at my father, who sat dabbing his mouth with his napkin which he then proceeded to fold self-consciously and meticulously before finally placing it beside his empty plate. Instead of his usual cold and supercilious smile, for the second time in a matter of weeks, he looked utterly lost. His gesture was so clearly unexpected that he himself seemed to be aware of how uncharacteristic it was and of how much it contrasted with what we had all come to expect from him. Again no one quite knew how to react. This was definitely uncharted territory.

Fortunately, the prospect of a couple of weeks on a foreign beach had really begun to work on Elena and, unable to contain her excitement any longer, she let out a whoop of delight. She jumped up from the table, ran to my father and threw her arms around him.

Oh Papa, it will be wonderful, won't it, she said.

She began interrogating him about where and when we would go, what we would see and what Yugoslavia was like. Then she broke loose and ran off to find her atlas. Uncharitably, my mother and I were, at first, a little suspicious about my father's motives.

But in the weeks leading up to the trip and in fact for the entire holiday, my father was totally unlike the person I had known him to be for as long as I could remember. I could see why my mother had married him; his charm, his urbanity and his open smile could be totally disarming.

That this was only a temporary thaw in the ice age that quickly followed did nothing to diminish the reality of my father's good intentions at the time. It was like a remission from a dreadful disease. We were all surprised and happy that it had happened and desperately sad when it didn't continue.

Ultimately, his relapse seemed to be the necessary catalyst for the catastrophic events which followed and he seemed to emerge as merely a pawn in some greater, more protracted, game.

*

By definition, a priori judgements have the twin characteristics of necessity and universality, neither of which can be found in conclusions from experience (in other words, experience presents us with no more than contingent truths).

*Kant, however, came to the conclusion that there were **some** features of sensory experience which could not be accepted as empirically given. In other words—there **were** a priori elements involved in sensory knowledge. This led inevitably to his famous distinction between appearances (phenomena) and things-in-themselves (noumena). The argument:*

> *If the world we confronted were one of things-in-themselves, a priori knowledge of it, even in a very restricted sense, would be quite impossible. The fact that we have such knowledge is proof that the objects of our knowledge **are** phenomena or appearances.*

*It, in fact, proves no such thing. If the basis on which we have a priori knowledge is dependent on making the distinction between phenomena (or appearances) and things-in-themselves, then we can hardly say that the fact that we have such knowledge is proof that the objects of our knowledge are, as a consequence, phenomena. The difference between Descartes and Kant then is the difference between epistemology and ontology—**how** we know as against **what** we know.*

*

Initially my father's intention was to stay in Dubrovnik, which he had visited a few years earlier while at a conference in Titograd. But because we had left booking so late we were unable to find anywhere suitable to stay. Eventually, after a number of phone calls, my father was forced to make a reservation at a hotel, incongruously called the Hotel Belvedere, in one of the small coastal villages to the south.

Driving into Yugoslavia from Austria is like driving into the nineteenth century. The road surfaces are poor, agricultural methods are primitive and the people seem to be oppressed as much by the heat and dust as by their own inescapable poverty. Buildings appear to be on the verge of collapse and inland the people are sullen and taciturn.

But as you approach the coastal region of Montenegro, the countryside and the people seem miraculously to change. There is a new sense of vitality, of colour, a feeling of richness and warmth. The first glimpse of Dubrovnik from the surrounding hills is undeniably spectacular, with the bone-tinted buildings of the old city contrasting sharply against the deep blue sea of the Adriatic beyond. And the people of the region are also different. They are taller and darker, with high cheek bones and proud angular faces. The young women are particularly handsome and, if asked a question, have a habit of smiling enigmatically back at you with their dark, almost black, eyes before answering. But mostly it is their happiness which strikes you. To be on this part of the coast is to live within permanent earshot of laughter. It seems as natural as the sun shining or the trees growing.

When we arrived at the hotel after the short drive along the coast we were happily surprised at what, accidentally, a good choice it was. Originally the building had been a large two-storeyed family home but at some stage it had been converted into a small but comfortable hotel. It overlooked the town and from the first floor balcony, through the thin blue-grey foliage of the trees outside, you could see the beach stretching out beyond the rooftops below.

Elena and I shared a bedroom which was separated from my parents by a small sitting-room, a bathroom and

84

a toilet. The walls were covered in old-fashioned wallpaper and the high ceilings were panelled in wood. It was sparsely furnished but comfortable nevertheless. On the wall next to the shuttered windows was a faded photograph of a family standing in front of the house long before it had been converted into a hotel.

It took us no time to settle in and before long Elena and I were wandering around the town as if we had lived in it for years.

Early in our stay—it must have been the third or fourth day because I recall we had already discovered an idyllic spot at the far end of the beach where Elena and I used to swim and which we had begun to think of as our own— I remember being awakened one morning by a thin shaft of flickering sunlight which penetrated our room through a crack in the shutters over the window.

Drowsily I moved my head out of the line of fire and looked across to Elena in the bed opposite. In the half-light I could see her lying there on her back. She had kicked off her sheets and the buttons of her nightdress had come undone so that her left breast was now exposed. I lay watching the slow rise and fall of her breathing. I could see where the line of her developing tan shaded into the paleness of her breast and I could also make out the small, flat, dark circle that surrounded her nipple.

As I watched I realized I had never really considered Elena as a separate being before. She had always been someone who was just there, who was simply my sister. But now, in the half-light, I suddenly caught a glimpse of the image of the young woman she was on the verge of becoming. For the first time I registered how beautiful she really was. It was as though I had never even seen her before, as if for years I had been anaesthetized, insensitive to what had grown up around me. I could not take my eyes off her, off her perfect face, her lips, her slender arms and hands, off the contours of her body beneath her nightdress.

Quietly I slipped out of bed and went to the window. I unlatched one of the shutters and pushed it slowly open so that the room began to fill with light. I turned and stood leaning against the wall watching her sleep. I felt its coolness against my back. Outside a faint breeze filtered through the leaves and, as I watched, Elena's nipple began slowly to contract. I was fascinated as it changed shape, transforming itself from a smooth, even flatness to a textured, dark hardness.

As I stood there I wondered why, in all I had read, no one had written about the pain I now felt in my heart. What was it about this sudden and unexpected confrontation with Elena's emerging beauty that made the experience so agonizing, so overwhelming, so physically wrenching? Everything I had ever read about love, or desire, or beauty expressed itself in such abstract terms, so abstract in fact that, in reality, it had meant nothing to me at all. Why had no one mentioned this **physical** tearing, this sick rending I felt in my soul? It was as though, unable to raise my hands quickly enough, I had suddenly been blinded by the glare from some accidentally perceived truth, the exact nature of which remained undisclosed to me. For the first time in my life I felt absolutely isolated. I became aware that between whatever it was that Elena seemed to incarnate and my own being there existed some mysterious and unbridgeable gap.

She began to stir and I slipped quietly out onto the balcony. I stood there with my eyes closed, warming my face against the sun. Then I heard her voice.

Wolfi…Wolfi? Where are you?

I'm out here on the balcony.

What time is it?

Half past six.

Oh God, she said, we have to get up. Otherwise we'll be late.

I heard her get out of bed and creep up behind me. She reached up and covered my eyes with her hands. I could feel her body pressed lightly against mine.

Penny for your thoughts [woran denkst du gerade]? she said.

I was just thinking about you in fact, I said.

Thinking what?

Nothing in particular. Just thinking, that's all.

She released her hands and came around beside me, shielding her eyes from the sun. Then, squinting, she leaned on the railing, her wrists turned outwards and yawned. A shiver passed through her body. She stretched and once again I could see her body outlined against the soft material of her nightdress.

Come on, she said. Let's have a shower and go and get some breakfast.

By the time we were sitting at our table it was still only a little after seven. We waited impatiently for our breakfast to arrive, already anxious to be out walking along the white sand. Our mornings had become charged with a peculiar and inexplicable sense of expectancy, as though we both sensed that each of our destinies were in some way linked to the clear light and cool water of the small peninsula at the far end of the beach.

Through the window we could see groups of people already making their way down the narrow lane towards the sea, including a few whom we now recognized. Elena seemed more agitated than usual as she watched the trickle of passers-by and when our coffees and hot bread rolls arrived she exclaimed loudly: At last!

She immediately broke open a roll and spread it with butter and some of the locally produced apricot jam with which they came. She took a large gulp from her cup of coffee.

Um, she said, shrugging her shoulders. Isn't this great.

She took another bite from her roll and with her tongue licked the sticky excess from her fingers. As she ate she half rose from time to time to get a better look at whoever was coming down the lane-way on their way to the beach. I watched as her eyes found and followed a boy about my own age whom we had seen the day before on the beach. She stopped chewing until he disappeared from view and then smiled to herself. She took another sip of her coffee and looked up at me.

What are you looking at?

Nothing, I said.

Yes you were. You were staring at me. What for?

I wasn't staring. You're imagining things.

I'm not and you were. But I don't care.

She wiped her hands on her paper napkin and threw it at me.

Come on, she said. Let's get our things and go.

Our favorite spot, at the far end of the beach, was sheltered by three old and very stunted olive trees. Beyond these, the rocks curved out in a long finger into the sea just far enough to form a shallow basin of cool clear water.

As we walked along the beach several of the older boys turned their heads to follow us as we passed, or nudged one of their less attentive companions who then turned to look our way. Occasionally one of them whistled or yelled something incomprehensible at us.

When we arrived at the olives there was already somebody swimming in the small bay. I recognized him immediately as the youth Elena had earlier watched so attentively as we ate breakfast. It was still early and the sunlight appeared to dance on the surface of the water and from where we were standing we could look down on the boy's strong form magically suspended in the shimmering transparency below. Elena, too, had noticed him.

She placed her basket on the ground and took her beach towel from her shoulder and carefully laid it out. She stooped to adjust one of its corners and then stood, crossed her hands in front of her and, gripping the hem of her loose cotton dress, with one swift flowing movement of her arms, lifted it high into the air. For a moment or two she held her body in a shallow arc as she stretched higher and higher with her raised arm. It was as if she wanted to shake off any lingering drowsiness she may have felt from our early start. The contours of the muscles in her legs were visible as they tightened beneath her brown skin and I remember being close enough to see a few tiny curls of dark hair caught beneath the elastic of her costume and the flexed tendon of her leg. With one arm held high and the other arched to fluff her hair into a new disorder her breasts appeared flattened against her ribcage, but as her arm came down in a wide arc to fling her dress towards her basket I watched fascinated as they regained their former fullness. She ran her fingers around the bottom of her costume and then stood for a few moments with her hands on her hips. It seemed absurd to think that we had sprung from the same blood, that we shared so much in common and yet were so utterly separate.

All of this could only have lasted a matter of instants. It was as though I had been mesmerized by this vision of Elena reaching out for the sun, a vision which now repeated itself in my mind—her arched body, the wisps of dark hair, the sinew in her thigh and the contrast of her red costume against her honey-coloured body.

Elena's voice intruded suddenly into my reverie and I turned back to catch what she was saying.

Wolfi...Wolfi, what's the matter with you? Please come here, won't you, and put some cream on my back.

She lay on her towel and as I began rubbing the clear liquid into her shoulders she squirmed with delight.

Oh it's cold, it's cold, she cried digging her toes into the sand.

I watched her looking down to where the youth was still swimming. He would glide in a wide arc and then

90

flip over onto his back, holding his arms away from his body. Intermittently he moved them, driving himself forward. It was like watching a large eagle circling in the morning's heat, beating its wings occasionally to regain height. Then, with a splash, he rolled onto his stomach again and swam strongly to shore. He walked up to where his towel lay a few metres away. Standing on the sand he appeared more slender than he had in the water. But there was something about his leanness, something about the way he stood that suggested an air of self-assured sexual indolence.

Elena was still looking at him. We both sensed that it was no accident that he had been swimming nearby. I was sure he had watched us come here the preceding morning. It was also obvious that he knew he was being watched. As he finished drying himself he turned and looked over at us. He smiled and said hello.

His name was Alexis. His father was a short and talkative Greek who had come to Germany in the fifties and had eventually saved enough money to open an import-export business in Hamburg. He had married a tall Hungarian woman whose first husband had been killed in the last months of the war. She had a habit of resting her hand on his shoulder when they were out walking so that from behind they looked more like mother and son than husband and wife. In fact, I remember the day my mother and father, Elena and I ran into them for the first time in the crowded market place. I had recognized Alexis walking ahead of us with what I assumed to be his mother and younger brother and had called out to him. As the three of them turned I was quite astonished to find, instead of the young unblemished face I had expected, that I was looking into the gold-toothed smiling face of his middle-aged father. Alexis introduced our parents to each other and oddly enough they seemed to hit it off immediately. I heard Alexis' father explaining to mine that they had been coming here for years because he couldn't stand what was happening to the Greek islands. Eventually we left the four of them at one of the outdoor cafés and we made our way through the narrow streets and up onto the ancient embattlements that once protected the town, from where we could look down to the water and part of the beach below. Further to the north, about ten kilometres away, we could just make out part of the old city of Dubrovnik.

As we stood looking out to sea, I could feel Alexis watching Elena out of the corner of his eye. She seemed to have grown quiet now that we were on our own. Suddenly Alexis pointed to a small boat far out on the horizon, barely visible through the heat haze.

Where? I can't see it, Elena said, shading her eyes.

He pointed again.

There, just below the horizon. It keeps disappearing from view. Here.

He put one hand on her shoulder and drew her to him so that she could sight along his outstretched arm. He bent his head to hers.

There, you can see it again now. See...

Oh yes. I see it. It looks so small. God, I'd be so scared out there on my own.

The three of us fell silent as we watched the tiny vessel bob up and down far out on the horizon.

After a few minutes we decided to make our way down to the beach. At the bottom of the stairs leading onto the white sand an old man with a mule laden with sugar melons was stationed waiting for thirsty passers-by. He gestured to us with a melon in one hand and a large shiny knife in the other as we came down. Alexis held up three fingers and the old man broke into a gap-toothed grin. As he cut our three giant pieces he babbled away to us in a language none of us understood. Then he handed us each a large, black-pitted crescent of red flesh and raised his fingers to his lips and kissed them smackingly. We went across to the wooden pier and sat with our legs dangling over the edge. It was warm and as we ate pale drops of sweet juice escaped from our hands, sending tiny ripples to momentarily disturb the image of the sun floating in the still water below.

A few days later, the three of us were sitting on the beach when Alexis suggested we go and have a look at a small cove he had discovered on the other side of the rocky peninsula. Since we had nothing better to do we packed up our things and prepared to set off. The sun was already high and once we left the shade of the olive trees the heat quickly became quite oppressive.

Instead of making our way directly over the top of the rocky outcrop we headed inland towards a sheltered little path where Alexis said the going would be easier. We scrambled up the steep side of the exposed hill behind us until we reached the path he had mentioned and began to make our way along it towards the bent and twisted trees that grew along the escarpment of the ridge opposite. Once we had reached these we sat down for a few minutes to rest. Around us the air pulsated with the noise from thousands of invisible cicadas in the trees overhead.

How much farther? asked Elena.

About half a kilometre. In a minute or so we'll be able to look almost directly down at the sea again through the trees.

We set off once more. Within about ten minutes we came to a small clearing where the path branched off.

This is where we go down, Alexis said. It's steep, so be careful. Half way down the path doubles back and from there you get a great view overlooking the little bay below.

We started the climb down. At the bend in the path the little cove suddenly came into view between the trees. Alexis, however, stopped abruptly in front of us and motioned with his hand for us to be quiet. At first I couldn't make out why, but as I looked across to the narrow band of sand opposite I saw a young couple lying in the shade of the escarpment not more than twenty metres away. They were making love. The three of us stood, silently watching, fascinated as the reverberation of the man's sharp thrusting shook the form of the woman beneath him. They were like two animals, he holding her arms pinned against the sand above her head, his upper torso held away from her, while she clasped his buttocks with her encircling legs and seemed to pull him with increasing violence into her. With each thrust her breasts quivered and she emitted a short, sharp, unidentifiable syllable. She lay there pinned, staring back up at him, her body arched to meet his.

Then, abruptly and without warning, it was over and he subsided onto one elbow beside her. As he lay there the noise from the cicadas seemed to die away. It was as though we had suddenly been engulfed in a strange and palpable silence.

Clearly it was impossible for us to go down now and we turned to make our way quietly back up to the path above us.

None of us said a word until we arrived back at the olive trees. When we did, Alexis mumbled something about having to get back. He stood facing us awkwardly for a moment and then turned and started walking slowly across the sand towards the town. A few minutes later we followed him in silence ourselves.

*

The statement that every event has a cause carries strict necessity with it and therefore cannot be grounded on an inductive survey of empirical evidence. Causality for Kant and Hume is a relation between successive events—a cause is an event that regularly precedes its effect. In other words, it is an invariable antecedent.

While we admit events are necessarily connected, one must not, however, conclude that causal connections can be established a priori. All causal propositions are synthetic and empirical. There is then a nexus between logic and causality. In nature, in the real world, causality exists as an empirical syllogism. It is fundamentally metonymic.

Kant was prepared to accept that all experience is experience for a subject. 'Whatever thoughts or feelings I have I must

*be capable of recognizing them as my thoughts or feelings.'
But for Kant, as has often been noted elsewhere, the subject
referred to here is not something substantial; it is merely a logical
requirement: 'In the synthetic original unity of apperception,
I am conscious of myself not as I appear to myself, nor as I am in
myself, but I am conscious only that I am.' This representation is
a <u>thought</u>—not an <u>intuition.</u> Here is what Kant himself had to say:*

> The original and necessary consciousness of the identity of the
> self is thus at the same time a consciousness of an equally
> necessary unity of the synthesis of all appearances according
> to concepts, that is according to rules, which not only make
> them necessarily reproducible but also in doing so determine
> an object for their intuition, that is, the concept of something
> wherein they are necessarily interconnected. [A107–108]

> Synthesis in general is the mere result of the <u>power of imagina-
> tion</u>, a blind but indispensable function in the soul [in dem Geist],
> without which we should have no knowledge whatsoever, but of
> which we are scarcely even conscious. [B103]

*

Like most childhood holidays, before we knew it our
holiday too was almost over. My father had decided to
leave on the Monday to avoid the weekend traffic and it
was already Saturday. We had not seen Alexis since the
episode of the lovers on the beach and in the interim Elena
had been moody and irritable, so I had spent the time on my
own exploring the nearby villages of Kupari and Srebreno.

But our last Saturday was market day and everybody
would be about. Despite this, all my arguing could not
convince Elena to shake off her lethargy and join me for
the walk into town. She just wasn't interested. Instead, my
mother offered to accompany me and we set off arm in
arm in the bright morning sunlight. She was wonderfully

happy and when we reached the plaza we decided to sit and have coffee at one of the sidewalk cafés and watch the people milling about the stalls that had been set up in the square overnight.

We had just finished and were about to go when I heard Alexis' voice call out to us. I turned to see him making his way through the crowd. When he reached us he said hello to us both. Then he asked if Elena and I would like to go to the movies that evening.

I didn't know they had movies here, I said.

Here the movies are an institution. You haven't experienced anything until you've experienced movies Yugoslav style. It's primitive but a lot of fun. Will you come?

Sure.

And Elena?

I think I'll be able to talk her into it. What time?

Meet me at seven-thirty outside the Plaza Hotel. It's on the far side of the square. Okay?

Okay.

I can't stay, he said retreating, I promised my father I'd meet him at the bakery in five minutes. See you tonight.

We watched him disappear into the crowd, paid for our coffees and then strolled leisurely through the narrow side-streets back to the hotel.

When we arrived I went up to our room. Elena was lying on her bed pretending to read.

Want to go to the movies tonight? I said.

Not particularly.

What a pity. Alexis will be so disappointed.

What do you mean?

Well, as it happens, I ran into Alexis in town and he's invited us to go to the movies. But if you're not interested I'll just have to go down right now and phone him to say you won't be coming.

I went towards the door.

You're a jerk [Du bist ein Arschloch], you know that, Wolfi.

She jumped up off the bed and threw her book at me but I was through the door before she knew it. I heard it thud to the floor behind me. Instantly I turned. The door flew open and Elena hurtled out. She managed to stop just millimetres from my face.

Changed your mind, eh?

She ran her hand up through the back of my hair and looked at me sideways with her dark eyes.

Well, it's just that I don't think one should ever rush into things, that's all. After all, it's not every day a girl gets the opportunity to go to the movies with a good-looking boy like you, is it?

Oh, I see. One moment I'm a jerk and the next you're behaving as though I were Prince Charming.

Well, I wouldn't go that far.

So I take it you're coming?

Uh huh.

That night, having said goodbye to our parents, we left the hotel to make our way into town. Out on the street I was reminded again of the strange meditative twilight of the region. It is quite unlike anything you could ever expect to experience back home. The buildings seem to glow with the heat stored from the day's sun. Overhead the sky seems to fill with a deep and luminous blue punctured by hundreds of stars of astonishing brightness. In the still evening air, as you pass, catches of conversation can be heard escaping from half-glimpsed interiors which, from a distance, look like delicate murals painted into the pink stone of the walls. Or the sound of a baby crying might drift down to you from one of the many side-streets above.

That night was no exception. Already there were quite a few people about. Men in singlets sat talking or smoking quietly on their doorsteps, groups of laughing people were assembling at the tables of the small, open-air family restaurants which during the day were the homes of the ordinary townspeople, and couples were strolling about enjoying the mild evening air. Occasionally someone nodded hello.

By the time we reached the square, the sky had become almost completely dark and a cool breeze had sprung up. As we approached the brightly lit area of the Plaza Hotel opposite we could see that most of the tables outside were already occupied. The flickering lights from the candles on the tables reflected eerily against the canopies of the umbrellas above them.

White-shirted waiters hurried back and forth with plates of food balanced along outstretched arms, while others wove their way expertly through the diners with trays of drinks held high above their heads. The sound of violin music filtered down to us from somewhere inside the hotel.

The entire area around the Plaza was lit by floodlamps mounted high on the building's facade and as we stepped into this arena of laughter and light Elena's simple white dress was transformed into a thing of dazzling radiance. It appeared to accentuate the slimness of her waist, while the unconcealable vitality of her tanned body beneath seemed, in turn, to amplify the radiance of her dress. The whites of her eyes sparkled in the shadows of her face.

A number of heads turned to follow us as we made our way through the tables towards the steps. Alexis emerged from the arched entrance to the hotel foyer and came down to greet us. He was wearing a loose white shirt and light cotton trousers and something about his easy confidence made him suddenly appear older. It was as though in the two weeks we had been here, the youth we had first seen on the beach had been fully transformed into a self-confident young man. He kissed us both on the cheeks and ushered us in through the hotel doors.

It might be better if we got our tickets now, he said, before it gets too crowded.

We made our way down the corridor to a makeshift ticket office and, after a short wait, bought our tickets. Then Alexis led us to a door at the far end of the hall through which we emerged into a large open-air courtyard. It was already quite full and people were laughing and talking loudly. On the wall of the building opposite hung what looked like a large rectangular piece of white sailcloth.

Is this it? I asked.

This is it. Movies Yugoslav style.

He laughed as I looked dubiously around. However, the more I looked the more it seemed to me to be the perfect space for an open-air theatre. The building was a

100

large, three-storeyed, U-shaped structure which occupied the entire end of the block of buildings overlooking the middle of the square. The base of the U was given over to the hotel's restaurant which spilled out onto the square itself. During the week the large inner courtyard served as a delivery area for the shops which faced the street. Broad, red-tiled eaves skirted the entire inner perimeter. Access to the courtyard was restricted to relatively small trucks because of the narrowness of the laneways between it and the wall of the building opposite. On film nights, these were partially barricaded off and a sentinel was posted at each end to prevent anyone without tickets from entering.

In the centre, rows of canvas deck chairs had been set up and already many of these were occupied. Not only were there holiday-makers here, many of the audience were locals. Large slack-faced women sat knitting, while groups of older men in ancient suits and gaudy ties stood sipping small glasses of apricot brandy under the eaves. A table with a projector on it had been set up in front of one of the second-floor windows, while at the back of the theatre a number of other windows gave directly onto the restaurant's kitchen. From here you could buy a range of hot food or coffee as you watched the film or during one of the many intervals.

Have you eaten? Alexis asked.

We nodded.

Then let's find ourselves some seats. There's going to be a mad rush for them any minute.

After we had sat down Elena, who had barely uttered a word, turned to Alexis.

101

What have you been up to? she said. We haven't seen you since...Well, what I mean is, for days.

I went to Titograd with my father. God, what a depressing place. Have you been there?

No, she said. My father went there years ago, but we've never been there.

Alexis went to say something else but was cut off by three short blasts from what sounded like a car horn and people began noisily scrambling for their seats.

I'll tell you later, he yelled.

The crowd was incredibly rowdy, their laughter and shouting resounding across the inner space. Everyone was in a festive mood and the place was packed. There were still people standing under the eaves as the lights dimmed. The stars brightened in the dark square of sky above us.

The projector flickered into life. It took a few moments to stabilize before a fuzzy image appeared on the screen. As the focus was adjusted the close-up of a label advertising the locally produced apricot brandy came into view. But something was drastically wrong. The sophisticated young Yugoslav couple featured in the advertisement appeared to be spewing the nation's favorite drink back into their glasses as though it were vile-tasting poison. The locals, who knew the advertisement well, erupted into waves of laughter as some clichéd endearment was transformed into what sounded like someone being violently ill and the high pitched cackle of an old woman in front of us kept setting them off again. The culmination, however, was reached when the handsome, tanned, sophisticated seducer of a thousand women, having emptied his glass gravity-defyingly

102

back into the bottle, turned to the audience and, with his face in close focus, smiled, then belched obscenely out at us. This had the locals rolling around in their chairs as though they had drunk gallons of the stuff themselves [als ob sie selbst total besoffen waren].

There was a short pause as the laughter died down and then the main feature started. From what I could make out it was a melodrama, the plot of which was too convoluted for me to follow. Even the locals didn't appear terribly interested in it. They were more excited by a couple of young daredevils who ran the gauntlet of the barricades on their noisy motor scooters with their girlfriends riding pillion on the back. A collective cheer would erupt as the wall in front of us lit up and one, or sometimes two, of them sped noisily through, while the guards posted at either end looked on helplessly. Each time the crowd would settle back down for a few minutes until the next young blood came racing through, and each time a cloud of smoke and petrol fumes would drift slowly up through the flickering light of the projector.

Between reels there was an interval to allow people to get something to eat or drink. We waited in the queue for a few minutes and came away with hot fresh rolls stuffed with spiced chicken meat and mustard and cups of steaming black coffee. Alexis was in high spirits. Apart from Elena's slip, the incident on the beach was not mentioned. It was strange how different Alexis now appeared from the youth who had so awkwardly turned away from us that day to walk back to town. When he fell silent I watched him out of the corner of my eye looking at Elena intently. She had completely cheered up and was clearly enjoying the noise, the food, the people and, most of all, Alexis' attention.

The film had barely recommenced when I felt the first large drop of rain splatter against my face. I looked up to see that the stars were now largely obscured by masses of fast-moving cloud. Fat globes of water were beginning to plummet through the projected light and land smackingly around us. At first they came sporadically, but within minutes they turned into a downpour which sent us running for shelter under the eaves. Here we huddled while the rain streamed down in front of the screen. The gutters filled quickly and soon began to overflow. The lights came up and through the thin curtain of water that cascaded down in front of me and the thick veil of the downpour in the centre, I could see an irregular row of half-lit faces under the eaves opposite. Occasionally someone looked skywards, catching the light more fully. Others, the men, were half obscured under the brims of their hats. Their cigarette ends glowed intermittently, followed by thin ghostly masses of white smoke which slid fleetingly up and over the roof into the night. No one made any attempt to leave, enjoying the sense of intimate solitude. As I looked along the line of faces opposite, I suddenly saw Elena and Alexis huddled between two old women with scarves drawn tightly over their heads. I had thought that we were together but clearly I had been mistaken. As I watched I could see Alexis saying something to Elena, his hand slightly raised in emphasis. Elena nodded her head. I turned to try to make my way through the crush of people but had gone no more than a couple of metres when, as suddenly as it had started, the rain stopped. Now I understood why no one had left. These summer evening downpours obviously only lasted a matter of minutes and most of the audience, who I now saw had taken their collapsable chairs with them, began to resume their places. Because the stone courtyard retained its heat the area would soon be dry and here and there little plumes of steam began to rise from the isolated air vents in the pavement.

When I reached the spot where Alexis and Elena had been standing they were gone. I looked back to where we had been sitting, stupidly thinking for a moment that perhaps they had gone back to our wet seats. But the few chairs that had been left out in the downpour had been collected and stacked against the walls to dry. I looked through the crowd and still could not see them. Cursing, I decided to see if they were out at one of the tables in the square. A number of the crowd, having been entertained enough for one evening, were leaving and I joined those who chose to go through one of the laneways at the end of the building rather than through the congested corridor of the hotel.

Out in the dimly lit street I turned towards the bright lights of the plaza and followed the dispersed silhouettes of the people in front of me. The external pillars of the building cut deep shadows into its facade and the pavement ahead of me glistened in the reflected light. As I approached the corner a breeze caught the hem of a white dress and sent it billowing diaphanously out for a moment from a doorway a little ahead of me before being smothered by a slim, brown, outstretched arm. I was sure it was Elena. As

I drew near I heard Alexis' voice earnestly saying something to her. I slowed down and moved closer to the wall. Alexis broke off as the small group of people in front of me walked past. Then I heard him say: But why not?

I can't Alexis. Not tonight. I've already told you, Wolfi will be looking for us already and I can't just disappear. What do I tell my parents when I get back. That I got lost or something.

Tomorrow morning then? After breakfast.

How?

Just say you're going for a walk.

What about Wolfi?

He doesn't go everywhere with you, does he? If he says anything, just say you want to go for a walk on your own.

I don't know, Alexis. It sounds risky.

Come on, Elena. Tomorrow's our last chance.

Okay, okay. But where will I meet you?

By the three olives.

But if I'm out walking, Wolfi might decide to go there himself.

Not without you he won't.

Okay, tomorrow morning then.

There were a few moments silence and then I heard Elena's voice again.

We should go and find Wolfi before he starts getting suspicious. He'll be furious as it is.

I heard their footsteps hurrying away and as I detached myself from the wall I saw them disappear around the corner into the arena of the restaurant's lights. I hurried across the street and made a quick detour around the perimeter beyond the tables and then cut back in so that I approached the building almost directly from the front. The waiters were still replacing seats around the tables and some of the diners had already resumed their places. Alexis and Elena were just about to go up the stairs into the building when I called out to them. For a moment they were unable to make me out as I walked through the tables. I waved and they came down the steps.

We've been looking for you, Alexis said easily.

So have I.

We thought you must have gone out when it started raining.

No, I waited, then went out around the back of the building when I found the corridor was too crowded.

Elena remained silent as Alexis invented some alternative reality to account for the truth of those few separate moments together.

Alexis suggested we get some coffee and have something to eat.

No, I've had enough coffee for one night, Elena said. There's a dance on back at our hotel. Let's go there and see what's happening.

When we got back there were still people sitting in the dining room. My parents were seated in the far corner talking to Alexis' father and mother. His father waved to us when he saw us standing in the doorway. Alexis pointed in the direction of the music coming from the far end of the corridor. His father smiled and waved us on.

But the dance was fairly dull and we sat for a time watching what was happening without any real interest.

None of us spoke much. We each seemed preoccupied with our own thoughts. I was trying to work out how I could get to the end of the beach the next morning without being seen. I looked across at Elena. She was watching Alexis, studying him, as he watched the dancers on the dance floor. However, since it was already late, we ended up saying goodbye to each other and after Alexis had left, Elena and I went up to our room.

The next morning, I awoke early. Elena was up already. She was obviously excited.

We were half way through our breakfast downstairs when my mother suddenly appeared in the doorway of the dining room. She looked upset.

We have to go, she said, her voice showing obvious strain. Omi has had an accident. She's broken her leg. They've just brought your father a telegram. We've decided to leave immediately.

Now? said Elena.

Yes now. As soon as we've packed. I'm sorry Elena, but we were going to leave tomorrow in any case and your father and I are both worried about your grandmother.

But we can't just leave like that. Not without saying goodbye to Alexis.

Okay, okay. Finish your breakfast and pack your things and then you can run over and see Alexis for a few minutes. But don't be long.

As soon as my mother had gone, Elena turned to me and said.

Wolfi, do me a big favour will you. Pack my bags for me. I've got to catch Alexis. I'll explain when I get back.

She jumped up and ran quickly to the door.

So, I thought to myself, if Elena was going to lose her virginity, it wouldn't be in the idyllic setting of an arc of azure water flanked by golden sands with the gentle heat of the morning's sun warming their young bodies. No, it would happen as a frantic embrace on an unmade hotel bed, without joy and more than likely without solace. And, what's more, I would have missed out on the opportunity of a lifetime.

I got up from the table and dragged myself slowly upstairs.

Fifteen minutes later, when I had barely finished packing, Elena returned. I looked at her as she stood in the doorway. She had been crying and was crying still. I went over to her and she embraced me sobbing.

He wasn't there Wolfi, he wasn't there, she kept saying.

*

*Now we are getting somewhere. When Kant says that, 'the original and necessary consciousness of the identity of the self is thus at the same time a consciousness of an equally necessary unity of the synthesis of all appearances,' he is specifically rejecting Hume's proposition that events are 'loose and separate'. Kant believed that if this **were** the case then not only would we be deprived of any insight into the **connectedness** of things, but we would have no unitary consciousness of any sort.*

> *The thoroughgoing affinity of appearances (the fact that appearances are capable of being connected in a single experience), thus relates closely to the ability of the observer to recognize himself as a single person with diverse experiences.*

There is in this then an element of consolation. It was, however, something existentialist philosophers came to reject.

They rejected it because they rejected the logical structures upon which it was based. Ironically, they moved back to a pre-Kantian position occupied by Hume. For Hume, man is a creature who is half sensual, half rational. This is man's central predicament. Sensual impulses are the determining factor in most of his actions and the role that reason occupies in a man's life is the role of a 'slave or servant of the passions'. Misunderstandings about existentialist thought transformed this into a pervasive nihilism. But, of itself, it is not entirely a bad thing. Goethe, for example, thought it offered the only salvation.

17

(Amongst the photographs included in Wolfi's papers is one of what in all probability is 'the new house'. It shows a large two-storeyed, free-standing building, quite imposing in its own right, its stonework pinkish in the mottled sunlight, set among a number of large trees. It has been photographed almost directly from the side, as though this were the view which confronted Wolfi as he stood leaning against the gate in the opening paragraph of what follows. Part of the balcony is visible although, for the most part, it is obscured by branches which hang low into the picture frame. In the background there is a high brick wall which appears to surround the house. In the foreground, the dark curve of its shadow sweeps up to intersect the left-hand edge of the photograph. Through this shadow a narrow path winds its way towards the front of the house. On the back is written: 'April '76').

I unlatched the gate, glad to be in the cool shade of the garden after the hot walk up the hill to the house. I leaned against it for a moment enveloped in the pungent smell of rich soil that rose from the freshly turned garden beds and the scent of jasmine that drifted down from the walls of the house above. I could hear music coming from somewhere but because of some acoustic illusion I could not identify where exactly it was coming from. It seemed to hang there, suspended in the luminous pockets of air that surrounded each translucent leaf of the canopy of branches above me.

As I emerged into the sunlight again I looked up to the balcony. Through the squat, rounded, stone shapes of the balustrade I could see Elena sitting back in a chair with her head resting against the wall behind her. She had her legs propped up on another chair in front of her. Her eyes were closed and from what I could make out, as I moved slightly to change my vantage point, she appeared to be naked. Because of the sharp angle, however, my view of her remained obscured and, in any case, as I stood there the music stopped suddenly and she began to stir. Before I could retreat into the shadows she bounced up from her chair and disappeared into her room.

I walked around to the front of the house, unlocked the door and went inside.

Anybody home? I yelled. Any body, I thought.

I walked into the kitchen and put the jug on. Just as the water boiled Elena came down the stairs.

Make one for me too please, Wolfi. I'm so drowsy.

She now had on a bikini top and shorts and I watched as she stretched her arms above her head. She turned her back to the kitchen bench, then hoisted herself lightly onto it. She chatted away as her drowsiness evaporated into unexplained rapture. She hopped down with a half-pirouette and distractedly began a series of stretching exercises. Occasionally she interrupted herself to make some point or other. Increasingly however, her focus changed from what she was saying to what she was doing. Slowly she raised her arm and looked along its outstretched length. I could almost feel the gentle curve of her breast where it merged with her flank. It reminded me again of that morning the previous year when I had awakened to see Elena lying there in the half-light, her breast exposed.

I think I'll go and finish cleaning up in the garden, I said.

She looked coquettishly at me.

Wolfi, I'm offended. You don't love me anymore.

She blew me a kiss, pirouetted once again and ran chuckling up the stairs.

This was typical of the way Elena behaved at the time. It was as though she were well on the way to becoming fully aware of her erotic potential and of the devastating effect that this would have on the men around her, but was still a little unsure about how this effect could be achieved. I seemed to have become the guinea-pig for her experiments. She appeared to delight in teasing me and to enjoy my obvious confusion.

Elena's behaviour, then, became part of what characterized the feeling that surrounded the new house and part of what increasingly troubled me. The other part of course was the state of my parents' relationship, which had begun to deteriorate again and the toll this was now taking on my mother's sanity.

Out in the garden, I began raking up the pieces of ivy I had trimmed from the wall the previous weekend. The day was warm and I soon began to lose myself in the mechanical rhythm of what I was doing. Elena had come back out onto the balcony and stood looking down at me as I wheeled the barrow out from under the trees to the pile of rubbish at the far end of the house.

I had been working for perhaps half an hour, enjoying the garden's smells and the music which again filtered down from Elena's room, when I heard the muffled sounds of voices coming from the other side of the wall. I stopped to listen. It sounded like they were arguing. I pushed the wheelbarrow against the wall and by stepping into the tray I could almost see over the top. I reached up, gave a light spring and hauled myself up to sit on its lip. By grasping the lowermost branch of one of the plane trees I was able to turn and look down to the path that ran alongside the wall below. About ten metres away, heading slowly towards me, were two elderly stooped combatants dragging a reluctant dachshund on a leash. Despite the heat they were both wearing overcoats and while she wielded an open umbrella in one hand he carried a cane in the other. Every few paces they would stop and as she menaced him with her umbrella he was forced to defend himself with his walking stick.

Nothing happened, Lotte. Nothing, nothing. You **know** nothing happened. Nothing ever happens. Tell her, Püppchen.

The dog looked guiltily away.

Fifty years ago also nothing happened. And after fifty years, ach Du lieber Gott, suddenly she's standing there on the street. Heinrich, she says. Heinrich Vogelschein. And after fifty years a little peck, that's all, a little peck.

You wanted that something should happen.

When?

When when? Then when, Heinrich du Arschloch. Fifty years ago what you wouldn't have given to get your rocks off with Gertrude Tannenbaum.

Lotte, such language I've never heard. You should be ashamed.

I watched them pass beneath me and continue up the street looking like two characters out of a silent movie. I turned to get back down and looked across the five or six metres towards Elena. She had gone. Suddenly I felt dizzy. Instantly my brain reeled through an entire scenario which set my whole body trembling. I grasped the smooth bough of the plane tree tightly to steady myself as I contemplated what had just raced through my mind.

My head was level with the bottom of Elena's balcony and by pulling myself up so that I stood on top of the wall I could just see through the double doors into Elena's bedroom opposite. Cautiously I stepped off the wall and climbed a little higher into the tree until I discovered a comfortable perch which gave me what could only be described as a bird's eye view of almost her entire room.

114

The reason that the plan which had instantaneously come to mind now appeared so tantalizingly feasible was that I knew that in summer Elena kept her balcony doors open at night so that she could enjoy the cool evening breeze. As I climbed down I realized that I had not been this excited since the morning of Elena's thwarted assignation with Alexis on the last day of our holiday the year before.

That evening the meal seemed to drag on unendingly. Barely a word was spoken. The old tension had returned. The only noise came from the ticking of the clock on the mantelpiece as it scythed the oppressiveness into neat, one-second blocks. Eventually, I knew, something would have to give. I tried to escape by concentrating on a vision of a lighted square of window, a lighted square into which I would soon be gazing. The meal finally drew to a close and I excused myself and went upstairs. I went over the notes I had made that day. Rather than being unable to concentrate as I had anticipated I seemed instead to achieve a new state of lucidity.

One of the formal problems of any kind of logical investigation, I realized, is the problem of methodological circularity—the rules of inference which the completed investigation hopes to formulate and justify must be employed during the course of the investigation itself, so that its result is the product of the application of the rules to themselves. This kind of circularity is difficult to get around. It is possible, I realized, to say then, as Kant had said, that if the basis on which we have a priori knowledge is dependent on making the distinction between phenomena and things-in-themselves, then the fact that we have such knowledge is proof that the objects of our knowledge are, as a consequence, phenomena. This statement I recognized was also epistemologically circular.

Just after eleven I heard the door to the bathroom across the corridor close and the shower being turned on. Elena would be in there for at least twenty minutes so I leisurely packed up my things and jotted down a few points I would have to follow up in the morning. Then I went quietly downstairs.

After I had pulled the door of the house closed behind me I stood for a moment waiting for my eyes to adjust to the relative darkness outside. Gradually I was able to make out details in the garden around me. The night was warm and I began to feel quite exhilarated. I quietly made my way around to the back of the house where a weak light from the open doors of Elena's bedroom illuminated the irregular pattern of leaves of the trees opposite and sculpted diffuse blocks of shadow into the shrubbery below. I stepped up onto the wheelbarrow, reached up to the lip of the wall and pulled myself up.

Moments later I was comfortably seated four or five metres above ground on a thick, smooth bough with my back leaning against the arch of an adjacent branch. There, a short distance away, directly across from me, was Elena's room, bathed in a soft light from her bedside lamp. I listened to the night fidget around me while above the sky seemed to breathe in slow, regular waves of luminosity. Behind me, in the distance, I could see the shape of the dimly lit church spire.

The bathroom light flicked off and almost immediately Elena appeared in the doorway. She was wearing her red bathrobe and had a towel wrapped around her head. She switched her radio on and I heard the opening bars to Debussy's *L'Après-midi d'un faune* reach out into the darkness towards me. She pulled up a chair and sat in front of her dressing-table. Her back was to me but I could see the reflection of her face and shoulders in the mirror in front of her. She undid the towel around her head and started drying her hair, cocking her head sideways as she did so. From time to time she stopped rubbing and shook her head. Her hair was not long and she was soon finished. She tossed her towel across to her practice rail and sat flicking strands of hair away from her face. She leaned forward pouting her lips, turning her head from side to side. She seemed to be examining her reflection intently in the mirror. Then her two hands appeared at her shoulders and, grasping the edge of her bathrobe, they pulled it slowly down behind her. The muscles of her back flickered into view. She pulled her shoulders back and her inflated ribcage and breasts suddenly appeared in the mirror. Gone was the shading of her tan into the modest paleness of the previous summer. Now she was evenly tanned all over. Obviously she had been spending her afternoons sunning herself on her balcony for some time. She sat there, her breath held, and rotated her body slowly. She drew her hands up over her breasts and across her nipples. Then, with the tips of her fingers, she lightly traced the outline of each breast against her ribcage below.

She stood and let her bathrobe fall away. She twisted from side to side again, shamelessly admiring her faultless body and then, like some miraculous vision, turned to face

117

me, her hands on her hips. There in front of me stood an image of beauty incarnate. Young, lithe, achingly beautiful. She looked back over her shoulder at her reflection. I was trembling as I watched her arch back on her toes. I clutched grimly at the cool trunk beside me, afraid I might crash to the ground. She turned and sat on the side of her bed, still facing me. In the soft light her young body seemed suffused with an inner radiance. She ran her fingers through her hair and then let herself fall softly back onto the bed. She bent one knee up towards her and reached down along her body with her hands. It took me a few moments to realize what she was doing. When I did I suddenly felt that the whole tree in which I was sitting had begun to shake and that all Elena had to do was to look out and she would see the mantle of leaves outside her window inexplicably shimmering in the moonlight. I watched her gradually surrendering to her passion. It was as though she were struggling with an invisible assailant, someone whom she was trying simultaneously to embrace and repulse. Unsuccessfully she tried to stifle her own cries as her body twisted and writhed like a thing possessed. It was like something catastrophic, indescribable, alien, inhuman almost. I squeezed my eyes shut, trying to concentrate, trying to work out what it really meant. When I opened them again Elena was sitting back at the mirror brushing her hair as though nothing had happened at all.

That night I lay for hours on my bed thinking about what I had seen before finally dropping off to sleep. When eventually I did, I dreamt I was sitting out in the tree again, watching Elena brushing her hair in front of her mirror.

She was still wearing her red silk kimono-style bathrobe and all around me, as though it were issuing from the leaves themselves, I could hear the rhapsodic melody of Debussy's music.

Then, in the moonlight at the far end of the house, I thought I glimpsed something move fleetingly through the shadows of the trees. I peered into the darkness. A silvery form flickered into view and was instantly gone again. I rubbed my eyes. Perhaps I was seeing things. I looked across at Elena. She was still sitting in front of her dressing-table mirror. I pinched myself to make sure I was awake. I was sure I was. I looked back to the end of the house just in time to see what appeared to be a faun-like figure glide noiselessly through a patch of pale moonlight and into the shadow cast by the balcony. I could see a pair of moonlit feet slowly making their way along the base of the wall of the house. Then, against a triangular patch of serrated-leafed ivy which in the moonlight looked as though it had been sculpted from hundreds of tiny sheets of burnished silver, appeared the phosphorescent shape of a naked youth. A soft mysterious light seemed to dance across his body and along the muscles in his arms and legs. He turned momentarily towards the garden and I glimpsed his face. It was, of course, Alexis.

He looked up towards the balcony and whistled the three-note melancholy call of a nightingale into the night. Elena hesitated for a moment, listening intently. He whistled again, and Elena stood, turned and ran to the balcony.

Alexis, she cried. Alexis, Alexis. Oh, how I've longed for you.

119

Elena. My darling Elena.

[You have to remember, this **was** a dream.]

He looked around desperately for a moment.

Is there a ladder or something I can use to get onto the balcony? he called softly.

There should be a wheelbarrow by the wall I think. No, no...to the right a little.

My heart sank.

Yes. Here it is, I heard him say.

In the moonlight I could see Alexis' half-aroused sex nodding heavily, like some thick-witted accomplice not quite sure what was going on but pretty excited about it nevertheless. Quietly he positioned the wheelbarrow under the balcony and like a giant ghostly cat hauled himself swiftly up and over it. They stood apart for a moment, bathed in light, before clasping each other in their arms. Elena's bathrobe fell away as Alexis' head bent to kiss her breast. At the very instant his lips closed over the dark bud of her nipple a large drop of rain splattered against my cheek. Within seconds it was teeming down. Elena and Alexis seemed oblivious to the rain as they stood there exultantly embracing each other. Finally Elena broke free and, taking Alexis by the hand, she pulled him through the open doorway into her room. She closed the doors and, unfortunately, drew the curtains.

I sat there in the rain for a few minutes, soaked and dazed by what had happened. Then I carefully lowered myself from one slippery bough to another and hung suspended for a moment or two before dropping into the garden below. I made my way back towards the front of the house. To my dismay the lounge-room light was on and through a small gap in the curtains I could see my mother sitting at the piano playing softly. Then she stopped and sat staring at the music, just staring. A shiver passed through my body as it registered the cooling dampness of my wet clothes.

On the porch I undressed and wrung as much water as I could out of them, then quietly I opened the front door. My mother had begun playing again and I could hear the sound of the piano faintly. For a horrifying moment, as I made my way noiselessly through the entrance hall, I imagined myself encountering my mother naked on the stairs. But in the event I made it back to my room without incident.

In the morning, when I awoke, I could have sworn that my clothes were still damp.

Why is it I can get **nothing** to stabilize, no order to coalesce? If only I could recall everything I had ever read. Instead, the more I throw myself into my work the less I remember. It's as if in an effort to achieve a perfect tan I had spent hours out in the sun only to find that a week later I have begun to peel.

I sat ensconced in one of my Omi's large, floral-patterned armchairs, disconsolate.

Although she looks much younger, my Omi, my grandmother, is in her seventies. She is small and grey-haired and has mischievous, unpredictable eyes. She is impatient and has a habit of finishing the sentences of the person she is talking to and then asking some apparently quite unrelated question. One often has the impression that a conversation with her is really a series of randomly connected fragments not subject to any prevailing sense of logic. People who do not know her well find this disconcerting.

On first appearances her apartment is light, open and stylish. In reality it is an impossible mixture of nineteenth-century Viennese conservatism and anarchic modernism. Most of the furniture she inherited from her parents and in its new surroundings it seems hopelessly caught between a sense of unquestioned cultural superiority and offended dignity as it unfashionably clings to memories of a quieter, more unified past. Any real sense of nostalgia however is completely banished by the chaotic splashes of colour which decorate the walls. My Omi is a passionate collector of modern art. It is an obsession with her. Unfortunately these pictures are also a source of constant pain to my father. They are tangible evidence of the undiscussed relationship that exists between my grandmother and Gerhard Liebermann, faculty colleague and Professor of Art History at my father's university and twenty years my grandmother's junior. We have no modern art works at home, nor does my father ever accompany us on our visits to the local museum.

One has the impression that her apartment belongs to a much younger woman: someone, perhaps a successful independent businesswoman in her forties, who has consciously yoked together these disparate elements in the hope of creating some shocking new decorative harmony, someone who has just popped out for a moment and whose return is imminent. The presence of my little grey-haired

122

grandmother seems then to add yet another contradictory note to the overall design.

The self-willed, chaotic personality of her youth has mellowed into an energetic, sharp-witted pragmatism. She remains the only person who can constantly out-manoeuvre my father in an intellectual discussion, who, to her glee and his exasperation, is able to reduce everything to the original and irrefutable status of their relationship as mother and son. She simply refuses to accept that the world is accessible to rational debate and, given that this is so, maintains that it is patently absurd to conduct any argument according to mutually agreed-upon rules of logic. To her, causative effect is an illusion—'ergo' simply does not exist and should be banished from the language. You can't burn the cake at both ends, she is fond of saying.

What is worse, however, is that she used to turn up uninvited to official university functions, announce who she was and, if she thought my father was being particu-larly unbearable, she would wander from group to group explaining to them how, when my father was a little boy and Wittgenstein and Moritz Schlick came to dinner, he used to get them mixed up.

Guten Abend, Herr Doktor Professor Schlick, he would say looking up at Wittgenstein with his hand outstretched.

Schlick thought this was a tremendous joke.

See, he would say laughing. What did I tell you Ludi? What did I tell you! Ah Theochen, Du bist mir wirklich lieb [Ah, my little Theo, I think you're really sweet].

And look at him now, she would say. Calls himself a logical positivist, bah!

Poor old Moritz.

You can imagine how infuriating this was for my father.

She is also an incredible snob and at times she peppers her language with wildly colourful and occasionally obscene French, English, Italian and even Russian phrases. Sometimes, particularly when she wishes to annoy my father, she will impersonate the family's former Jewish housekeeper.

As I sat there she stood opposite me looking at the image of a large print in a chrome frame newly hung over the mantelpiece. It consisted of a series of broad black brush strokes against a white background. She wanted to know what I thought of it but I wasn't really interested, my mind was elsewhere. She walked back up to it and made a minute adjustment to the way it was hanging. I had half an urge to lift my head to smell one of the flowers amongst which I seemed to be sitting. I could hear her chatting away in the distance. I had to get myself out of myself, I thought. Out of what was becoming an obsession.

Pardon, I said.

Mother well.

Yes, she's fine. You asked me already.

She laughed and turned to look at me.

How about some coffee? she said after some moments.

Sure.

A few minutes later she returned from the kitchen carrying an ornate silver tray with two delicate china cups full of black coffee. In the centre of the tray was one of her outrageously flamboyant creations for which the name cake was just not appropriate. I had to laugh.

Wow, that's incredible, I said. What's it called?

Jugendstilkuchen. I got it from my new art-deco cookbook. Do you like it?

It's fantastic, I said.

This cheered me up somewhat and as I sat there talking to my grandmother I became aware that she wasn't saying anything of real consequence at all. Instead she seemed to be waiting for me to pluck up enough courage to broach the subject of what had so obviously been bothering me. But how on earth could I tell her about what had led to my life becoming permeated with a sense of strange and relentless erotic presentiment—that I could be sitting on a bus staring absent-mindedly out of the window when the fleeting glimpse of a tanned calf muscle or the momentary arch of an eyebrow would suddenly send a succession of vivid and disturbing images racing through my mind. And just at the moment when I thought one of these crises had passed I would glance innocently across at the patterned trunk of a plane tree and off I'd go again. But I felt that if I didn't tell someone soon, I would go mad.

Now Wolfi, the cake, you hardly touched it. You got something the matter with you. A boy your age should eat. Aren't you happy?

Oh Omi, I think I'm going crazy, really, I'm going crazy.

Only two things drive a boy your age crazy. Either you got a girlfriend who don't love you or you don't got a girlfriend who loves you.

You're too romantic, Omi. It's not that. Well, not exactly that.

Then what's the matter?

I'm eighteen, I said.

So?

I looked at her desperately.

I'm eighteen and I still haven't slept with a woman. It's driving me crazy. How can I call myself a man if I haven't slept with a woman?

I told her I saw the world divided into those who had and those who hadn't. Making love for the first time, actually holding a woman in your arms, well it must be like crossing some invisible barrier, like entering some other cosmic dimension, like being born or dying. I flung my arm out in a wide arc. She sat there patiently listening to me until it seemed clear to her that I had finished.

This is serious, she said. Or perhaps she said, Are you serious? I can't remember. When I look back on this conversation with my grandmother I must admit I feel utterly foolish that I could have taken the business of sex so seriously. And yet whenever I **have** gone to bed with someone new, I have still had a faint echo of the feelings I described so clumsily to my grandmother that day.

She excused herself and went into the kitchen and closed the door. I could hear the muffled sound of her voice and a few minutes later she returned.

It's all arranged, she said, handing me a piece of paper and a sizeable sum of money.

Here is the address of someone who'll look after you. Her name is Andrea and your appointment is for two o'clock tomorrow. You have all afternoon, so take your time. She's very pretty and I hear she's very good at what she does. Think of it as part of your education.

But Omi, the money?

Money, money, Wolfi. What's money. You have to live. Enjoy yourself, just enjoy yourself. No more of this moping about.

I kissed her on the cheek.

Now, I have some things to do so you'll have to run along, okay?

She showed me to the door and I kissed her again on the forehead and said goodbye.

*

Where are we? So Kant distinguished objects and events as they appear in our experience from objects and events as they are in themselves, independently of the forms imposed on them by our cognitive faculties. The perversion of the 'real' or essential nature of reality by the act of perception is central to his philosophy. All we can ever know, he thought, are phenomena.

On the other hand, Hume's empiricism was attacked for its phenomenalism, that is, for the view that physical objects, as well as human beings, are no more than collections of their observable properties. 'Observable properties' in this context refers exclusively to sensory qualities. Hume held that all concepts derive directly from sensory experience and, moreover, that all nouns naming physical objects refer to concepts that can be completely analysed into simple concepts referring to sensory qualities. This is what had so bowled Wittgenstein over [hatte ihn wirklich umgehauen].

In the twentieth century the whole situation, however, was inverted. Phenomenologists claimed that phenomenological statements were non-empirical. What they describe are 'phenomena'. And what are phenomena? Incredibly, phenomena are now 'essences'. And what's more, they are intuited! What they are definitely not are particular observable objects by reference to which empirical statements are confirmed or denied. Phenomena have turned out to be noumena—things-in-themselves. This is even more paradoxical given the fact that Husserl insisted that phenomenology was descriptive. This distinguished the method of phenomenology, he thought, from the established practice of philosophy which deduced what must be true of the world from prior assumption, instead of looking at the world and discovering what it is like. It looks as though we're back where we began.

*

Like many major European provincial centres the inner-city business district of G. is expanding. Warehouses, old hotels and some of the larger former residences which used to surround the area are being transformed into professional suites, exclusive boutiques and expensive apartments. It was into one of these elegant tree-lined streets opposite Hindenberg Park that I turned the next day. I had not known what to wear and in the end had opted for my Sunday best, and now as I walked along the street looking for the number written on the piece of paper in my hand I felt, as you can imagine, both nervous and conspicuous.

Number 36 was an imposing six-storeyed brownstone building which two hundred years ago must have looked quite grand indeed. A small flight of stairs led up to a rather formal entrance which was flanked by two new salons retailing exclusive fashion for women. The designs could not have been more different and the mannequins in the display windows seemed to have been deliberately arranged to give the impression that neither would have been seen dead in any of the other's so-called 'creations'—an arched shoulder here, a head thrown back there.

Five to two. This was it. With my heart pounding I made my way up the flight of stairs into the plush foyer of the building. Music filtered down from some invisible source in the ceiling through the large polished leaves of the ferns dotted about the place. It was quite busy—men in suits and efficient-looking women were coming and going. The lift opposite me opened and another small wave of noisy success brushed self-importantly past me. I waited for a rather distinguished-looking gentleman carrying a black leather briefcase and wearing a bowler hat [eine Melone] to enter the lift before I too got in. We stood for a moment facing back into the foyer until we both realized that neither of us had pressed the button for us to ascend. Simultaneously we reached for the same floor and our fingers collided momentarily. I mumbled an awkward apology, he raised his eyes and the doors hissed shut.

When we reached level 4 each of us appeared as reluctant as the other to leave the lift first. What if there had been some dreadful mistake? What if he thought **he** had an appointment with Andrea at two? What then? As we slowly walked down the corridor shoulder to shoulder I could feel myself beginning to sweat. We passed suite 2. Suite 3 was next and there were only four suites to a floor.

Suite 3. I stopped, fully expecting my temporary companion to stop too, but fortunately he continued on. I glanced at my watch. Two minutes to two. I took a deep breath to regain my composure and my confidence began to return. After all, I was here for an almost professional consultation. Certain matters would be discussed and Andrea, I knew, had been fully briefed about the exact nature of my problem. A suitably lengthy visit had been arranged. What could be simpler?

As I stood there looking at the sign on her door I was impressed by just how professional the whole arrangement was. In gilt letters the sign read: 'A. Rudlinger and Associates'. I realized just how naive I had been. Why, in this day and age, shouldn't a business retailing sins of the flesh be organized like any other consultative enterprise.

I adjusted my tie for the last time and knocked forcefully on the door.

Come in, a female voice called from the other side. It's open.

I turned the handle and strode confidently in. Directly opposite me sat an attractive young woman at a desk. In front of her was an electric typewriter and in her hands she held what was obviously a leather-bound appointments book. To her right was a low, glass-topped coffee table upon which several glossy fashion magazines were carefully scattered. Beside these stood a single long-stemmed rose in a glass vase. Behind the table was a large comfortable-looking sofa. On the wall above this was an equally large modern print which I recognized as one my Omi also owned.

Sonderborg, I said, half to myself.

Bravo, the young woman cried as I turned back to look at her. She had taken off her glasses and now sat smiling up at me.

I have an appointment for two o'clock, I said. My name is Wolfi...ah Wolfgang Schönborn.

She replaced her glasses and picked up the book again.

What time did you say your appointment was for, Mr...

Schönborn. Yes, um...Two o'clock.

There must be some mistake Mr Schönborn. I don't seem to have you listed for today.

She quickly checked the days either side. My heart began to sink.

When did you say you made your appointment?

I didn't. My Om . . My grandmother made it for me... yesterday. She said everything had been arranged...

Just a moment.

She picked up her phone, pressed a button and spoke into it:

Herr Rosenthal, sorry to disturb you. I have a young man here who says he has an appointment for two o'clock. You didn't by any chance take an appointment yesterday did you?

There was a short pause and she replaced the receiver.

Who was your appointment with Mr Schönborn?

I was just about to answer when what must have been Herr Rosenthal appeared through a door behind her.

What seems to be the problem, Mr...?

Schönborn. Wolfgang Schönborn.

I see. Well then, who was it you were supposed to see?

Andrea, I said.

By this stage my palms had begun to sweat with the growing realization that something was dreadfully, dreadfully wrong. I suspected my grandmother of some grotesque practical joke.

Andrea? he repeated.

131

He looked at me for a moment and then leant down to whisper something in the young woman's ear. He rose and stood gazing at me again for a few seconds with a look almost of anguish. Then he turned and walked back into his office. A series of what sounded like suppressed sobs issued from behind his closed door.

The young, infinitely desirable receptionist looked seriously up at me.

Is it true that your grandmother made your appointment, Wolfi?

Yes, I said.

Wonderful. Just wonderful, she replied enigmatically.

She smiled up at me and I smiled down at her. I shuffled a little on my feet.

Well Wolfi…I don't know how to say this, but this is suite 3, level 4. Rudlinger and Associates are interior design consultants. Andrea is waiting for you in suite 4, level 3. Down the corridor, downstairs, first door on your left.

She got up from behind her desk, walked to the door and opened it.

There's a good boy. Don't take it too badly. Enjoy yourself…oh, and Wolfi, say hello to your Omi for me.

As I walked to the door she touched me lightly on the shoulder.

Out in the corridor I forced myself to walk normally, reining in an urge to run, to flee as fast as I could down what now appeared to be a never-ending tunnel closing in around me. How could I have made such a complete fool of myself? 'Rudlinger and Associates are interior design consultants…' Mensch! The events of the last few minutes ricocheted through my head, while an echo of suppressed laughter reverberated around me. I imagined them retelling my story for years to come—towards the end of drunken dinner parties. He would barely be able to get the words out for laughter. Tossing himself back in his chair, wiping the tears from his cheeks.

And who, who...who made the appointment, Mr Schönborn? My grandmother, he says. Can you imagine that? There he stood, like a schoolboy, cap in hand...and he says—my grandmother!

The laughter crashed around the walls again as I waded on. I glanced back over my shoulder. The beautiful young receptionist was still standing there outside her door. She smiled faintly and her hand appeared to rise slowly and wave to me, a wave full of nostalgia, as though I were boarding a ship about to leave port for some unknown and mysterious destination. And now as I stood at the railing looking down at the girl I loved, I knew we would never see each other again.

On the landing I leant against the wall and rested for a moment. I wiped the dampness from my forehead and fanned my face with my hand. I looked at my watch. It was two minutes past two. I was stunned. I felt like I had been in there for hours. I watched as the seconds ticked over. Three minutes past two. I began to feel vaguely reassured— I was hardly late at all. I wouldn't even have to explain why I had been delayed. I could still arrive at Andrea's door as though nothing had happened, or perhaps nothing more than a few minutes wait for a slow lift. My confidence began to return.

The door to suite 4 was, of course, unadorned. After a moment's hesitation, I knocked. Almost immediately a young woman appeared in the doorway.

I have read of instants in which the protagonist of a novel, by Proust or Joyce for example, suddenly experiences a powerful visionary moment of epiphanal insight, triggered off by some chance occurrence which transports them from the world of the mundane into a world in which everything is bathed in a luminous halo of light, a light in which all that had previously seemed completely random or purposeless instantaneously coalesces into a unified whole, and that the apprehension of such a moment becomes, for the protagonist, a truly mystical experience. As I stood in the doorway looking into Andrea's eyes, I experienced such a moment, an instant of rarefied insight suspended in time. Here, standing before me, was a slightly older but no less beautiful version of my sister Elena. Here were the same dark impetuous eyes, the same full smiling mouth, the same irrepressible sensual vitality. In Andrea, however, the fledgling coquette had given way to a look of knowing delight. I felt simultaneously exhilarated and ineffably serene [unbeschreiblich gelassen], as though my life to date had all been heading inevitably towards this moment of apocalyptic summation. I sensed also that the young woman who now took my arm and gently led me into the room, knew and understood this.

I followed her to a large couch covered in white, heavily textured material and she invited me to sit down. She put some music on and then came and sat near me drawing one leg up under her. She rested her arm along the top of the couch. I remember thinking how its smooth texture and soft even colour contrasted with the material of the lounge below.

She was simply dressed—a light, loose-fitting blouse tucked into a brightly coloured cotton skirt, both of which seemed designed to simultaneously reveal and conceal her youthful body beneath. A single-stranded silver necklace followed the undulations of her neck and this was complemented by a pair of beautiful silver pendant earrings, one of which now oscillated slowly from her right ear. Apart from a trace of subtle blush to her lips and cheeks, she appeared not to be wearing any make-up. Her hand reached up to brush a strand of dark hair from her forehead. She smiled at me.

You are a very attractive young man, Wolfi, she said. We shall enjoy each other. We have all afternoon, so there's no need to hurry. Omi tells me it's your first time.

I shrugged and nodded, opening my hands to her as if they contained some invisible gift. What could I say?

We shall take things slowly—as if you were beginning to learn to play a musical instrument.

I tried to concentrate on what she was saying. I watched her lips moving. I wondered how many men or women could remember the first breast they had kissed or the first lips they had touched. I was determined to register every detail, every sensation, every breath I took in Andrea's presence. If only I concentrated, then time would never dispossess me of this, the ultimate of all experiences.

Andrea got up and walked into the kitchen where I watched her prepare two drinks. She came back to sit down again and handed me mine. We touched glasses

135

and I sipped the slightly herbal-tasting cold clear liquid. She placed her drink on a small table beside the sofa and resumed her former position. She certainly seemed in no hurry and merely sat half-smiling, looking at me.

I felt myself relax. My gaze began to wander about the room, absorbing more of this strange creature from the surroundings in which she lived. Her apartment was elegantly and comfortably furnished. The walls of the living room were wall-papered in a deep red, the effect of which would have been overwhelming were it not for a number of large paintings which seemed to pierce the red plane against which they were suspended. Again some of them reminded me of paintings my grandmother owned. Against the wall behind me was a bookshelf with a surprising number of books in it, mostly on art and art history. The rest of the wall was covered with photographs. There was also a doorway which, I presumed, led into one of the bedrooms. At the far end of the living room there was a row of windows which looked out over the tree tops to the street below and the park opposite. In front of the windows and parallel to them was a long, very modern-looking wooden table. On it sat an ancient stone bowl with a large fracture in its rim and this was flanked by two simple fluted vases. Each of these I remember contained a single yellow chrysanthemum. I continued my sweep around the room, lingering for a moment on a small bronze figurine of what at first appeared to be an old woman leaning on a walking stick, but which closer scrutiny revealed to be a decrepit blind man groping his way for breasts, two oh my God, beautiful bra breasts faint nipples. Concentrate, concentrate.

Your blouse? I said.

She shrugged her shoulders.

Look at me, Wolfi.

My confusion began to mount. What did she mean by 'me'. Her eyes? Those infinitely revealing and yet infinitely mysterious dark wells into which I now gazed. Wasn't this what people meant when they said look at me. Or did she mean her smiling mouth, or her neck perhaps? Or was it the two dark centres of her breasts which were now outlined beneath the translucent fabric of her bra? What was 'me' when images of Elena kept floating up into my consciousness? And in addition to this there was the overwhelming power of Andrea's physical presence which set my whole being trembling. Andrea's physical presence—what did this mean? Her body? Her beautiful, young, irresistible, heavenly body? This flesh and blood. Was this 'me'.

She moved forward, nearer to me. My heart began to race and my head to spin. I couldn't concentrate on what was happening. She took my hand and ran the tips of my fingers across the small hard swellings of her still concealed breasts. She reached up behind her back with my hands, drawing me to her as she did. She lightly brushed my lips with hers, then bent her head. I felt her tongue graze the lobe of my left ear. I could hear her breathing become momentarily suspended as she released the clasp behind her. She drew away slowly to free herself fully. Again she took my hands and traced the curve of her breasts along her rib cage in a long slow arc. For the first time in my life I felt that strange pliant weight. She arched her back and pulled my head down to her chest.

137

Kiss me, Wolfi. Let your tongue glide over my nipples…
That's it, that's it. Ah, that's soooo nice.

I felt them change shape, grow harder. I wanted to call time out, get myself together, slow things down. I felt I was beginning to lose consciousness. Instead she pulled my head abruptly away and stood, dragging me to my feet. She undid my tie, then unbuttoned my shirt and pulled it playfully out of my trousers. She was laughing as she grasped it in her two hands and, in one fluid movement which ended in an embrace, pulled it open and down my back. The cool softness of her body and the two small nodes of pressure against my chest began to enflame me [mich zu entflammen]. Her face arched up and she gave me a long, full kiss. Then she pulled away until our lips barely touched and instead, merely brushed caressingly against each other. I felt as if each tiny cell in my body had come to life and now reached out after that lingering, infinitely intangible touch. She let the tip of her tongue glide lightly across my lips and then kissed me again. I watched her eyes close as she seemed to lose herself in the warmth of our embrace.

Then she broke free and pushed me sharply in the middle of my chest so that I toppled back onto the sofa. She bent down and grasped my shoes in her hands and, with a flick of her wrists, sent them sailing over her head. She knelt and roughly pulled my knees apart. She undid my belt. Now off with these, she said as she worked at my trousers with a combination of playful fury and mock ineptitude. I felt increasingly mesmerized by the intricate pattern of arcs, ellipses, crescents and parabolas her restless nipples etched into the retina of my sensual being.

These celestial mammary trajectories fascinated me and even then I remember thinking that perhaps some infantile primaeval urge had been suddenly resurrected from my subconscious—that perhaps during those early post-natal months of incoherent visual stimuli there was not some primitive biologically encoded mechanism which caused every tiny putti-like hand automatically to reach out after the random tracery of those blurred orbs in search of sensual gratification. Could it be that the smooth, dark-centred fullness of a mother's breast became, as it were, as archetypal 'madeleine', condemning man to a more or less hypnotic trance whenever they, or something else in the natural world, inadvertently resonated with the oscillation of this inchoate erotic stimulus? Who knows, perhaps Galileo's interest in pendulum motion could be traced back to an early image of a richly coloured areola suspended before his smiling, chubby little cherub face.

Andrea was clearly enjoying this well-choreographed prelude to the more serious and heady exploration of her sensual geography that was to come. Having succeeded in loosening my trousers, she had gathered them in a large concertina'd bundle around my ankles and now commanded me to raise my legs. She stood and, with one swift unravelling, cast them over her right shoulder in a long tumbling trajectory which was prematurely interrupted by a hat stand in the corner, where they hung for an instant with one leg bizarrely outstretched before slumping into a configuration of surrealistic dejection.

Of course, by this stage I had reached an obvious state of arousal and Andrea knelt between my knees again and slipped my impeccably starched and newly purchased underwear expertly off.

Io sono gentile, ma tu non sei un gentile. Ma è bello, molto bello, she said.

She cradled me in her hands and began talking to me as if I were a third person, admiring me as though I were a prized possession. Then I watched as her head slowly bent and she raised me to her lips. I know this sounds ridiculous, but that moment of exquisite, breathtaking contact became for me a moment of sudden and transcendent philosophical insight. For the first time in my life, with Andrea bent tenderly over me, I became conscious of the real implications of the Hegelian dialectic—the implicit, irrefutable duality of the world, the polarity of human thought, the constant apposition of thesis and antithesis, noumenon and phenomenon, body and soul, reason and passion, Io e lui. The whole of Western philosophy seemed to me to be paradoxically defined by this strange and exciting ritual, as if it were, so to speak, inextricably linked to the male-femaleness of human existence, to this, the most fundamental of human dichotomies.

It was difficult to imagine, so natural and spontaneous was her behaviour, that this was all probably an act, an act she was paid to make appear as fresh and uncalculated as possible. Even in my state of heightened sensory intoxication I was still aware of how theatrical much of what she was doing was. For a long time I was to wonder whether her motivation had been purely financial or not. It wasn't until some months, or perhaps even a year later that, as I walked through the busy central shopping area of G., I felt someone touch me lightly on my arm and I turned to see Andrea's smiling eyes looking into mine.

Wolfi, she said a little breathlessly. How are you? I was just sitting over there having some coffee when I saw you walking by. Would you like to join me? I would be so glad if you did.

We went back to her table and she ordered another coffee.

I'm so happy to see you, she said. That day was such a wonderful day. You know, I felt I was really doing something for you. I kept putting myself in your position—saying, now if it were me what would I like? I wanted you to live forever with a memory of your first sexual experience that you'd never forget. I even half expected to see you again, but as time went by I became less and less sure about whether you **had** enjoyed me...

She hesitated for a moment, looked slightly flustered and then said.

Did you enjoy me, Wolfi?

I told her that that day had been one of the most wonderful days of my life. I related what had happened before I arrived, what a fool I had made of myself, the look of disbelief on the receptionist's face when I told her my grandmother had made the appointment and what a sensation I had caused when I eventually arrived home that night. She wiped the tears of laughter from her eyes as she dwelt on the images my words conjured up in her mind.

The conversation became more intimate as we recalled some of the details of that day. She said how startled I had looked when she had said, Non sei pagano, ma sei bello, and had started caressing me with her tongue, repeating what her fingers had so deliciously done, and how, at the end of one long tongue-tickling caress, she had gently eased me into her mouth. I remembered her teasing me like this for some minutes. Then, suddenly, she had stopped!

Now you have to do the same to me, she had said, and she stood up, her hands on her hips. She held her head high, looking down at me with eyes as cool and dark as moonlight shimmering on a summer sea. I knelt before her, unzipping her light skirt and let it fall to her feet. My cheek grazed her hip and I slipped my fingers under the slender piece of material which was all that remained to conceal her nakedness. Even as I write I can still vividly see, centimetres away from my face, her dark tangle of pubic hair emerge. I can see the moulded form of her sex and the mysterious folds of flesh which conceal her intricacy within.

She drew me up, pressing her open mouth against mine, twisting her lips, engulfing me.

Then she broke free and fell back onto the sofa.

Have you ever seen a woman's sex before? Andrea asked.

[Hast Du jemals zuvor das Geschlecht einer Frau gesehen? fragte Andrea.]

I shook my head.

Kneel down then.

As I did she raised her legs. I could glimpse nestled between the dark declivity of two longitudinal ridges a small inner fissure surrounded by two glistening, soft, petal-like pink folds. Compared to my own sex hers seemed strange, complex and mysterious. She reached down with

142

both hands and by placing her finger tips along these two ridges and slowly drawing them apart she magically, as though everting some rare and exotic fruit, revealed herself to me. It was as though she had suddenly blossomed and where previously her sex had seemed so hidden, so innocent, the full, intricate, yet still mysterious terrain of her sensual being, with its subtle shadings of the most delicate rose blush to its full, dark, plum-coloured fringes now appeared exposed before me. For some reason totally unknown to me I thought of falling autumn leaves reflected in an Oriental lily-pond glazed by a pale night light.

Then, with one of her fingers, she pulled back on the short ridge formed by the intersection of her petal-like inner lips to reveal a tiny, paler, glistening pink bud.

Wolfi, she said, you see this little spot. I want you to run your tongue lightly over it. If you bend your head down and wrap your arms around the tops of my legs you'll be able to pull me closer to you. And if you hold this little fold of skin back with your lips you'll be able to draw me into your mouth and caress me with your tongue.

She reached her hands behind her knees and pulled them towards her chest, making it easier for me to bend down and kiss her. I placed my thumbs where she had and, cautiously, pulled them apart. Magically her sex blossomed again. This was incredible. I leaned down as she had told me to do. She shivered as my lips touched those dark petals and, tentatively, like someone testing the water with their toe, I pushed them open with my tongue. I looked up to see my reflection swimming in Andrea's moist eyes.

143

I remember thinking how utterly extraordinary all of this was. These whorls and eddies of pink flesh were like a tiny mirror of the universe to me. Inscribed within them seemed to be some inscrutable, unfathomable truth about the world. If only one could unlock their intricate pattern.

I bent down again and resumed my exploration of her with my tongue. My confidence grew as I began to locate that tiny pale bud with increasing accuracy. Each time I did so I felt her catch her breath and push herself harder against me. Her warm heady fragrance enveloped me. Then a curious and unexpected thing happened. Her sex began to change shape! Under my mouth everything, I felt, had started to become more prominent, more rigid. Unbelievably, that tiny bud now seemed to reach out to me after each caress! She began to writhe against me.

Don't stop, don't stop Wolfi, she whispered.

I began to feel an extraordinary sense of power hearing her moaning, and as I glanced up I saw her running her hands lightly across her breasts. Images of Elena glimpsed between the dancing silhouettes of dark pendulous leaves came flooding back [Durch tanzende Silhouetten dunkler herabhängender Blätter flüchtig gesehene Bilder von Elena überschwemmten mich noch einmal]. Her young body glistened.

Suddenly she grasped my head and pulled it sharply against her. Sie rieb sich in mein Gesicht [She ground herself into my face]. Her whole body seemed to coil, like a crossbow being cocked, and then she exploded in a series of sharp percussive shudders whose aftershocks coursed through her entire body and set her breasts quivering against the luminous air above them.

Oh God, oh God, she whimpered.

As these aftershocks finally began to die away, her body began to relax. I watched as the contours of her sex slowly began to resume their former shape. I felt awed by the power of her ecstasy. She had seemed projected for a moment into another dimension, a dimension in which the normal laws of cause and effect, of time itself, seemed held in abeyance. This violent implosion was almost frightening, as though she were matter encountering anti-matter. I sensed the strange otherness of this creature whose sexual response seemed to manifest itself in every corpuscle, every cell, every nerve of her body, and against which my own largely localized response seemed puny and inconsequential. I felt that this difference symbolized the mystery and essential unknowability of woman. And yet I also knew that from this day on I would be irresistibly drawn to and fascinated by this process of a woman's withdrawal into a world of private ecstasy, the crossing of whose border was so shatteringly manifested [dessen Grenze zu überschreiten eine so überwältigende Wirkung hervorbrachte]. I kissed her lightly again, but she gently pushed me away.

No, no Wolfi. Wait. It's too sensitive. You have to wait a moment. But you were wonderful, really wonderful. Come and kiss me.

I came up beside her and she wrapped her arms around me and gave me a long, languorous, affectionate kiss.

Wonderful, wonderful Wolfi, she said again dreamily.

145

I felt elated and proud as she absent-mindedly caressed my back. I lay alongside her, one hand playing with her dark hair. The other lay across her breast tracing the rise and fall of her breathing.

We must have dozed for a few minutes and I awoke to feel her stirring beside me. She got up a little unsteadily and stretched her arms up behind her head. I watched her sleepily. Here was a nymph, someone who didn't belong to this world. She belonged to another world, the world of myth. This was the world into which she was projected in her moments of ecstasy, into the realm of the gods.

She yawned, gave a slight shiver and disappeared for a moment into the bedroom. She returned with two soft towels, one of which she threw to me.

Come on, she said, let's have a lovely hot shower and go to bed.

The water reinvigorated both of us and as I ran the soap over her back and chest she squealed with delight.

God, it's ridiculous, she said. When I make love I'm totally okay. Any other time I'm unbelievably ticklish. Crazy isn't it.

She let the water run over her head for a few seconds, then turned the shower off. We dried each other and she wound her towel up around her head and we went back out into the bedroom. She pulled the covers down and told me to get in. I lay there with my head propped up on my elbow as she went back to her dressing table and sat in front of the mirror to dry her hair. Her slender back and torso in half profile accentuated the curve of her breasts. I thought she was incredibly beautiful. I could see her face in the mirror and from time to time her reflection looked fleetingly across at me and smiled.

She finished and came over and slid in beside me. I could feel myself absorbing the warmth radiating from her body. She kissed me and rolled onto her back pulling me over on top of her. She opened her legs, reached down and guided me into her. Her arms and legs encircled me as we began to rock slowly back and forth.

Slowly Wolfi. Slowly, slowly.

She kissed me again, lightly, grazingly, infinitely softly. I looked into her face to catch a glimpse of a fleeting smile pass across her lips as she closed her eyes. It was a look of ineffable nostalgia, as though suddenly she had become aware of the transience of her own youth, of her own ephemeral beauty.

It was already after six when I said goodbye to Andrea, and forgetting that it was Wednesday and that my grandmother would be at my parents' for dinner, I had caught the bus to her apartment. It was only after I had climbed the stairs and breathlessly knocked on her door that I realized my mistake so that by the time I arrived home, having been obliged to wait twenty minutes for another bus, it was getting on for eight and the evening meal I knew would be well underway.

When Omi came to dinner, dinners were formal. The table was set with candles and flowers and my mother spent the entire afternoon giving the silverware a thorough going-over. But what really characterized these meals was the truly magnificent set of bone china that was used exclusively for such occasions. It had been handed down to my Omi by her mother on her wedding day and, in turn, had been given to my mother when she married my father. Now it would be laid extravagantly out. Its use, however, merely added to the already considerable nervous tension which surrounded these meals. It was as if each piece had been sanctified, and while none had ever been broken in its 150-year history the slightest harshness of contact inadvertently produced between spoon and bowl or knife and plate was enough to have my father menacingly glower in your direction. Its use seemed to be my father's only real concession to stupidity, as though he were deliberately tempting providence by allowing these hallowed objects to be desecrated by the heathens with whom he was forced to live. Perhaps this is an exaggeration, but, in any case, my early childhood memories of these meals are coloured by a feeling of oppressive terror as I observed out of the corner of my eye my father's set jaw and scowling forehead.

Omi on these occasions, however, was the source of an apparently deliberate and constant clatter. She would flamboyantly wield her knife and fork momentarily above her head as she emphatically made some point or other and then would swoop down to batter and attack whatever lay on her plate. My father was never able to disguise the look of pained incredulity on his face when my grandmother made some particularly horrendous gesture. But this just seemed to fill her with a sense of malicious delight, a delight that expressed itself, sometimes for no apparent reason, in the spontaneous eruption of her high-pitched laughter, as though the desperate absurdity of it all had suddenly overwhelmed her.

My entrance into the dining room where my family was gathered around the meal table and the scene that followed must have been truly sensational. My father, seated at the head of the table and impeccably dressed in top coat and bow tie, despite the heat, was caught slightly stooped as he lifted his spoon to his mouth. His lips had already begun to pucker, reaching out for the now suspended yet still steaming broth, a few tiny droplets of which escaped the rim of his spoon and elliptically sped around to their nadir where, momentarily, they looked like liquid nipples suspended from Andrea's now proverbial breasts, before releasing themselves back into the bowl from whence they had come. Tiny beads of perspiration had formed or were forming on my father's forehead due to a combination of the rather sultry night and the proximity of his head to his already mentioned soup bowl.

The fact that they were eating soup was a bad sign. It meant that they had waited for me to arrive home and when I had failed to appear would have been ushered to the table with some exasperated remark by my father.

Omi sat to my father's right and as I entered she gave a quick half-smile in my direction, glanced at my father and continued eating. Elena sat opposite her. Both her forearms rested on the table and in her hand she held her empty spoon. She too glanced quickly at me over my mother's head and then looked rapidly around the table, first at my grandmother, then at my father and then back at my mother who faced away from me and was obviously still unaware of my presence. She was in the midst of saying something to my grandmother when she caught my father's eye. He sat back in his chair and lowered his hand. My mother turned and gazed anxiously at me. I looked alternately at each of their faces, smiling. The clock on the mantelpiece continued ticking. I rose a little on my toes.

I am a man, I announced.

My mother's anxiety gave way to a look of perplexity. My father's expression remained unchanged. I was ecstatic. Still beaming, I repeated what I had said, enunciating each word clearly.

Ich–bin–ein–Mann!

Omi, who had been watching my father out of the corner of her eye from the moment I made my announcement, turned to me and smiled. Then in a perfect imitation of my father's pedantic voice she asked me the very question he had asked me a thousand times before.

Yes Wolfgang. But how do you **know** you are a man?

Seven words was all it took. Seven little words and that veil of incomprehension was whipped forever away.

I have just slept with a prostitute, I proclaimed.

[Ich habe gerade mit einer Prostituierten geschlafen.]

The scene which now unfolded was as though the detailed depiction of the family gathering in the eighteenth-century painting which hung on the wall behind them had suddenly come to life. My mother slumped to the table, overbalancing the water-jug which stood beside her left elbow, sending it crashing against the base of one of the silver candelabra, spilling its contents as it did so and breaking a large fragment from its delicately fluted lip. She cradled her head in her arms and began to sob. One had the impression that the water which had now reached

150

the overhanging edge of the white lace tablecloth and had begun to drip in a quick syncopated patter to the floor issued not from the overturned jug but from my mother herself. Elena rose to comfort her but produced instead an even more violent convulsion of tears as she laid her hand across my mother's shoulders.

My father's expression, in the meantime, continued unchanged, but as my mother's sobbing subsided he looked down at the table, momentarily appearing as if he were about to say something. Then he looked up again, picked up his napkin, began to fold it, decided against this and threw it instead into the middle of the table. He shifted his chair back, rose, adjusted his coat, took one look at us all, turned, and walked out.

Omi just sat there looking at me, a beatific smile on her face.

I turned myself and went up to my room.

We were never to use that ancient crockery again.

Later that evening, as I lay on my bed thinking about the day's events, I heard a soft knocking at my door. I got up and opened it. Elena stood there nervously.

Can I come in for a minute, Wolfi?

I gestured with my hand for her to enter and I pushed the door to. She sat on the edge of my bed and I sat in the chair beside my desk. Neither of us spoke as she looked around my room as though for the first time. I asked her how my mother was.

Oh she's fine now, she said, although she keeps muttering something about her poor baby.

She laughed.

God, what a night, she said as if to herself. And then again: What a night.

I watched her hesitate for a moment as she formulated something in her head.

Wolfi, she asked tentatively, tell me about it...

What?

You know. You and the prostitute. I mean, what was it like? How old was she? Was she attractive?

I told her more or less what had happened, leaving aside the role my grandmother had played and how much Andrea had looked like her. She just sat there, occasionally smiling and drawing her shoulders up and pressing her hands together as she imagined some minor detail to herself.

God, how did you have the courage? she said when I had finished. You must have been crazy. And then to come home and announce it! To stand there and say: 'I am a man'. I mean, what a sensation.

She stood up and did a little pirouette with her arms clasped about her.

Oh Wolfi, that was so romantic. Wunderschön war es.

As I walked her to the door she turned suddenly and embraced me, kissing me on the mouth.

You're a hero Wolfi, she said. A real hero.

After that night things were never to be the same.

*

Philosophers since Descartes had been accustomed to maintain that all knowledge is based on the contents of one's own mind. Idealists like Bradley and phenomenalists like Mill took as indisputable the fact that the existence of the objects of *perception consists in the fact that they are perceived. Mach however denied that what is immediately perceived **is** a state of mind. Descartes had presumed, wrongly according to Mach, that in being aware of 'representation' we are simultaneously aware of the act of representing to ourselves. This is where Husserl's phenomenological analysis of mind enters. It is an attempt to intuit directly the essence of various mental acts. The end point of all this however is that we can know nothing except our own mental states. There is no such thing as an external reality which exists independently of the mind which perceives it.*

*There is no such thing as X, asserts that there **is** such a thing as X which does not exist, against which all things that do exist in some way fail.*

Should this read:

*There is no such thing as, X asserts that there **is** such a thing as X which does not exist, against which all things that do exist in some way fail.*

This is more logical.

18

(I must confess that even before I had reached this point in my first reading of the material Wolfi sent me, I had already begun to suspect that there was more amiss in Wolfi's family than either the breakdown of his parents' relationship or the unsatisfactory relationship between him and his father. My suspicions were intensified when I discovered between the previous bundle of papers and the next a photograph

153

carefully wrapped in a sheet of newspaper. It was a photograph I recognized instantly.

Now as I sit looking at it, looking at Elena standing there with Anya supported on her hip, it is Anya's **eyes** that immediately strike me. They are almost unnaturally blue, unnaturally intense. In my mind I can see an image of Wolfi as I saw him for the first time, standing nervously outside the door to my room in Heidelberg. I see **his** intense blue eyes, and then through them, I see Elena on the beach. I see the wisp of pubic hair poking out from beneath her swimming costume. I feel Wolfi registering her as a separate being for the first time.

Returning to the photograph, I look first at Anya's face and then at Elena's—and back. The resemblance is unmistakable. Behind Elena's smile she seems to be laughing, as though at some shared secret. I reread the inscription: 'Viele Grüsse von Deinen zwei Lieblingen' [A big hello from your two little darlings].

For a long time I sat trying to reformulate conversations I had had with Wolfi, trying to piece together chance remarks that might have confirmed or denied what I had begun to think. I tried to recall when Anya had first come up in our conversation, what exactly **had** been said. I felt as you would feel if, as a reader, you were now forbidden to go back to the conversation that took place the day she actually was first mentioned. And yet I cannot be sure that this **was** the first time. I simply cannot remember.

Moreover, it did not end there. It wasn't until I had begun to rewrap the photograph and the phrase 'sexuelles Verlangen' [sexual desire] caught my eye that I took a good look at the piece of newspaper in which it had been wrapped. It was a page torn from the issue of *Die Zeit* dated 12 June 1982. On it was reprinted an interview with the Latin-American writer Ramon Fernandez together with the last half of one of his short stories. I have translated this from the *Die Zeit* article **not** from the original Spanish. An alternative version can be found in Fernandez's collection *Internal Exile and other stories* [Hoddard & Co., New York, 1984]. It would be years before I was able to confirm that its inclusion had been no accident.)

RAMON FERNANDEZ

ZEIT *Sein eigener Gefangener [Internal Exile]* **has received a lot of attention for its startling beginning...**

FERNANDEZ The view of Inocenta as a child, an angelic vision?

ZEIT Yes. Some commentators however have felt that the transition to Placido's point of view in the latter half of the story is too obviously symbolic of the fracture in the relationship between Inocenta and Placido that follows.

FERNANDEZ Yes, perhaps you are right. But remember, Placido never actually stops loving her, and in a sense, it is his actions, his withdrawal, which forces Inocenta to act as she does. Initially the story was quite different...quite different. Perhaps now, as you say, it is a bit heavy handed.

ZEIT Different in what way?

FERNANDEZ Well the story, you know, began as a commission for Olivares...

Placido left he was still a boy. In any case, he arrives back in Charada and is standing on the station platform looking across at the little township beyond, thinking to himself that nothing much has changed. You know, the air is still hot, the sun oppressive, the same flies buzz about his face, the shadows still fall in their old familiar patterns. He sees the station-master, a certain Don Miguel Fernandez [laughs]—a little joke between Olivares and myself—so he sees Don Miguel walking along the platform towards him and he says hello to him. I can still remember writing: 'Buenos días, Don Miguel replied. But he uttered the words coolly, without affection.'

And you see, Placido is hurt. It does not occur to him that **he** has changed, and that this long-time family friend, a man who had showered gifts on him as a child, has simply not recognized him.

Similarly, when Placido arrives at his mother's house later that afternoon, the young sister he left behind ten years earlier has developed into a beautiful young woman. Their meeting, and the scene which followed with his mother, struck me then, and still does, as being absolutely authentic. Placido enters the house without knocking.

At the sound of his footsteps, a young woman stepped into the hallway from the kitchen.

Yes? she said, her voice faintly anxious.

Placido stared hard at her face.

Amaranta, he said. My little Amaranta.

Yes, she said again, her voice trembling. Then she whispered: Placido?

He smiled.

Placido. She repeated the word slowly, incredulously, then turned and ran to the back door.

Mama, Mama, she called. Come quickly.

She waited a moment, clenching and unclenching her fists. Then she ran back to where Placido was standing and he swept her up into his arms and embraced her. She was sobbing.

Placido, you're back, you're back. She pulled her head away to see his face. I don't believe it, you're back.

She kissed him elatedly, joyfully, on both cheeks.

With her still clasped to him he walked to the door and pushed it open. His old mother was walking through the yard wiping her hands on her apron. Half a dozen chickens scattered in front of her like noisy scraps of paper caught in a gust of wind.

When his mother stood before him he released Amaranta. She stayed beside him, her arm around his waist, her head leaning against his shoulder. For a moment, the world seemed to grow silent. Then his mother spoke.

So, you've finally come home.

She wiped her hands again.

The two of them stood looking at each other. Then, slowly, his giant hands reached down to her and he picked her up and held her to the sun. Her lightness frightened him. This tiny woman who had struck fear into his soul as a child now seemed to him a child herself.

And there is a moment, later, four years after his return to Charada, four years in which the vision of a child singing in the choir has begun to haunt him, that he realizes he can stand it no longer.

So one hot summer evening, while his mother and Amaranta sat talking on the dimly lit verandah, he went to them and, without saying a word, kissed first

159

> Amaranta and then his mother on their foreheads. His
> mother could still feel his lips against her skin as he
> disappeared into the night.

All of that had to go.

ZEIT   You sound disappointed.

FERNANDEZ   Yes, in a sense I suppose I
am. Those moments are like memories for me,
memories that just weren't good enough. There is a
sense of personal nostalgia about them. It's difficult
to explain. I guess it's just part of what the real
difference between life and art is.

ZEIT   And what's that?

FERNANDEZ   Editing! [laughs]. But in a way it's
true. I mean, what you're going into in a novel or
short story is an alternative world where you're
completely in control, whereas life is mostly not
being able to control anything. It's also quite
comforting to be in the position of making all the
right moves and if it's not right no one knows about
it. You just start again.

ZEIT   You're serious?

FERNANDEZ   Absolutely. It's one of the reasons
I enjoy writing for the cinema. Here you have this
ludicrous situation in which real people, actors,
clamour to play roles from a world that initially
exists solely in your head. It's insane really, people
wanting to get inside your head...But that's another
issue. Where were we?

**ZEIT   I'd like to put a question to you about
form. You have been criticized for consistently
breaking down the conventions normally
associated with the short story. How do you
react to such criticism?**

FERNANDEZ   I think it's largely irrelevant. For me

160

a narrative, in its telling, naturally inscribes its own centre, a point about which the narrative tends to 'gravitate' as it were. All I do is refuse to allow this centre to stabilize. This is not to say that there are no patterns, no conventions, no structures to my narratives. They are just not the ones you'd normally expect to find. Technically then, the challenge for me is to give enough suggestive detail to allow these patterns of narrative implication to appear without, at the same time, committing myself as an author to any definitive articulation of one or other of these. Besides, *Internal Exile* is hardly unconventional.

ZEIT   No, but you would have to admit it is atypical.

FERNANDEZ   Relatively atypical, yes.

ZEIT   In *Internal Exile*, the breakdown of the relationship between Inocenta and Placido is particularly movingly told, from the almost childlike reverence Placido experiences in the face of Inocenta's physical beauty and, on her part, the awakening of her sexual desire, to the eventual gulf which separates them as it becomes obvious that Inocenta cannot fall pregnant. And it is through Inocenta that we feel Placido's silent, hopeless rage, his sense of powerlessness in the face of the cruel blow fate has dealt him. We see him turn away from her. He becomes, literally, his own prisoner, exiled within himself. Yet it is exactly this that has led some commentators to see the story as a political allegory that Inocenta represents your homeland at the time of the revolution and that Santiago and Placido, two brothers with

161

houses adjoining, represent the forces, neither intrinsically good nor bad, struggling to gain control.

FERNANDEZ Yes, but this is an aberration. This is **not** reality, you know. I mean, it's ridiculous. It annoys me that people still read hidden political agendas into my work.

ZEIT But what about Chavez's music?

FERNANDEZ Chavez's music is different. I used this episode from my country's history because it had for me the feeling of a universal truth. There was something mythical about it, something about its paradoxically fictional content that transcended temporal and historical reality. Placido himself is like this for me. That's why they're linked at the end. I disagree, by the way, with your statement that neither is ultimately good or bad. Remember too, that music and Inocenta are indissolubly linked as well. It is her voice which reaches out continually to him across the vastness which separates them. The only time the perspective changes to Placido's in the entire first half of the story is when he is returning in the train to Charada and the image of Inocenta singing in the choir suddenly reappears in his consciousness:

> He saw again the slight frown appear on her face as their eyes met, saw her lips falter, saw her profile as she looked away, glimpsed again the slenderness of her body as she made her way self-consciously out through the sunlit archway of the tiny church and into the nothingness beyond.

In the film, one can still hear the voices of the children singing as this scene dissolves to show an image of Placido's face staring impassively out through the compartment window. For Placido, Inocenta is like music—something that is always there, that inhabits him, yet always remains for him unknowable, ungraspable.

Ramon Fernandez
Sein eigener Gefangener
und andere Erzählungen
Kreuzer Verlag, 224 Seiten. DM12.50

---

night after returning from a trip far along the coast, Inocenta came to his bed again and re-aroused in him the passion he had felt for her in the first few weeks of their marriage. They made love in a strange and frenzied silence. Afterwards, as he lay there in the darkness exhausted, he felt Inocenta's weight rise from the bed and inexplicably steal away from him.

Six weeks later a telegram was delivered to him in the hotel of the small town of Aguila. It read simply: 'Choose a name for your son'. He had been overjoyed. He read and reread the telegram. A son. At last, a son!

Two days later when he arrived home, the joyful embrace he had imagined as he and Inocenta shared their happiness together for the first time became instead a moment in which they stood separated from each other, he in the doorway holding the telegram in his hand, she on a chair by the stove, sewing. Each remained looking at the other, each unable to move.

Neither came to the other that night. Instead, they both lay awake in their isolation, wondering where destiny would take them from here.

The child, a boy, was born a month early. Nevertheless, he was strong and healthy and Placido had been overjoyed to have a son at last. But the gulf which separated them remained. It was as though he were recovering from a long illness. Time, he told himself, would eventually heal the wound they shared in common.

*

Two days before his son's third birthday, Placido found himself in the town of Coyoacán, sitting in the office of Carlos Rivera whom he had not seen for ten years. He was growing impatient. He had waited all morning for his friend to arrive from the capital. Inside it was hot and muggy. He watched the ceiling fan turning in slow, insolent circles. Outside it was raining. Even the rain was hot.

When Carlos's young secretary brought him the news that the bridge at Tostada had been washed away and no one would be arriving from the capital that day, he sat for a moment wondering what to do. He watched the girl putting papers into the cabinet by the door. Under her dress he could see she had small, hard buttocks, like those of a boy. He wondered idly if she was Carlos's mistress. He stood up, said goodbye to her and left.

He walked across the main street in the rain and from there continued under the eaves of the shops opposite to the post office. He would stay another day in Coyoacán awaiting his friend. He wrote out a telegram to Inocenta: 'Delayed. Return Friday. Placido.'

Then he walked back to the small bar opposite his friend's office. He had been sitting there for not more

164

than five minutes when he felt a hand on his shoulder. He turned to see Carlos's smiling face.

Carlos? They told me the bridge had been washed away.

He laughed.

You should know a little washed-out bridge wouldn't stop Carlos Rivera from seeing his old friend.

They went back to his office. The girl he had seen earlier was still there. As soon as they entered, Carlos ordered her to bring them two coffees. He eyed Placido watching the girl as she left. He gave a strange high-pitched laugh.

I see nothing's changed, Carlos said, making an obscene gesture. That girl will do anything for me. You want her for the afternoon?

Before Placido could answer, the girl returned.

Margarita, Carlos said.

Yes, Don Carlos?

Don Carlos, Don Carlos! Do you hear that Placido, Don Car-los. I like that. Come here Margarita. I want you to meet an old friend of mine. Placido, **Don** Placido Alvarado—Margarita.

Placido smiled at the girl. She smiled faintly at him and then stood uneasily looking at the floor. Carlos was standing behind her. He raised his cupped hands to his chest and bounced them up and down. He threw back his head and rolled his eyes.

Fan-**tas**-tico, he said.

The girl looked around and saw what Carlos was doing. Carlos turned to her.

165

Margarita has the most fantastic tits, don't you Margarita. Why don't you show my friend Don Placido your tits.

She glanced quickly at Placido.

No, come on Carlos. Leave the girl alone.

No, I insist…Margarita, show my friend your tits—now!

He moved menacingly towards her.

She turned to Placido and began slowly unbuttoning her blouse. When she had finished she parted it slightly so that Placido could just make out the inward curve of her breasts. Dissatisfied with this, Carlos reached out and pulled her blouse violently down her back.

Now hold your head up high so that my friend can see your face.

She looked at Placido with a look not of humiliation but of defiance, challenging him not to find her beautiful after all, as if to say, no one, not Carlos, not him or anybody else could strip her of her dignity.

Carlos quickly grew bored with Placido's lack of interest and impatiently dismissed the girl.

What's the matter with you? What happened to the good old days? Don't you like women anymore?

Sure, he said.

He walked over to the window and looked out. The clouds had begun to break up. Great shafts of sunlight lit up the facades of the buildings opposite.

Is there a train to Charada tomorrow? he asked.

There's one at eight to San Domingo. In the afternoon from there you can get the mail train to Charada.

166

He thought for a moment. If he took the mail train he could be home by eight the next evening.

When he left Carlos half an hour later he walked back to the post office to send the second telegram that day to Inocenta. But when he got there he found the line was down. He would have to wait until the morning.

That night he dreamt that Margarita came to him. They made love, slowly at first and then, like two animals, they were clawing at each other. She bit and scratched him, pulling his hair with a wild, fiery passion. Then, with a start, he was awake and Margarita was gone. He lay there blinking, disoriented. He could feel the cold, wet perspiration of his shirt clinging to his back. He felt the rough stubble of his face. Outside, through the curtains, he could see it was already light. Still dazed he looked at his watch. Seven-thirty. Seven-thirty! He could not believe his eyes. That only gave him half an hour. He lay staring at the ceiling.

A few minutes later he staggered out of bed, looked at his face in the mirror and decided a shave would have to wait. He searched through his bag for a clean shirt and with it half-buttoned up sat on the side of the bed and pulled on his boots. He remained sitting there for a moment. Why hurry, he thought, he wasn't expected home until tomorrow. If he missed the train he missed the train.

But in reality, he knew he had made up his mind to go and a few minutes later he descended the hotel stairs and once again emerged into the thorny sunlight of another day. He glanced at his watch—a quarter to eight. He had plenty of time.

It was only at the ticket office, when he asked for his ticket to the capital, that he realized how really **happy** he was to be going home. Home to Inocenta, home to his young son.

Seating himself in the empty compartment, he smiled to himself. Home at last. He enjoyed these return journeys. For him they meant the return to his centre, the end of an unidentifiable yearning in his soul which began the moment he left Charada.

He suddenly realized how weary he was of all this travelling, how much this endless trekking from one town to the next had been a need to get away from something he could not face in himself. He could see the day when his love for Inocenta would be rekindled, when once again they would live together as man and wife, and he would re-experience that strange animal fierceness to which Inocenta had surrendered herself in the first year of their marriage.

Distractedly he watched as the occasional farmhouse approached then receded through the window of the carriage. It occurred to him that he could not remember leaving the station, so lulled had he been by the rocking motion of the carriage and the repeated, hypnotic rhythms of the wheels. When he got back he would ask Santiago if he could once again manage one of the plantations near Charada. This life of continual travel was no life for a man with a young son.

He arrived at the capital a little after twelve. The mail train for Charada didn't leave until after two. When it did it would wind its way slowly up into the mountains, until eventually an hour, perhaps two, after sunset it would stop briefly at Charada before continuing on into the night.

And when Placido did board the mail train for Charada, it was once again with the feeling that there existed some mysterious, unfathomable force which guided the world. In a toy shop near the station of San Domingo he had found the perfect gift for his young son. It was as though fate had led him to it. He knew already the delight he would experience watching his son unwrap it. It would be like unwrapping part of history. He felt its comfortable weight resting on his knees. He smiled to himself as, with a jolt, the train started to move.

But at Carmelo, Placido was awakened by the harsh crackle of the platform loudspeaker, the same loud-speaker that years before had advised passengers that the war had finally ended. He looked at his watch. Four-thirty. He tried to concentrate as the message was repeated. For some reason they were going to be delayed. He asked the young boy sitting opposite what the problem was. He shrugged his shoulders. No sé. He did not know. One of his companions leaned out the window to talk to the conductor on the platform.

A tree has fallen, he yelled back to them, grinning.

The conductor said something else and the youth slumped back into his seat.

How long will it be? someone asked.

He doesn't know. An hour, maybe two. He says for us to stretch our legs. He slapped his forehead in a gesture of feigned exasperation.

169

Placido could see that some of the passengers had already begun to disembark and the group of youths opposite got noisily up. The carriage began to empty. Drowsily he looked across at the old woman sitting adjacent to him. She was staring at him intently. She grinned conspiratorially as his gaze fell to two large cloth-covered packages at her feet. Her tiny head with its hair pulled back and the crevassed texture of her face reminded him of the puppet figures he had seen as a child whose heads had been carved from walnuts. When he looked across at her again she beckoned him with one thin bony finger. At first he was at a loss to know just what it was she wanted of him, but as he slid along the carriage seat towards her she looked quickly around, raised her finger to her lips and slowly lifted one of the cloth covers. Beneath was a wire cage. Inside sat and then stood a magnificent, jet-black rooster. it looked back at him with the same restless eyes of the old woman. She lowered the cloth again and threw back her head in an inaudible laugh. This was no ordinary rooster. This, he knew, was a fighting cock—a champion. She raised her finger to her mouth again and pursed her lips. In return he lifted the clenched fist of his right hand to his chest and smiled. Then she pointed to the package on his lap. He held it up and she nodded. So this was what she wanted, he thought. Slowly he pulled the present he had bought his son out from its bag and held it up for her. He opened its lid and a tiny soldier carrying a drum rose from its centre. He turned the box towards himself and saw the solitary figure multiplied endlessly in the mirrors behind it, as though it were now proudly standing at the head of a whole battalion of tiny soldier-drummers. He cranked the handle and the familiar march tune which had become their national anthem, first under the dictatorship, and then again, in sensational circumstances, after the revolution, began to play.

Chavez, the old woman said, clasping her hands together and raising her eyes heavenwards.

Every man, woman and child knew the name Chavez, the man who had been transformed overnight from a despised traitor into a national hero.

And one day he would teach his own son the story of how this tiny elf of a man had been compelled by the military dictatorship to compose a national anthem for their country and how after the revolution he had been denounced for acts of treason against the people. He would tell him of how eminent scholars, noted musicians and distinguished conductors had all testified against him, claiming his music embodied the 'oppressiveness of the overthrown regime' and the 'regimentation of the human spirit'.

He would tell him how he had been at his trial, how he had seen Chavez standing there openly, sometimes uncontrollably, laughing at their testimony, but saying nothing. His behaviour had scandalized the court. The presiding judges had had to call repeatedly for order. After all the evidence against him, apparently conclusive, had been heard, Chavez, still beaming, was asked if he had anything to say before sentence was passed. He did. He asked that an orchestra be brought before the court to hear the offending piece. After a long discussion his request was agreed to and the court adjourned.

The next day an orchestra was assembled in the courtroom and after tuning up, and with Chavez back in the witness stand, it began to play. Immediately tears of laughter began to stream down his face. He slapped his knees with glee, bent double and hooted as the march changed tempo, chortled to himself as though he'd been told the funniest joke of his life when the music modulated into a minor key and then, for the remainder of the piece, stood before the court red-faced and trembling with barely suppressed laughter. Everyone, including the judges, thought his mind had become unhinged.

Finally the last notes died away. It was some time before Chavez could pull himself together. The three judges sat there outraged.

Is that all you have to say for yourself? one of them finally asked.

No, your Honour, he said. With the court's permission I would like to ask the orchestra to play the piece again.

Again! said the judge.

Yes, your Honour. But this time with one change. I want them to play it backwards from the end. And slowly, very slowly.

A murmur passed around the crowded courtroom. Was this a joke? Was this man really mad? The players looked at each other with puzzled expressions on their faces and then at the music.

Absolute silence settled over the courtroom as the musicians took up their instruments again.

Slowly, hauntingly, a single cello began to play. A stark, seven-note melody of ethereal beauty floated up to fill the air above their heads. It rose and rose, and then seemed to hover, to stagger, and then to die away. Then a chorus of violins repeated this motif in a long lingering answer until finally the whole orchestra was swept away by the music, drowned in an elegiac hymn of such haunting tenderness that each person in the courtroom, from the chief presiding judge to the most humble peasant, felt shamed, shamed to the soul that they had called this man a traitor. It was as though in his music Chavez had incorporated their entire history, their suffering, their defeat, their tragedy and, ultimately, their victory such was its greatness.

When finally the last note had sounded a strange silence had settled back over the courtroom.

This was the story Placido would teach his son. And now as he began to wind the handle in the opposite direction he heard the melody he had come to know so well, and he watched as the tiny soldier-figure turned and seemed to stagger, first once and then again, after a battalion of tiny tired and battle-wounded soldiers returning home before him.

When the train reboarded it was six in the evening. He looked up at the sun. He would be by Inocenta's side, all being well, he thought, by nine-thirty.

But when he stepped down from the train at Charada it was already after ten. He had been the only passenger to get off. He poked his head into Don Miguel's office.

Buenas noches, Don Miguel.

Ah, Placido. Cómo estás?

Muy bien, Don Miguel. Muy bien.

173

He waved his hand.

Adios.

Adios, Placido. Adios.

He walked, his bag slung over his shoulder, up through the darkened side-streets that would lead down the hill on the outskirts of town to his home, to Inocenta and to his young son. He heard music coming from a gramophone in one of the houses as he passed. Out of the darkness a voice called softly, Buenas noches, Placido. Buenas noches, Doña Isabel, he called back into the night.

When he began walking down the dirt track that led to his and his brother's house he could see that his own lay in darkness and only a solitary light burned in his brother's. This would mean that Inocenta had gone to his mother's again. He would sit for a while drinking coffee with his brother and discuss with him his plans to stay at home.

As he stepped up onto the verandah he heard a muffled cry. There was no mistaking that sound. He would recognize it anywhere. It was the sound of a woman making love. He hesitated for a moment, smiled and turned to go. So, he thought, Santiago was not the celibate bachelor everyone believed him to be.

Then he heard the cry again. Clearly this time. A short breathless, single syllable. He stood looking across at the darkness of his own house. Then it came again, that same horrible, familiar sound. No, he said to himself. It could not be. Then, unmistakably, he heard her laugh. Inocenta. No! His whole body, his whole soul screamed into the infinite darkness above him, a never-ending, silent No. He felt his legs go weak beneath him. He clutched at one of the verandah posts, felt its cool rough texture against his cheek. He heard their voices again, their subdued laughter.

He half stumbled down the steps of the verandah. He felt sick, delirious. Like a dead man he walked back up the road beneath the dark vault of the sky, insignificant against its vastness. All around him he heard their voices, the ecstasy of their love-making. Inocenta's laugh echoed through the void. In his mind's eye he could see her, see her head thrown back, her full mouth smiling, her white teeth flashing, her eyes closed. He thought of his son. His son? He lifted his arms in a powerless rage against an invisible, malevolent God above him. He felt like falling to the ground, beating it with his fists until they bled.

When he arrived at his mother's house a light still burned in the kitchen. The front door was ajar. A mosquito coil glowed on the window ledge outside.

He pushed open the door.

Quien es? his mother called.

He saw her appear in the lighted doorway.

Placido?

He walked past her to the far end of the corridor, felt for the key in the drawer until his fingers found it and opened the cabinet door. He took his father's rifle from its rack and loaded it with two bullets from the box on the shelf beside it.

Placido? He felt the tremor in his mother's voice. He walked past her again. He felt her hand brush the sleeve of his shirt.

175

Outside the night was still. He knew she would stay standing there, that she would hear the muffled echo of the shots from the surrounding hills. First one, then a few seconds later, another.

For the second time that night he walked down the hill towards a bright rectangle of light dancing in the blackness of the valley beneath him. He felt the weight of the rifle in his right hand, heard the crunch of gravel beneath his feet.

As he stepped softly back onto the verandah a first breath of cool air stirred the dark stillness. He stood looking at the compressed plane of light less than a man's length away from him, listening. The room was quiet. Perhaps they had already fallen asleep. Perhaps they always left the light burning. Perhaps Inocenta had already gone back to her own room. He watched as a corner of the pale thin curtain fluttered momentarily and then hung limp.

Then, imperceptibly, he heard a sound, unidentifiable, like the frame of a chair settling under his own weight. He heard Inocenta's voice, soft, languid.

Slowly, far out from the wall, he felt his body being drawn along the verandah. Through the window a tall vase filled with red flowers came into view. Above it, a series of photographs in thin wooden frames hung on the wall. One showed his mother and father on their wedding day outside the old church of Charada before it had been pulled down. Another, he recognized, would be the one his father had taken of himself at the entrance to the mine. A corner of an old-fashioned bed appeared. His feet passed silently through the pale sliver of light cast onto the verandah. Then, through the thin transparent veil of the curtain, he saw his brother Santiago's smiling face. He was lying on a pillow, his arms outstretched, reaching up to touch Inocenta's lips. She sat straddled across his naked body rocking gently.

Placido stood in the darkness watching them, watching his brother looking up at Inocenta's angelic face. He saw his hands descend to encircle her waist. The breeze parted the curtains in a shallow arc, momentarily unveiling the two lovers before settling back against the window frame. He raised the rifle to his shoulder.

When Placido fired the shot that instantly killed his brother, Inocenta's body gave a short involuntary shudder. In that instant, she felt the muscles that enveloped Santiago's sex contract around him and as his head slumped to one side, she felt his body stiffen, then felt the dead man's life being drained from him in a series of short sharp spasms within her.

Placido raised the rifle again. He saw Inocenta's face turn towards him along the barrel. He felt his finger against the smooth, polished arc of the trigger. He had expected Inocenta to cry out, to flee. Instead she sat there, mesmerized, looking unseeingly out into the darkness at him. He looked into her eyes, into the wound that had begun to bleed in her soul. She raised her arms to her breasts to hide her nakedness from him. He watched her turn back to his brother, watched her head sink slowly over his body until her forehead rested on his chest.

Then he heard voices coming down the hill behind him. There were people running, shouting. Lights flickered in the darkness. He lowered the rifle and leaned back against the verandah rail.

Now as he looked impassively across at Inocenta standing beside his tiny mother in the crowded makeshift courtroom, standing only metres from where they had been married, he felt a certain sense of solace settle over him. His life had come full circle. No longer did he feel that somewhere, at some particular moment in the past, years ago, he had lost his way. That he should be standing here in this courtroom, waiting for a judge to pass sentence on him now seemed inevitable. This thought comforted him. He felt strangely euphoric.

The judge rose and cleared his throat. Placido's gaze floated over his sad, embarrassed face, over the faces of his mother and Inocenta, over the faces of the crowd turned expectantly towards him and up towards the small blue square of sky set high in the wall at the far end of the church. Up it floated until he felt as light as the light itself. He could hear Chavez's music playing. He felt his body dissolving, scattering in the wind. Somewhere, in his soul, he was rejoicing.

*

We simply have to face the fact that the reality Kant discusses is different from our reality. The realm of the senses for him was the world of nature, the world of Goethe's Werther, of Caspar David Friedrich's romantic vision which saw man as part of a pure and untainted universe, dwarfed by its majesty. Today, arguments about the existence or non-existence of a world independently of the mind that perceives it are irrelevant. Nor is it still valid to talk of the perversion of the essential nature of the external world through the act of its perception. Kant's natural world has been, at best, conquered or, at worst, displaced by the human imagination. Our reality is literally a construct of the human mind. This is what so distressed Wittgenstein on his visit to New York in September 1946. New York for him represented an entirely man-made [menschengebaut] reality, a gross and barbaric projection of the human imagination. The world, he felt with horror, had become literally a metaphor for the mind. The distinction between the real and the imaginary had simply ceased to exist. New York was his Armageddon. After his years of isolation in Norway he felt overwhelmed by what confronted him. He left the city having stayed there for less than two days and never referred to his visit again.

It is impossible then to do as Alexander would have us do:

to de-anthropomorphize; to order men and minds to their proper place among the world of finite things; on the one hand, to divest things of their colouring which they have received from the vanity or arrogance of mind; on the other, to assign them along with minds their due measure of self-being (as) one finite thing amongst others, not the ruler and lord of the universe.

It is far too late for that.

Erich Maiberger, The Transcendental Dilemma, Lügner Press, p.78.

19

BERLIN
Das Leben als Kino.
Life as Cinema.

Karl's fingers grip the pliers and he tears a short section of protective plastic coating from the wire. He twists the bared strands together tightly, pushes them into the fuse-box and screws it securely into place. Then he replaces the safety cover. In his overalls, with his eyes squinting in his lean face, he could be mistaken for a terrorist. In fact, the whole group of us look like terrorists.

There, that should do it. Try the switch.

As the lights come on a collective cheer goes up.

Let the bastards figure that one out.

I had moved to Kreuzberg about a month before, into a graffiti-covered building which had been earmarked for demolition. But like many other buildings in the area, it had been occupied by squatters before the demolition order had been carried out. Now, because of a loophole in the law, it could not be torn down. To do so the owner had to prove it was uninhabitable and since the group had moved quickly most of the windows were still intact, the toilets had not yet been sledge-hammered and the floorboards were still in place. To make it uninhabitable the owner had to gain access to the building and again, because the law now considered the building to be tenanted, if he tried to gain entry by force he was technically trespassing on his own property. The group who occupied the building, most of whom belonged to one of the local experimental theatre companies, were not about to invite him in.

Normally, of course, we would not have had a leg to stand on. The authorities would have just turned up one morning and thrown us into the street. But because there had recently been a number of violent demonstrations protesting against the critical shortage of accommodation in Berlin, such forced evictions were no longer politic.

Pressure was being put on local councils to buy buildings such as ours and convert them into low-cost accommodation. So, for a time, there was a stalemate while the council negotiated to buy a building it couldn't afford and in which it really wasn't interested in the first place. From time to time the owner would turn up accompanied by three or four councillors and they would pace up and down on the broken concrete outside, gesturing to one another as we looked down on them from our second-storey vantage point. And then, exasperated, they would leave.

But things seemed to be on the move again. The electricity supply, which someone had reconnected some time previously, had now been permanently cut. They had dug the line up. A hurried meeting had been called of the ten or so of us who occupied the building to decide what to do. Perhaps the time had come to find somewhere else to live. It was Karl however who suggested boring a hole through the common wall of the still legitimately tenanted block of flats adjacent to us and tapping their electricity supply.

After a brief discussion it was decided that he and one of the others whom I did not know would enter the block of flats disguised as council workmen to see if this were possible. According to Karl, nothing had been simpler, with the result that once again we had lights, hot water and heating—at least for the time being.

It had been a major triumph and a small group of us went back to Karl's room to celebrate. Those who came included Marianne, a tall independently minded, unusual-looking woman in her mid-twenties and Vladan, bearded, intensely serious, in his early thirties. I had only met him in passing but from what I had heard he had defected to the West while touring with a Czech theatre group about six months previously. There was also Irena, young, pretty, naive and two others whom, to tell you the truth, I hardly remember at all. I had seen Karl and Marianne together often and assumed that they were lovers but, once again, I wasn't sure of the exact nature of their relationship.

When I recall the short sequence of events that took place in Karl's room that night, I'm sure that Karl's every gesture, so apparently natural, had been carefully calculated. Even his room seemed to function in some strange, complicitous way. It was significantly different from the rooms the rest of us occupied. The building, after all, had been on the condemned list for some time so everything was in a fair state of disrepair. The moulded plaster ceilings of once elegant apartments had begun to sag and crack. Sections of faded wallpaper hung in tired curls from many parts of the walls exposing the stonework beneath, tiles were cracked or missing, sinks and baths had corrosion stains of varying degrees of intricacy etched into their enamel surfaces and, in most cases, carpets had been ripped up leaving a layer of fine dust covering the floorboards beneath.

Karl's room had probably not been much different when he moved in. But now it was conspicuously clean, corners of unstuck wallpaper had been torn away leaving a flat, if collaged, surface and the dust had gone. Through the doorway to the bedroom could be seen a large comfortable-looking bed. In the main room, which also served as the kitchen, was an old sofa and a couple of old armchairs. Against one wall stood a battered table and a number of wooden chairs in poor condition. Hardly unusual. But on the table were an electric typewriter, a cassette player and a number of cassettes, a couple of expensive-looking pens, a gold watch, a small bronze statue and a number of new records. This was only the start. He also had an impressive stereo system, one entire wall was covered with books [most of which looked new] stacked into a makeshift bookshelf. His electric jug was new, his cooking utensils looked new and, unbelievably, he had a microwave oven and a small fridge!

Watching Karl emerge from his overalls was like watching a strange metamorphosis. By comparison with the rest of us he always seemed meticulously dressed, which is to say his jeans were clean, his shirts were pressed and he often wore a red scarf rakishly tied around his neck.

This calls for champagne, he said.

He reached into the refrigerator and pulled out two bottles.

This should do, he said, inspecting the labels. He reached up into the cupboard over his head and got down half a dozen glasses, champagne glasses. He may have even said something about them being genuine crystal. He smiled as he expertly uncorked the bottles and poured the champagne. It was only when Karl jovially handed one to Vladan, who hesitated slightly before accepting, that I began to sense the air of increasing tension in the room.

Vladan, who was sitting at the table, placed the glass of sparkling liquid on it without drinking any. Karl picked up his own glass, raised it and said: 'Nasdrovie' [Russian for 'cheers']. Each of us, except Vladan, took a sip. I watched Karl looking at him, clinically, dispassionately, as though he were little more than some curious form of insect life. Marianne glanced quickly from one to the other.

I'm hungry, Irena said, oblivious to all this. Got anything to eat, Karl?

Look in the fridge. Take what you want.

Irena got up to go to the fridge.

What's the matter, Vlad? French champagne not good enough for you.

Vladan didn't reply. He just sat looking at the bubbles rising in the glass on the table. He ran his finger around its lip.

Jesus, Karl, where do you get this stuff?

Irena was kneeling in front of the fridge. The door was wide open and it was clear that the fridge was well stocked. She began taking items from it and examining them.

There's a fucking feast in here. Look at this—smoked salmon, caviar, camembert...marinated dates, marinated dates? I don't believe this.

184

Prefer some Russian caviar, Vlad. Might make you feel more at home.

Lay off, Karl, Marianne said.

He turned towards her.

Well if it isn't left-wing chic come to the rescue of the sensitive but oh so silent proletariat. And speaking of come to the rescue, I hear left-wing chic has developed a, how shall I put it, a taste for Russian c-c-c-caviar.

Instantly Vladan was on his feet and his glass of champagne swept up and burst against Karl's face. His mouth twisted with rage and he was breathing heavily. Karl began mopping his face with his scarf.

Dear me, it looks like you spilled a bit, Vlad, Karl said amiably. Like a top-up?

Vladan turned disgustedly away. He picked up his coat and looked across at Marianne.

Are you coming?

She hesitated for a moment before hopping down from the table. Vladan walked to the door, opened it and turned back to her again.

Well?

She picked up her bag.

You're an arsehole, Karl, she said, you know that. Why couldn't you just leave things as they were?

Vladan disappeared through the doorway and Marianne made to go after him, but as she reached the door Karl was by her side. He gripped her high on the arm. They stood looking at each other for a moment before she twisted free. Karl turned back to us. We were all too stunned to move.

185

Why don't you all just fuck off, he screamed. Go on, get out...Are you deaf? **Out!** Jesus fucking Christ.

We picked up our things and left. The door slammed to behind us. Moments later the sound of breaking glass echoed up the corridor. In my mind's eye I could see the slow-motion image of a bottle of champagne exploding against the wall of Karl's room.

After this incident I was to discover that the small group who shared the building were about equally divided in their opinion of Karl. There were those who, even given his unpredictability, were fiercely loyal to him, claiming that despite his apparent wealth and ostentation he never refused them money, food, coffee, books, whatever. And it was true. What was his was yours. He was almost lavishly generous. This is what Vladan hated about him, quite apart from the fact that Marianne refused to stop seeing him. To Vladan, Karl was a fraud, a charlatan, someone who had grown up a spoilt kid and still had a rich father in the wings who dropped around every month or so with money for him, and whom it amused to indulge his son's whim to slum it with the lower classes. Karl, on the other hand, made it obvious that he hated Vladan's self-righteousness and the self-congratulatory moral hypocrisy that allowed him to denounce the 'evils of capitalism' and yet, at the same time, enjoy its comfortable oppression. What was indisputable, however, was Karl's commitment to the theatre.

For reasons that were never clear to me, in the weeks that followed, Karl and I became close friends. Despite this, it still remains difficult for me to give an adequate account of him. He was quirky, tangential, quick-witted, superficially

186

erudite and secretive. Whenever I was with him time seemed to accelerate. You never knew where you'd end up. One day, for example, we were sitting at one of the outdoor cafés along Kudamm (the long main avenue that passes through Berlin's central business district) with the Kaiser Wilhelm Gedächtniskirche in the background. It was busy and we had been forced to share a table with an older, business-suited man who sat reading his newspaper, occasionally sipping his coffee. A young, attractive-looking waitress took our order and I watched as Karl's eyes followed her back into the café.

God, what I wouldn't give to have her sit on my face, he said wistfully [sagte er wehmütig].

The old guy opposite coughed into his coffee, looked up and frowned.

What about Marianne? I said.

No, Marianne doesn't dig women.

She came back with our two coffees.

She's gorgeous, he said when she had gone.

Did you know, he said, in ancient Babylonia every woman was obliged to sacrifice her virginity by prostituting herself in the temple of Ishtar. Have you read Herodotus?

No, I said.

He launched into an epic discussion about the rise of the romantic conception of love, from the heroic hedonism of antiquity to the subsequent identification of sin with the carnality of woman by religion. He went on and on, sweeping through the dark ages, through the medieval courtly love tradition and its idealization of feminine beauty until, finally, we arrived at what he called the 'bourgeois-ification' of love through marriage at the end of the eighteenth century. It was a great performance. I watched as the old guy opposite began to revise his opinion of Karl.

But now, he said, all that has changed. It's so difficult these days having a relationship with someone you know. All **we're** left with is the existential despair of anonymous sex—again and again.

I couldn't tell whether he was serious or not.

You know, he said, the thing I like most about Marianne is her sex. It's so rich, so full. Every time I look at her I think of the opening word in the movie *Citizen Kane*.

I laughed.

No, seriously. Have you ever seen the film?

No.

Well, the opening scenes show the incredible domain of Charles Foster Kane's Xanadu. It starts with an illuminated window, you know, in the distance. All around, the screen is almost entirely black. The camera moves slowly towards the window. Other forms begin to appear. Barbed wire, cyclone fencing and then, looking up against an early morning sky, an enormous iron grillwork. Through this and beyond you see the fairy-tale mountain tops of Xanadu, the great castle a silhouette at its summit, the little window a distant accent in the darkness.

Karl seemed to sketch an image of Xanadu in the air above us as he spoke.

There follows a sequence showing the facade of the castle, emphasizing its ludicrous combination of architec-tural styles, its alligator pit and so on. A great ape is outlined against the dawn murk. He is scratching himself slowly, thoughtfully, looking out across the estates of Charles Foster Kane. Then there follows a long shot of Kane's huge bed, silhouetted against the enormous window.

There is a dissolve. The year is 1940. A snow scene appears on the screen: gigantic snowflakes cascade down over an overly picturesque farmhouse. There is a snowman and the jingling of snowbells. The camera pulls back showing the whole scene to be contained in one of those glass balls you can buy in toy shops and novelty stores everywhere. A hand—Kane's hand—which has been holding the ball, relaxes. The ball falls out of his hand and bounds down two carpeted steps and falls from the last step to the marble floor below where it shatters.

You hear Kane's old voice utter the opening word: 'Rosebud'.

Karl repeats the word in a cracked and shaky voice.

Ro-se-bud. Of course, in the film rosebud appears to be a reference to Kane's childhood sled. But in actual fact using it to open the film was a brilliant move by Orson Wells. You see, it's a sexual pun—the opening word, the word that opens. Rosebud was Randolf Hearst's pet name for his young mistress's blond-haired genitalia.

You're kidding?

No, amazing isn't it.

He paused for a moment.

Want another coffee?

You just want another look at her.

So?

Don't let me stand in your way.

189

He caught the girl's attention and once again she came over. A few minutes later she returned with two more coffees.

She reminds me of my sister, I said. Not to look at, but her mannerisms, her age.

I told Karl of my own experience with Andrea and how watching Elena masturbating while perched up a tree had led to it.

She masturbates up trees?

No, I was up the tree. She was in her room. You're not taking me seriously.

Sorry.

You don't think it was perverse of me?

What?

Well, watching my sister masturbate.

That depends, he said. There's a big difference between eroticism and perversity. I've thought about it a lot. Do you know what the difference is?

No, what?

Well, eroticism, he said leaning forward, eroticism is when you use a feather, and perversity is when you use the whole chook!

He burst out laughing. Even the old guy, whom I'd forgotten about and who had apparently been following the entire conversation, started to laugh.

You're too much, Wolfi. You know that. But it's true in a way. I mean, it's all a matter of degree isn't it.

He laughed again.

God, you think that's perverse. Catherine the Great of Russia died when the harness supporting the horse that was

190

being lowered onto her broke and it fell and crushed her. Apparently she'd outgrown her interest in men as lovers.

I don't believe you.

It's true, it's true, he said smiling. Incredible, but true.

He glanced at his watch.

Holy shit, it's two-fifteen. I've got an audition at two-thirty. Come on, let's go.

We got hurriedly to our feet. Karl picked up the bill and handed it to the old guy, thanked him profusely and while he stared after us open-mouthed, we made off. When we reached the corner at Joachimstalerstrasse Karl stopped and turned to me.

Wait here until I get the car, he said. I'll be back in a couple of minutes.

Before I could say anything he had gone.

A few minutes later a sleek black two-door BMW pulled recklessly to a stop beside the kerb.

Don't just stand there gaping, Karl yelled. Get in!

I went quickly around to the passenger door. It was still open when, with the rear tyres screaming, he gunned the car into the middle lane. He shifted quickly and effortlessly through the gears.

I didn't know you had a car, I said, strapping myself in.

It's new, he said, adjusting the rear-view mirror. He glanced at his watch.

Nice, I said looking around. Very nice. How long have you had it?

Not long.

The car was moving quickly now as he wove it expertly through the traffic. I began to think that perhaps Vladan was right. Perhaps Karl was a fraud after all. One day I could see myself knocking on his door and there would be no answer. Karl would simply have disappeared, finally bored by the pretence of living a bohemian life. And twenty years from now perhaps one or two of us might make the connection between Karl X., head of some huge multinational firm of Industrial Chemicals and the Karl whose hands now calmly gripped the wheel of the speeding black BMW.

I was suddenly jolted back to reality as we swerved wildly to avoid a car stopped at a set of traffic lights in front of us.

I grabbed for the dashboard to steady myself.

That was a red light!

So?

We were going very fast now. The radio was on. The music was up. They were playing Nina Hagen's hit 'Superboy'.

He glanced in the rear-view mirror, muttered something, then looked quickly left and right.

Just hang on for a bit will you, he shouted. I have to make a detour.

Instantly the car braked hard and with the tyres howling Karl flicked it left through a tiny gap in the stream of oncoming traffic which I swear was smaller than the proverbial eye of a needle. We hurtled into a narrow side-street.

Jesus, I said.

He pushed the car hard through the gears. My heart began to race. Up over a stomach-wrenching rise we went.

A blur of faces turned to watch us as we passed. The car's nose dipped. Hard right and right again. Over the music I could hear the suppressed roar of the engine as he took the car to its limit.

What the fuck are you trying to do, Karl, I yelled. Get us killed?

He didn't answer. Instead we shot back out across three lanes of autobahn in a truly spectacular high-speed slide. He adjusted the rear-view mirror again and laughed. He did a drum roll across the steering wheel in time to the music.

Superboy, he mimed.

When we arrived, Karl parked the car a couple of blocks from the theatre. We got out.

Aren't you going to lock it? I said.

He stood looking at me for a moment.

Jesus, Wolfi. Do I have to explain everything?

He walked off up the street shaking his head.

When we got to the theatre the auditions were already underway. Karl nodded to a tall thin haggard-looking man pacing up and down in the foyer of the old theatre. He ushered us into the darkened auditorium. Inside there were about twenty other people dotted about the place towards the back. Four rows from the front were seated the panel of three who would make the eventual selection. We watched as a young, spot-lighted woman gave a transparently heart-rending performance of tragic despair. One trembling hand was outstretched in a gesture that reminded me of Grünewald's Isenheim crucifixion, her fingers twisted agonizingly skywards. Her other hand clutched at her peasant blouse. Her face contorted in a spasm of grief. A ripple of suppressed laughter passed through the audience.

Why? she was sobbing. Why, why?

She mopped her brow with her forearm and stood transfixed by some point on the floor. Suddenly she looked up at us and tore open her blouse. She clutched at her breasts.

How am I to feed my children? she implored.

There was a loud guffaw from the far side of the theatre. This only seemed to increase the anguish on her face. Her eyes rolled wildly, farcically. I could see the shoulders of one of the judges shaking with suppressed laughter.

Mein Herz [my heart]...Mein Herz...brecht, she cried.

There was another loud burst of laughter at the unintended pun. She fell to the floor. Now there was open laughter. Even the judges were laughing. The girl got up, looked desperately into the auditorium, and then ran from the stage.

Karl explained to me how the selection was made. It was on the basis of an improvised piece. Topics would be drawn from a hat or a box and the candidate had two minutes to think about their topic, one minute to give an introduction to the piece if they needed it and three minutes to present it.

Like hers was probably grief or sorrow, something like that, he said. But it could be anything—an anorexic bus, an honest politician, a TV set, the colour blue...anything.

An actor's name was called. The tall nervous-looking fellow we had met outside made his way down to the stage.

One of the judges held up what looked like a pack of cards to him. He selected one. He was asked to announce his subject to the panel.

He looked at his card.

Empörung [Indignation], he said.

You have a preparation time of two minutes starting now.

The spotlight began to dim.

Hang on, he shouted. Mach' das verdammte Licht wieder an [Turn that bloody light back on].

What's the matter, Herr Bruer?

What's the matter, Herr Bruer? he mimicked with obvious sarcasm. What do you mean what's the matter? This is a fucking farce. I've been an actor for ten years, five of those with the State Theatre Company and never before, **never** have I had to put up with such an amateurish load of shit as this in all my life.

He began tearing the card up into little pieces as he walked towards the edge of the stage. The spotlight followed him. When he got to the stairs leading down into the auditorium he threw the pieces up over his head and they showered back down on him like confetti.

You're entitled to a second draw, Herr Bruer.

Shove it up your collective arses, he yelled.

He stormed up the aisle and the door to the foyer crashed to.

Karl started to clap. Others, hesitantly at first, began to join in. The members of the panel realized they had been duped. One of the judges stood.

Would someone ask Herr Bruer to come back in please.

A young woman got up and went out to get him. A few seconds later she returned.

He's gone.

Gone?

Yes, gone, vanished, verschwunden. I think he was serious, she said.

Then it was Karl's turn.

He went down to the stage and selected a card.

Your topic please.

Spannung [Suspense], he announced.

He sat down on a chair at the back of the stage. The lights dimmed into semi-darkness. When they came up he got quickly to his feet and strode to the front of the stage. He spoke rapidly, gesturing as he did so, showing us where things were located.

At the end of this introduction, he said, I want the lights out for fifteen seconds. Now I want you to imagine you are looking at a film set of a café. There is only one table. It is covered with a piece of black and white checked material. On the table in a silver ashtray a cigarette is burning, a thin trail of white smoke rises towards the ceiling. At the table are seated a man and a woman. She is wearing a black, loose-fitting evening dress in the style of the late thirties.

Karl's hand seemed to rest on her shoulder as he looked down on her.

Beside her a man is sitting. He is wearing a tuxedo. The action has been frozen and his right hand is suspended over the table. He could be reaching for the cigarette but we cannot be sure. Both their faces are obscured by a TV

camera which hovers over the table. On a screen behind
them is projected what the camera sees. It shows the
burning cigarette. When the lights come up the camera
is going to pan up and away from the table and move to
a point adjacent to the man's head so that we see what he
sees. And what he sees is that as the woman moves forward
her right breast, with its pale pink nipple, appears outlined
against the inner darkness of her dress. They are about to
be joined by a third person. Okay—lights!

The theatre darkened. Silence.

Even when I got back to my room later that afternoon Karl
was still not home and none of the others had seen him.
It wasn't until a couple of days later that I caught up with
him and by that time he had not only found out that he
hadn't got the part but he had had another falling out with
his own theatre group. Again it was over the same thing—
what they saw as Karl's moneyed arrogance.

When I did see him he was sitting alone in Maximilians.

Mind if I join you?

It's a free country, he said without looking up.

I sat down. He looked pale, jittery. The waiter made
his way over to us.

So, what'll it be? he asked.

Just a coffee, thanks.

Don't you ever drink anything but coffee?

I went to answer.

No, don't bother me with the boring details.

He turned to the waiter.

Another coffee thanks.

197

I'm sorry to hear you didn't get the part.

Win some, lose some.

Who did in the end?

Our despairing woman got the lead female role and some complete unknown got the male lead.

You're joking. But she was dreadful. You said so yourself.

Yes, that's what I thought at the time but apparently she was brilliant. What I didn't know was that she was playing the role of dissatisfied customer. Her soup was cold. She had apparently improvised the entire scene using quotes from Brecht, which is why her final line broke the audience up. It had been deliberately farcical. Thanks.

He paused as the waiter placed my coffee on the table.

But tell me, what happened after I left?

I recounted how, in that fifteen seconds of darkness, I had gone quickly over the details of the scene he had created in my mind. The table, the cigarette, the man and the woman sitting there and the image of her breast appearing on the screen behind them. So much so that when the lights came up I had the momentary impression that the entire scene he had outlined was there on stage. But of course there had been nothing. Absolutely nothing. No Karl, not even the chair he had been sitting on. Just empty space.

Cretins, he said.

We sat in silence for a few minutes.

Tell me, he said suddenly, why did you give up your Ph.D.?

His question took me by surprise. Karl had never asked me anything about my personal life before, at least, not without my having mentioned it first.

Well you know, I said, it's like Wittgenstein compared a proposition to a solid body that restricts the freedom of movement of others. A tautology—for example, he is here or he is not here—leaves open to reality the whole of logical space. No restriction is imposed on anything. A contradiction on the other hand—for example, he is here **and** he is not here—fills the whole of logical space and leaves no room for reality.

So?

Well, central to my thesis was Kant. But eventually I got to the point that whenever I thought of Kant all I could think of was Andrea. Perhaps it's the English, I don't know.

I see, he said laughing.

I thought for a moment about what I was going to say next, then plunged in.

While we're on the subject of true confessions, I said, and I know it's none of my business, but what gives between you and Marianne?

You're right, Wolfi. It's none of your business. Besides, I wouldn't have any misplaced ideas about Marianne if I were you.

Why not?

You know what she calls you behind your back.

No, what?

Karl's little clown.

Really?

Uh huh.

I sat there thinking about what Karl had said. It certainly tallied with Marianne's reaction to me which was one of barely disguised disdain. Fuck her, I thought.

Well, if that's the case, while I'm at it, do you mind if I ask you something else?

What?

What **does** your father do?

What do you mean?

Well, you obviously live pretty well and you don't work. The money must come from somewhere.

I have never in my life seen anyone get to their feet as quickly as Karl did. For a moment I thought he was going to up-end the table.

Not you too, he shouted. You complete fucking arse-hole, Wolfi.

The pleasant hum of café conversation gave way to an uneasy silence as heads turned our way. An espresso machine hissed in the background. I sat uncomfortably looking up at Karl, half-expecting him to throw the remains of his cup of coffee over me. The waiter was already making his way over to us but as he reached our table Karl turned and roughly brushed him aside.

You don't have to tell me, he said. I'm going.

People turned to watch him leave, then went back to their coffees and the noise level resumed. The waiter began clearing the table suggesting as he did that perhaps it would be better if I left as well.

I didn't see Karl after this for some weeks and in any case I was busy myself. Then one day to my amazement, when I answered a knock on my door Karl was standing there smiling.

Wolfi, he said.

Karl?

Aren't you going to invite me in?

I gestured for him to enter.

We're having a party on Saturday night to celebrate the opening of our new play and I need some help to do the shopping. Want to come along?

Now Karl **never** allowed anyone to shop with him. It was one of the things he was secretive about, so my curiosity was aroused.

When? I asked suspiciously.

Can you meet me tomorrow at ten?

Sure, okay.

Well, that's settled, he said. See you tomorrow then.

He said goodbye and left.

Later that day I was to have a real find. At the State Library I discovered the original programme notes, dated 12 October 1925, to the Berlin performance of Pirandello's play *Six characters in search of an author* in which Marta Abba herself had actually starred [deren Hauptrolle die Marta Abba selbst gespielt hatte]. I was ecstatic.

Next morning I was still thinking about my discovery when I knocked on Karl's door. It was five past ten. Knowing Karl's impatience I wasn't surprised when no one answered. I knocked again and was just about to make off when I heard a series of muffled coughs and heavy footsteps approaching the door. It opened and I was confronted by a short, exceedingly fat, bearded man in his fifties. A wave of putrid-smelling smoke which seemed to fill the room seeped past him. In his hand he held a cigar. He coughed hoarsely.

Ah, you must be Wolfi, he said grasping my hand. Come in, come in. Karlchen will be back in a minute.

I went in.

Sit, sit, he said indicating one of the armchairs while he himself stood wheezing for a moment. He was huge. I could see the buttons of his shirt straining against the soft bulk of his enormous belly. He was wearing thick glasses, the type that make a person's eyes look twice as large as they really are, so that as he stood there gulping for air he looked like some enormous, bearded toadfish dressed in a suit and a hat.

I'm terribly sorry, he said. Gustave Aloysius Klebbermann at your service.

He reached into his inside pocket and retrieved a small white business card. He trundled over and handed it to me beaming. It read:

TX-FK21264	Tel. 691196
Klebbermann Securities International	
G. A. KLEBBERMANN	
Frankfurt New York Hong Kong	
Paris Tokyo	

I went to hand it back to him.

Keep it, keep it, he said, waving his hand. You never know when you might need it. Karlchen's told me so much about you.

It was only then that it struck me who this monument to fat was. He was Karl's father! Somehow I had expected

202

someone more distinguished, more urbane. Instead this mountain of flesh, while obviously successful, was gross and more than a little repugnant.

You don't mind the hat, he asked suddenly, pointing to a perfectly ordinary if rather old-fashioned business hat on his head.

No, no. Not at all. It's very nice, really. What else could I say.

He picked up his cigar from the ashtray, bending over it cautiously as if he were wearing a truss. It wouldn't have surprised me if he was. He inhaled deeply on his cigar, spluttered and wheezed obscenely for a moment, then smiled at me.

The stairs, too many stairs. Just arrived. Always like this for the first fifteen minutes.

He manoeuvered himself over to the other chair, backed himself awkwardly up to it, bent his knees slightly and, raising his voluminous trousers a little, let himself fall slowly backwards into it. I winced as the chair strained under his enormous weight. He settled back into it. The smoke from his cigar was beginning to make me sick. There was an awkward silence. He leaned forward slightly.

Karl, he said in a confidential tone.

I had no idea what he was talking about.

Karl? I said.

Yes, Karl. Can't get used to it. Wear a hat all the time. Well, almost all the time if you know what I mean.

He laughed knowingly at me. I began to think that perhaps he wasn't all there. We fell silent again.

Kahl! I almost shouted.

203

He jumped noticeably in his chair.

You mean kahl—bald!

I started to laugh.

I'm sorry, Herr Klebbermann. I don't mean to laugh, but I thought you meant Karl Karl.

I pointed meaninglessly to my head. He looked at me weirdly.

Speaking of Karl, I said. Where is he? You said he'd be back in a minute.

Yes, yes. Of course. He's just parking the car. Said it wasn't safe. New you see. Mercedes 450...SE...blue. Couldn't go back downstairs myself. Not as young as I used to be.

With this he reached again for his cigar and, finding it had gone out, fumbled for his cigarette lighter and relit it by discharging half a dozen lung-fulls of acrid smoke into the room.

Best cigars in the world, he said. Havana grandes. Sure you wouldn't like one?

No, no thank you. Perhaps I should go and look for him.

No, sit, sit. He should be here any minute. Besides, I have to be off myself in a moment.

Then why did Karl have to park the car if you're going almost immediately yourself? I asked.

Ah yes. Very good question Wolfgang. Very good question. Karlchen told me you were a sharp young man. Young men like you we could use in our firm.

Suddenly, and with surprising agility for a man his size, he heaved himself up out of his chair and with three quick strides was looming over me. He was breathing hoarsely. Beads of sweat had begun to form beneath the brim of his hat. He took another puff of his cigar, brushing the smoke from his face with his great bear-like paw. He looked menacingly down at me.

Yes, Karlchen told me a lot about you, he rasped. You call yourself a friend. You're nothing but a hypocrite and a traitor to my Karlchen.

He held his cigar dangerously close to my face. I tried to get up but he kicked my feet sharply out from under me and I fell back into my chair. He started to cough, uncontrollably, hideously. His eyes bulged. He clutched at his chest and turned away from me, his great body bent double, his enormous buttocks quaking millimetres from my face. I saw his hat fall to the floor in front of him. A hand returned to his side, clutching his glasses and a white handkerchief. He was making a frightening, inhuman, horrible sound.

Herr Klebbermann!

I went to rise again but it was too late. The great trembling mass of his body had begun to topple backwards. I raised my hands in a futile attempt to protect myself as he came crashing down on top of me. Instantly the hoarse coughing gave way to a high-pitched laugh and I felt a pair of wet lips kiss my cheek.

Ah Wolfi, you were terrific, terrific.

Karl!

Gustave Aloysius Klebbermann at your service.

He could hardly get the words out for laughter.

God, I haven't had so much fun in a long time. You should have seen the look on your face: 'You're a traitor and a hypocrite to my Karlchen'. But you deserved it. You deserved it, you arsehole.

He got up. Suddenly he was tall again, his trouser cuffs up around his calves.

Come on, let's go. God, these awful cigars. You know, I spent three or four minutes before you arrived furiously puffing to get the room full of smoke and then when you knocked I couldn't find my glasses. For a desperate moment I thought you'd gone. And then later, when you said kahl, I thought you'd recognized me.

He picked up his hat and replaced his glasses. He made for the door.

Aren't you going to change? I asked.

No. I said we were going shopping. The fun has just begun.

On the crowded bus into town Karl created a fuss by insisting that a pretentious-looking woman in her forties give her seat to his son because I had a heart condition and, as anyone could see just by looking at me, I was severely mentally retarded. So I sat all the way into town until we got to our stop at the Kaufhaus des Westens.

In *Midnight Cowboy* there is a scene in which Jon Voigt and Dustin Hoffman as Ratso almost get run over by a car as they cross the street. The car screeches to a halt just centimetres away from them and the limping Ratso turns, bangs its bonnet and yells: 'Hey, I'm walking here, I'm walking here'. In a subsequent interview Hoffman claimed that this scene was real and unstaged. It had actually happened that way when they were shooting, and he liked it so much that he left it in.

206

Karl's departure from the kerb, however, was carefully calculated to allow the driver of a smart new Mercedes coupé just enough time to bring the car to a nose-diving stop. But it **was** close and Karl wisely chose not to acknowledge the driver's abuse, continuing instead in the direction of the KDW.

God, that was close, I said when I had caught up to him.

Yes, for a moment there I had the horrible feeling he hadn't seen me and with this fat-man suit on I would have been flat out getting out of the way.

Instead of going into the KDW as I had expected we headed around the corner to one of the nearby supermarkets.

I thought we were going to the KDW.

Some other day, he said. Today is food shopping day and it's easier if we go somewhere where there are fewer store detectives, particularly if we're together.

What do you mean, if we're together? I said, offended.

Well, take a look at yourself. You look like a political terrorist and in the KDW they'd never let you out of their sight. Together we look so incongruous that it's suspicious. On my own, dressed like I am, I'm just another successful Spiessbürger.

Because of Karl's bulk we had difficulty getting through the turnstile. I could see one of the young cashiers looking at him with obvious disgust as Karl, with what I now recognized as exaggerated slapstick, somehow managed to get one leg caught either side of the turnstile bar. He was stuck. The manageress had to be called and after some moments of pushing and shoving at the bar between his legs, during which Karl claimed the manageress was trying to touch him up, he was freed.

I went to get a trolley and rejoined Karl in the first aisle where he stood balancing several boxes of cereal precariously in front of his huge belly with one hand, while attempting to pile even more things on top with the other.

It would have been easier to shop if you'd changed. How do you expect us to lug bags of groceries back to the bus when you can hardly walk as it is?

I reached up to put the boxes of cereal into the trolley but he pushed my hand roughly away.

What do you think you're doing? You get these.

He handed me a list.

I can look after what I've got, he said.

Suit yourself, I said. But four boxes of cereal! What kind of party is this?

He went to answer.

No, no. Don't bother me with the boring details, I said.

I walked off in search of the first item on the list. Two aisles later I caught a glimpse of Karl awkwardly manoeuvering himself between the other shoppers and their trolleys, stopping occasionally to rest his legs and to arch his back in the futile gesture fat people make in an attempt to redistribute their weight. As we passed I noticed that all he had added to his pile were a couple of jars of caviar.

What do you do, spread it on your Rice Bubbles, or have you and Vladan made up?

He just pushed past me without saying a word. I watched him as he waddled up the aisle reaching for the occasional thing off a shelf. I saw him bump into another shopper and nearly lose all of what he was carrying.

A short time later we passed again and still all he was carrying was four cartons of breakfast cereal. Still I didn't understand.

Change your mind about caviar on your Rice Bubbles? I asked.

He just rolled his eyes.

Then I saw him do it. His right hand reached out and took two jars of coffee off the top shelf. He laid them precariously on top of the uppermost box of cereal, trying to keep one of them in place with his chin as he shifted his weight a little. His right hand came away from the top of the box still holding one of the jars. He looked at it for a moment as if he were reading the label and, deciding against it, turned to put it back on the shelf. The whole thing was totally natural. But when he turned back to me the jar he had been cradling beneath his chin had disappeared. I looked dumbly for a moment at the blank space where it should have been. He caught my eye. He grinned and raised his eyebrows once again as if to say: 'Finally, you understand.' I half ran up to him and, without being too obvious, scrutinized the top of his shirt. A narrow band of stitching was all there was to conceal the spring-loaded flap beneath. As if to show me how easy it was, he took another item off the shelf, placed it on top of the cereal and by reaching across to scratch his other shoulder, swept it into his cavernous stomach. I started to laugh.

That's fantastic, I said.

Not bad, is it, he said nonchalantly. I'm about half full. I've got most of the things you've got, although you could give me your shampoo.

You mean I've been wasting my time?

No, some of those things, like the yoghurt for example, are too risky for me. I had a nasty experience with yoghurt once. No, some of that lot we'll pay for.

But despite this, now that I knew what Karl was up to, we went on a spree. Dried figs, imported nuts, real coffee, camembert, exotic biscuits, truffles, chocolates, ridiculous things really. Around the aisles we went, intoxicated by the daring transparency of it all.

When we had finished, there was still enough room for a bottle of champagne to celebrate. By this stage, Karl really did appear to be having genuine difficulty walking and when we made our way to the cashier, having ditched the boxes of cereal, all we were carrying in fact was a six-pack of toilet paper. I looked like the solicitous son helping his asthmatically overweight father as I supported him with one arm. As she gave Karl his change he pointed to me and said: 'Diarrhoea'.

Back on the streets Karl stopped for a moment and grasping his huge belly in his hands he appeared to shift it from side to side.

Jesus, this is heavier than I thought, he said. And I think one of the straps is twisted. Where's the nearest bus stop?

He was now definitely struggling under the load and we were forced to stop every twenty or thirty metres while he tried to make himself more comfortable. Finally we arrived at the bus stop where we were able to sit for the five minutes it took before ours came along. I helped my poor suffering father aboard.

Back home, we were hardly in the door to the building when Karl took off his coat. I could now see the contraption he had strapped to himself. It consisted of a large, hemi-spherical container made of fibreglass, the back of which was more or less shaped to his body. A harness attached to the top passed over each of his shoulders and was reattached at the container's base. The front was a master-piece. It consisted of a fake shirtfront, collar and bow-tie and, as I had guessed, a spring-loaded flap concealed behind some fancy stitching.

Help me off with this, will you, Wolfi. This bloody strap's killing me.

Underneath, his T-shirt was bathed with sweat.

This is fantastic Karl. Where'd you get it?

The props people made it up for me. I got the idea when we did *Wilhelm Meister* last year. It was a natural progression really. I'd been shoplifting for years using big coats but it's too risky. Now I've a character who's beyond suspicion and despite what you saw today, normally I'm very careful.

I looked at him for a moment.

That explains the books, I said.

Of course. Man does not live on marinated dates alone.

And the other things?

No, not directly. I'd look pretty stupid trying to fit a microwave into my stomach. But watches, jewellery—anything there's a ready market for. Mink coats...

You're joking.

He looked at me. He wasn't.

Jesus! I said. The possibilities are almost limitless.

211

Uh huh. All you need is a little imagination, that's all.

Once back in his room I watched him carefully emptying the contents of his stomach onto the table. It was only then that I realized how systematic he had been. He stood there marking things off a list in his hand. When he finished he glanced at his watch.

Eleven-thirty already. Okay Wolfi, that gives us about four hours to do the rest. Want to try your hand?

Me?

Sure, why not?

I shrugged my shoulders.

Okay, sure. I'll try anything once.

He went into the other room and returned with another less sophisticated stomach.

You can use the Mark II version. I'll use the prototype. Not as advanced technically, but its capacity is greater. Male or female?

Male or female what?

Do you want to go as a male or a female? God, Wolfi, it's probably the only time you're going to get a choice. So what's it going to be, man or—he pouted his lips and fluttered his eyelids—woman.

Ah...male, I think.

Oh you brute you. Now you jus go on an git yoself undresst an don't you worry bout lil ol me. Ahs bin aroun men all mah life an ah've seen **everythin**.

He strutted over to me and started undoing my shirt buttons.

Oh, oh. Ah thinks ah got maseff a ticklish one heah.

You watch too many B-grade movies, you know that, Karl.

I started to undress while he began rummaging through a pile of clothes in the bottom of his wardrobe.

What I was wearing should fit you, with a few minor adjustments. And seeing as you want to be a man I think I'll go as a woman. Besides I'm sick of being a man. Women have so much more fun.

Ten minutes later we were putting on the final touches. Karl looked utterly convincing in an ugly, frumpish sort of way as he applied lipstick to his mouth in front of the mirror. He was wearing a bulging little floral number and when he got up he looked like the sort of badly dressed working-class woman one always sees at supermarkets, the type who takes things down from the shelf and short-sightedly examines them before putting them back, muttering in disgust. He tied his scarf around his head.

Okay, he said. This is what you'll need to get on your first load. Now you've seen what to do. The best idea is to pile up a few bulky items in front of you and place what you want on top. It'll fall in under its own weight, or you can brush it in by reaching across yourself, or by blowing your nose or whatever comes to mind. You'll soon get the hang of it. You alright? How does it feel?

Fine, it feels fine. But how do I look?

You turn me on, baby. No, seriously, you look great. But remember, your body's getting old and while you don't like to admit it you've gone to fat. You've been moderately successful in your life so you're a little conceited, self-satisfied. While you still try to hold yourself erect the superstructure of your body has begun to sag. Let your shoulders drop a bit and think of your spine as fixed so that if you go to look at something to your left then you're more likely to turn completely by moving your feet rather than twisting from your neck or spine. Here, put on your hat and glasses and have a look at yourself in the mirror. No, no. Don't stride. Your hips are less flexible now and you're carrying more weight. You're **not** young any more, you just remember being young. Look, as the type of large-bodied woman I am, coming from the social class I do, I have to walk slightly stooped. My bum moves more because, even at my age, my pelvis rotates more than yours. But you have to move like this.

He straightened slightly, took a few steps, turned and came back. He did it so perfectly that, in his frumpy clothes, he looked like an old man dressed in drag.

Now, you try it...Not bad, not bad. Don't exaggerate too much. Just think yourself into the character of someone well past his prime. Okay, that's better. Now have a look at yourself in the mirror.

I was stunned. Instead of my own reflection I was looking at someone who could have been the brother of the man Karl had been an hour previously.

Okay, let's go.

Karl was Karl as we strode down the corridor and down the stairs. But as we emerged from the doorway onto the street, it was as though he had been instantaneously transformed into a working-class, bow-legged, pumpkin-arsed woman in her sixties. He was suddenly a head shorter than I was and beneath his scarf his face had gone slack.

214

He grasped his bag protectively to his side with both hands. I was tempted to laugh, but something in his portrayal went beyond mere caricature. His moist eyes seemed to have become preoccupied with trying to answer some question which wouldn't formulate itself properly in his mind, a question about the husband who had left her years ago or the son who had been killed in the war, or perhaps it was a daughter who had simply stopped writing. Her jaw moved back and forth as she chewed over the formlessness of her life. Here was someone old and lonely, and a little mad.

Each trip we went to different supermarkets and entered a few minutes apart. It was so easy, it was exhilarating. I experienced a strange sense of intoxication. In my disguise I felt invulnerable, as though I had stepped momentarily outside the normal order of things, or as if I had escaped the limits of my single existence. As I walked through the aisles filling my stomach with shoplifted groceries I felt invisible. Instead of feeling that life flowed through me as I used to, I now felt as though I were flowing unimpeded through life. What I was doing was so obvious, yet so obviously unseen, it was more than a little disturbing, as though I had become a metaphor for something far more unsettling.

From time to time I caught a glimpse of Karl talking to a jar of pickles or bent over the frozen goods section. I watched as a dark-haired little girl stared up at him, open-mouthed. As he caught her eye he slipped out of character for an instant and deftly flipped a small package up to his chest where it magically disappeared into his stomach. He beamed down at her. She looked self-consciously away, her tiny hand reaching up to tug at the hem of her mother's

215

dress. By the time she had been swept up to straddle her mother's hip and looked back, Karl was halfway down the aisle.

It was late afternoon by the time we arrived back after our last load and I was just doing up the laces of my shoes when there was a knock at the door. Karl was still in his dress which now hung in great folds about his body.

Will you get that, Wolfi, while I change.

I went to the door and opened it. A thickset balding man wearing dark glasses stood in the doorway. Before I could open my mouth he pushed me roughly aside.

Richter? he half yelled. Richter...Where's your friend? he said turning menacingly towards me.

Karl appeared in the bedroom doorway. He was still wearing his dress and his face had turned pale.

Very pretty Richter, very pretty. I won't bother asking you what you're up to, just tell your friend to go.

You'd better go, Wolfi, he said.

Are you okay, Karl? What's going on?

Just go, Wolfi, for Christ's sake.

He edged me towards the door.

But...

The stranger moved towards us.

He's going, he's going. Come on Wolfi, **go**. I'll see you later, okay.

He pushed me out into the corridor and pulled the door shut behind him.

When I dropped by his room a couple of hours later and knocked on his door he wasn't there.

216

A lot of people, most of whom I did not know, came on the night of the party. Karl's theatre friends had placed a number of trestles along the corridor and what amounted to a small feast had been laid out on them. Baths in some of the empty rooms had been filled with ice and the champagne, wine and spirits we had appropriated were stacked in these. Alcohol was the hardest thing for us to get in quantity so it was understood that everyone would bring at least something to add to the supply. A light show had been set up in the large empty room at the end of the building and one of the local bands had agreed to supply the music.

By ten o'clock the place was really rocking. The corridor was jammed with people, noise, flickering light and smoke. Karl however seemed to be avoiding me. Each time I caught sight of him, by the time I had pushed my way through the throng to him he had disappeared.

Later, when the crowd in the corridor had thinned a little as people either decided to dance or sit talking or not talking in one of a number of open rooms, I went looking for Karl again. I searched for him among the people dancing, without success. No one I asked had seen him for some time. Back in his room where it was quieter, a number of his friends were busy arguing about a recent retrospective at the Staatliches Kunsthaus which had caused a stir, but again he was not among them. I walked across to his bedroom door and pushed it open. A young couple were making love on his bed, her legs up over his shoulders. They continued on, undisturbed by my presence or the pale light that flooded across their bodies. I closed the door again and walked back out into the corridor. Marianne was leaning against the window sill opposite my room. I went up to her.

Have you seen Karl? I asked.

Why?

No particular reason. If you do though, could you tell him Karl's little clown is wondering why he's avoiding him.

I turned to walk off.

Wolfi, just a minute. Look, I'm sorry about the apparent put-down. But you know, you're a fool to hang around with someone like Karl.

And you're not?

No, I'm probably a fool too. But I know him better than you do. One way or another you'll end up getting hurt.

Sure, I said.

You don't believe me, do you? You know, the trouble with you, Wolfi, is that you wouldn't know the truth if it were staring you in the face.

I turned to go again.

You want to find your friend, try the first-floor loos.

She was right. I hadn't known what had been staring me in the face for months. A single, unshaded light globe was burning over the row of cabinets. Karl hadn't even bothered to fully close the door and when I pushed it open there he was, sitting with his head leaning against the wall, the needle still hanging from the bruised vein in his arm.

A few days after the night of the party Karl knocked on my door. He was unshaven and appeared agitated.

I need your help, he said.

218

He was hopping from one foot to the other, like a footballer trying to warm up in the cold. He wouldn't look me in the eye. I had never seen him in such a state before. I had just begun thinking that his behaviour must have been due to the smack he was shooting up when he suddenly became very calm. He turned and looked directly at me.

Are you deaf?

No, I answered.

Then what's the matter with you?

I could ask you the same thing, but then that'd be asking the obvious, wouldn't it.

But then that'd be asking the obvious, wouldn't it, he repeated in perfect imitation.

Come on Wolfi, let's cut the self-righteous petulance. God, anybody'd think you were a jilted lover. Boy loses hero.

You overestimate yourself, Karl.

Yes, but I always do. It's one of my more endearing qualities, he said with ironic sarcasm.

He started to get agitated again. His cheek muscle began to twitch as he stood there.

Well?

Well what?

Mind like a sieve. He threw up his arms. Why do I bother?

Don't do me any favours.

Once more, he became absolutely calm, a calm I recognized as suppressed rage. For the first time I watched myself watching him, clinically, as though I were watching a scene in a movie. In the background I could even feel that part

219

of me was frightened by what Karl might do, but mostly I felt completely detached. I knew that he would either turn and walk off down the corridor or grab me by the collar and punch me senseless.

A second or two passed. Then he faced me again.

It's like a game, isn't it, Wolfi.

What do you mean?

Well, we're both playing a little game. I've got a role and you've got a role. My role is first to recognize that we're playing a game and what the game is, because if you don't recognize you're playing a game it becomes self-perpetuating, doesn't it. The next step is to work out all the rules of the game. Having done that my role is then to do everything in my power to get what I want in the shortest possible time and at the minimum cost to myself—bend the rules, cheat, whatever. But playing the game is boring, and just at the moment I don't have the time. So let's stop playing it, eh. This of course is the most decisive move of all. So how about it? Stop playing hard to get, Wolfi, or just tell me to piss off and stop wasting my time.

That was rehearsed.

Sure. Why not? I've used it hundreds of times before. Never was very good at the whisper-sweet-nothings routine. You should try it sometime.

Okay, okay. What do you want?

You remember the guy who ah...dropped in after our shopping spree. Well, it's like this, I owe him some money.

I only have 80 marks myself, but you're welcome to it.

No, Wolfi. I don't think you quite understand. I owe him a lot of money.

220

Like how much?

2000 marks.

God, for a moment there I thought you were going to say 10,000 marks.

Yeah, well it might as well be. I have until six o'clock tomorrow. With these guys that could be literally if I don't come up with all or most of it.

What about your fat-man suit. A couple of watches, three or four fur coats.

Very funny.

Why not?

I've tried. I think they're on to me at the KDW. I nearly blew it completely yesterday. They're suspicious as hell. That's why I need your help.

I'm sorry Karl. I just don't have access to that sort of money.

No, no. I'm not asking you to lend it to me but to help me get it.

How?

Ever notice how many young kids hang around the Zoo Station loos at lunch time.

No, not really, but go on.

A lot of business gets done at lunch time in those loos.

What sort of business?

Businessmen's quickies. What the kids call 'cracking' it.

Cracking it?

Yeah, you know, having their butts fucked.

No way Karl. I couldn't. Not for you or anyone else. I'm not interes...

Karl's laughter cut me short as he realized what I was saying. I felt like a complete fool. I could just see him imagining me heroically bent, anxiously lowering my pants to expose my still virginal white bum, uttering a tentative plea to be gentle, and then squeezing my eyes shut as I waited for the first exploratory prod.

I started to laugh myself.

You're incredible Wolfi, you know that. Wait till I tell Marianne. Greater love than this hath no man than that he pull down his pants for his friend...God, that's a relief. What if you'd said yes?

He began laughing again.

No, what I had in mind was to roll one of these rich arseholes.

How do you mean?

You know, threaten to beat the shit out of him if he doesn't hand over his wallet. Take his cash and credit cards and work on from there.

Sounds risky to me.

Not if you're careful. I've done it once or twice before. They're usually so shit scared you don't even have to ask. Besides, there's not much choice, is there.

So what do you want me to do?

Just keep an eye out. I know the routine pretty well. The kids who are cracking it have a territory. There's usually about half a dozen of them and no one else operates their beat. Most of the customers are regulars who barely disguise what they want in any case. Occasionally there's a new-comer, so to speak. These kids have a sixth sense about a likely mark. It's uncanny really. The regulars are easy to pick, and sometimes even I can spot someone new, but these kids are amazing.

Karl's plan was for us simply to sit in the plaza and watch for one of the boys to be picked up by someone who looked loaded. We would then follow them down the stairs into the U-bahn station. I was supposed to keep watch outside the loos in case one of the railway cops came along.

What if someone turns up who wants to use the loo?

Would you? Look Wolfi, the only people who use them these days are homosexuals and junkies and now that the boys are working the place there are even fewer of these. And paradoxically, they're safer now. Hardly anybody gets beaten up anymore—it's bad for business. From time to time the authorities go on a blitz but for the most part they just turn a blind eye; who are they to stand in the way of ah, private enter-prize. That's what some of the kids call it you know, turning a blind eye. If someone should happen along, he's probably on the make. You should be able to stall him for thirty seconds by haggling over the price, or by asking him for money. Tell him the loos are closed, or just suggest it's not in the interest of his health to want to crap just at that very moment.

What about the kid?

Don't worry about him. I can be very persuasive when I need to be.

In the plaza the sun was shining and the air was warm. There were a lot of people about—singly, in pairs or small groups: business-suited men hurrying for lunch dates or business appointments, absorbed in speculation; lovers

223

strolling arm in arm, just enjoying the sunshine; smart-looking women in sunglasses and, of course, groups of street-wise kids.

Our boys were doing a brisk trade, so much so that Karl was worried. At times, two of them were gone at once.

Remember how I said these kids are amazing, how they have a sixth sense for spotting someone new. See that kid over there, the blond one. Karl pointed to a good-looking boy with blond hair who reminded me of Tadzio in Visconti's *Death in Venice*. One day I was watching them, you know, studying how they went about their business when this blond-headed kid suddenly gets up from the edge of the fountain where he had been sitting and walks quickly across the plaza, across the street and hurries along it for about fifty metres. Then he doubles back and begins casually walking towards a guy strolling arm in arm with what must have been his wife. The kid was looking in the other direction until the instant they passed. I swear there must have only been a microsecond's eye contact between them. He walks back to his friends without turning around. The guy walks on for a few metres, then glances quickly back over his shoulder. I watched his arm disengage itself from his wife's and they stopped and faced one another. You could see him talking to her and her nodding. He pointed to his watch and then to some destination further up the street. She nodded again. His right arm reached up to her shoulder and he bent slightly to kiss her on the forehead. She turned to go. His hand seemed to linger for a moment on her retreating shoulder, as though it preferred to go with her rather than be part of his betrayal. But his head had already turned towards the group of boys and his impatient eyes began searching for the object of his obviously undisclosed passion. He stood for some seconds like this, his hand half-beckoning, half-waving to a wife already lost in the crowd. At last he found what he was looking for and would have. He glanced in the direction his wife had taken while his body began hesitantly to move in the opposite direction, half aware it might run into someone walking across its path. Then he turned and made his way towards where this little blond god was seated. I got up myself and inconspicuously circled around to where their little group was gathered to try to hear what was said. You know, the guy wasn't even German. He was an English tourist! I tell you, these kids are amazing.

As I looked around at what was going on in the plaza it struck me that each instant seemed to imply a random cross-section in time, something completely patternless, but that if one could have photographed the plaza from high overhead with a time-lapse camera then, in the speeded-up film that resulted, a pattern would emerge. Tiny loci would appear, like microscopic encounters. Invisible scenarios were being enacted, the impact and significance of which might eventually be revealed by a frame-by-frame analysis of this constant flux. Perhaps even our own role in this complex drama would eventually have been unravelled from such a film, that is, of course, unless we had suddenly vanished in one of those crucial interstitial moments between frames.

A high-pitched girlish giggle a short distance away reminded me for a moment of Klaus Brambach's poem.

W.C.W. begegnet H.H.	*W.C.W. meets H.H.*
in Central Park	*in Central Park*
Die rosa Zungen	The pink tongues
drei junger Lolitas	of three young Lolitas
auf einer grünen Bank	on a green bench
nahebei	nearby
schleckten an weissen	licked at streams
Gerinne	of white ice cream
schmelzenden Eises	from
von	crisp cones
knusprigen Waffeln	held high
hoch gehalten	

I had never registered the obvious sexual content of these lines, but now as I watched the three young girls opposite us and heard their peals of obscene laughter I realized they could not be interpreted in any other way.

Here we go, Karl said, clutching my arm.

I felt my heart skip a beat. He was already standing. I got to my feet and looked across the plaza. There, by the group of boys, was a tall, well-dressed, dignified-looking man in his early sixties. He was grey-haired and wore a lightweight overcoat. From where we were he seemed almost jovial. Somehow I had expected that Karl would roll someone sleazier, someone less conspicuous. The terms of the transaction seemed to have been completed and one of the boys got up. It was only when the old guy turned to follow him that I realized he was leaning heavily on a walking stick.

For Christ's sake Karl, he's got a gammy leg. He's probably a bloody war veteran. You're going to mug someone who was an air ace in the Luftwaffe.

Shut up Wolfi. I'm not going to mug anyone.

We started to make our way slowly across the plaza.

I recognize this guy. He comes here two, maybe three times a week. Sometimes he just gets his chauffeur to pull up at the kerb and signals one of the boys to come over. Half an hour later he'll drop him back. Other times, like today, he'll send the driver on. If we were to stick around in half an hour you'd see him hopping into a blue chauffeur-driven Merc.

Yeah, hopping would be right.

Already I felt uneasy. Karl didn't bother replying. We watched as their heads disappeared down the stairs about twenty metres in front of us.

Besides, the fact that he's got a limp will give us more time to milk a few auto-tellers before he can call his bank to put a stop on his account.

Feeling guilty?

You just look after your end and I'll look after mine.

We headed down the stairs. In the pale fluorescent light of the platform there were fewer people about than I had anticipated but still too many to make me feel comfortable. In fact, now that we were down here I felt more nervous than ever. We walked quickly along the middle of the platform towards the long corridor which led to the men's toilets. As we had agreed I stopped in front of the entrance and got out my U-bahn plan. Karl stood in front of me, apparently talking to me but all the time watching our quarry over my shoulder as they made their way up the passageway.

Anybody there? I said, unable to suppress a tremor in my voice.

He spoke quickly, emphatically.

No, they're just about to reach the door. There's a bench two-thirds the way along the corridor. Sit there as if you're going through your timetable. I won't be more than thirty seconds. They're in.

I turned to go.

No, not yet. Give him a minute to get his pants down.

We stood there waiting. Time seemed to slow to a stop. Karl was incredibly calm, smiling, appearing to talk to me all the time he was analysing what was going on around him, calculating. I felt dazed. I could feel the cool dampness of my shirt clinging to my back. Karl smiled at me again.

You okay?

Sure.

Okay then, let's get this show on the road. Just walk slowly, don't hurry.

At the corridor seat he lightly touched my arm.

Well, here goes. Won't be long.

I watched him disappear through the door, saw it close noiselessly. I looked at my watch and sat down. One of the fluorescent lights overhead kept blinking on and off. Suddenly I felt sick. I couldn't believe that what we had talked about and what had seemed so unreal was actually happening. The reality of the nightmare was that I now felt trapped. It was as if by going through that door Karl had entered another world and would never return. And yet, at the same time, I could never leave because in some irrational way I was forever bound by my agreement to wait for him. I felt like a character in a novel written by myself who runs into a character in a novel written by himself. I would have to sit here for all eternity tortured by my fear that at any instant someone would come along the corridor and Karl would be caught. I looked down the narrow shaft, transforming each person who walked by its entrance into a railway cop. I could feel the sweat forming on my forehead as I tried to suppress the urge to surrender to some catastrophic hallucination.

I looked down at my watch. Nearly a minute had passed. I could now see two men talking on the platform as Karl and I had done. One, who had a briefcase beside his right foot, gestured with a newspaper as he made some point. The other nodded. I looked at my watch again. A minute and a half. He had said thirty seconds! I watched as the second hand moved inexorably towards two minutes. My sickening feeling began to grow worse. Something must have gone wrong. What if Karl was in trouble? He had said nothing about what to do if he didn't come back. Two minutes! Jesus, what to do…Two minutes fifteen! I got up and half ran to the door and pushed it open. The graffiti covered white-tiled washroom was empty. I ran to the other door, shoved it open with a crash. I looked down the row of cubicle doors. The one at the end was open. The old man's cane lay in the middle of the floor together with his coat. I could hear a young voice counting: One hundred and forty-six, one hundred and forty-seven…

Suddenly a blurred form shot out from the open cubicle, crouched, both arms raised. My hands went up in a reflex action. He straightened.

Fuck Karl, what are you doing with a **gun**? You didn't mention anything about a gun! Fucking hell.

I ran down towards him. The boy in the next cubicle had stopped counting and had begun to whimper like an animal. Karl tried to stop me reaching him, pushing me roughly in the chest. I fended him off and looked in. The old guy was slumped back against the toilet cistern. His trousers were down around his knees, his flaccid penis obliviously content as it nestled against the creped sack of his scrotum. But his face was a mess. Blood was trickling down his cheek from a nasty gash across his temple.

Fuck Karl, I think you've killed him.

Fucking hero. Some people just…

The outside door opened.

Come on.

Karl was past me in a flash and had scooped up the old man's walking stick.

Get the coat, he hissed.

As the door began to open he reached through the gap and brought the knurled end of the cane sharply down on the back of the skull of a man dressed in overalls. He slumped to the floor.

Jesus, Karl!

For Christ's sake, will you shut up!

He pushed me hard through the doorway into the washroom and towards the outer door.

Give me the coat.

He bundled it under his arm.

Walk, don't run.

230

As we stepped into the corridor two men turned the corner and started coming towards us.

Just keep your head down and keep walking.

They passed. I heard one of them laugh.

Karl began speaking quickly.

Okay Wolfi, there's a train about to leave. Get on it a few cars up and get off at the next station. Ditch your jacket before you do.

What about you?

I'll take the south exit.

At the end of the corridor I glanced back. The men we had passed were just about to go through the door. We separated and I walked quickly across the platform and got onto the train. I watched Karl weaving his way through the people on the platform, keeping close to the wall. Then he disappeared from view behind the pillar of the window. As the door hissed to I looked back to the entrance of the corridor. To my horror one of the men we had passed was already standing there, looking wildly up and down the platform. Suddenly he turned and broke into a run. The train began to move. For a short distance he kept pace with us as the train picked up speed. Out of the corner of my eye I could see the strain on his face as he brushed past people. Some of the other passengers had noticed him too and had begun to point. A few of them started to cheer. We began to leave him behind. I waited for the bright arch of the south entrance to come into view. As it flashed by I had just enough time to see that it was empty, except for a group of schoolgirls and, halfway up the stairs, a stooped little old lady in a dark coat. One hand rested on the banister while the other leant on her walking stick. Around her head she was wearing a red scarf. I smiled to myself. The train hurtled into the underground darkness.

I pushed my way past a number of other passengers swaying in the aisle and into one of the less crowded front cars where I found an empty seat and sat down. I now felt strangely exhilarated. It was as though what had happened represented some sort of breakthrough for me. I realized I had thought of Karl as being virtually invincible. He had been right. I **had** created a hero out of him. Yet things had gone horribly wrong. **He** had been wrong. How we managed to escape was a miracle. I resolved never to trust Karl to quite the same extent again.

I got off at the next stop. To my dismay there were two railway cops on the platform. One of them got onto the train. To get out I had to pass the other. It was impossible for me to reboard the train. That would have been just as dangerous. I caught up with a small group of people who had disembarked from the car in front of me and, walking as normally as my pounding heart would allow, I made my way towards the exit. His eyes quickly scanned our group and then moved on to the next. He was less than a couple of metres away when we passed but it was obvious he was no longer interested in us. I breathed a sigh of relief. I reached the turnstile and was just about to go through when I felt a large hand circle my upper arm and clamp tightly shut around it. I was brought instantly to a stop. I knew immediately all was lost and as I looked up I found myself staring into the face of one of the two men we had passed in the corridor.

232

While I waited for my father to arrive my life seemed to achieve a strange sense of serenity. All of the events that followed that catastrophic moment on the U-bahn platform seemed not to matter any more. What under normal circumstances would have been a harrowing couple of days now appeared in some way to be external, innocuous, unimportant. Things still happened of course, but it was as if I were cut off from them, separated, as though a wall of glass had been interposed between the external world and myself.

I watched myself being processed by the law: arrested, interrogated, searched, locked away and so on. Instead of being frightened or intimidated I suddenly became aware that something far more important was happening to me, something almost transcendent. I felt that if I concentrated hard enough I would be able to decipher the metaphysical static which surrounded my life, which in fact, surrounds all our lives but about which we are normally oblivious. To have this strange, background random noise, this celestial conceit of existence, suddenly become comprehensible made me feel wonderfully euphoric.

Perhaps it was this sense of euphoria which led to my initial lack of cooperation with the police. I simply did not care what happened to me. Initially I had told them my name was Wohlmann, a pretty common name really. When they asked me where I lived I told them that they should know.

What do you mean? they had asked.

Don't you read the papers, I said.

Wohlmann was a prominent government minister who was then under attack by the opposition for alleged misconduct: he'd been photographed consorting with a prostitute and the papers were full of it. Karl would have been proud of me and for an hour or two the police treated me with a certain nervous respect. However this soon gave way to outright anger once they had checked up on my story. I told them I had never said that I was **Gustave** Wohlmann's son, **they** had jumped to that conclusion.

Then they started asking me about Karl. I mean, they actually used his name. I must admit that this gave me quite a shock. I had forgotten about the kid locked in the cubicle and I could not recall having said Karl's name. In fact, I was sure I hadn't. Then they showed me a jacket and asked me if it was mine. There was no denying it so I said that it was. They showed me a letter. That really surprised me. I looked at it, turned it over. It was one Elena had sent me while I was in Heidelberg. I must have left it in one of the jacket's pockets. I told them it was from an old girlfriend, but of course they had checked up on this as well. As a result my father was on his way.

And it was actually my father's impending arrival which gave me my sense of serenity. Not because he would be able to rescue me from my situation but because I knew that, finally, we would have the showdown [Machtprobe] that had been written into our lives years before. Instead of my life being an unbroken stumbling from one unknown to the next, I could see a pattern beginning to crystallize. Something transcendentally deterministic had been set in motion and instead of feeling trapped by this I felt suddenly released. My whole trip to Berlin, which even to me had seemed a strange aberration, now emerged as having some underlying purpose and that purpose was to act as the catalyst for the final confrontation between my father and myself.

The next day he arrived. I had expected him to be tired and gaunt. But in a way I had also expected him to be relieved. I had, after all, not seen my father in over a year. I thought that perhaps in the intervening time he might have mellowed a little. Instead, when I was taken from my cell to the waiting-room he was standing at the far end by the window looking out. We both stood there for a few moments, me looking at him and he appearing to look out the window. I waited for him to select the move which would determine the direction our little game would take. But as he made no attempt to make this move I went to the chair by the table and sat down. I watched him standing there with his hands behind his back just as I had seen him do hundreds of times before. I watched a faint ripple pass along his cheek. He turned to face me, but still said nothing. I watched his eyes staring inwards as he decided what course to take. It was strange. He looked younger than I remembered him to be and I found it difficult to believe that this still young, still handsome man was my father. Again I caught a rare glimpse of that something which was almost dandyish about him, something which surfaced fleetingly from time to time from beneath his impeccably presanitized self-assurance. I could see the illusory hint of sensuality that had attracted my mother as a young girl twenty-five years before. I waited for the suspended cycle to break.

When he did finally look at me I knew immediately what direction the game had taken. I could see from his set mouth and his cool aloof eyes that any notion of the joyful embrace of a prodigal son was entirely mistaken. And yet I wished he could break out of his inhuman paralysis. Just for once I wished he could overcome his denial of something fundamental, something human, something which would have allowed our final reconciliation.

Whenever my father felt under threat he was inclined to become melodramatic or, alternatively, he would callously select his opponent's weakest spot, lunge, retreat and lunge again. There was always a sense of overkill, as though he were overcompensating for some perceived weakness in himself. In an intellectual argument this could be devastatingly effective. Now, as we stared impassively at each other, I waited for the first thrust.

It may interest you to know, he said, that your mother is in hospital.

Then came the calculated follow through.

She has cancer...She's dying. While you've been here indulging yourself in God knows what...

His voice became choked with rage. He raised his clenched fist.

And now this!

I felt numbed by the impact of what he had said. How was it that a few simple words, meaningless sounds in themselves, could suddenly make one feel so ill? How was it that they could suddenly crash unannounced and unwanted into your consciousness, instantaneously devastating the existing order of your life, leaving it irrevocably altered?

I hated my father for doing this to me. I wanted him to take back the words he had uttered, not to have heard them. I wanted to step out of this instant and go back to a point which led in some completely different direction. This was not the moment of inevitability I had meant. This was not the release I had sought.

Haven't you...

Shut up, I said. Shut up, shut up, **shut up**. I don't want to hear.

I was shouting. The guard had risen to his feet and stood nervously watching us.

Take me back, I said. I've had enough.

Two days later I was released on bail on the condition that I didn't leave Berlin, that I stay at the hotel where my father was staying and that I report to the police once every two days. They still had not found Karl and my own attempts to find out what had happened to the old man were greeted with an evasive silence. Because of my mother's illness a preliminary hearing had been set down for the following week.

The final confrontation did come two nights later. Against my father's wishes I had disappeared for the afternoon. He thought I had taken off altogether. Instead I had gone back to Kreuzberg, taking care that I was not followed, not that it mattered. When I got there the door to Karl's room was open and his personal belongings were gone. So was much of what else had been in his room. He had obviously gone. I went to my own room and packed up my papers and some other bits and pieces and put them into a bag. I knew I wouldn't be back. I called by to see Marianne but there was no one at her place either. Then I went to the theatre. Nobody had seen either of them for days. They had simply disappeared.

When I got back to the hotel around seven my father was waiting for me in my room. He was furious.

What are you doing here? I said.

Where have you been?

How'd you get in?

I asked you where you'd been.

What did you do, bribe the management?

Are you going to answer me?

Are you going to answer me?

Well?

Well?

We had reached a stalemate pretty quickly. But what he said then was completely uncalled for.

If it wasn't for you, he said, your mother wouldn't be in hospital at this very moment.

Are you accusing me of causing mother's illness? I shouted. **Me!** After years of your indifference. All you ever cared about was your bloody career. You never gave a damn about any of us. You were so caught up with yourself and what you were doing that you wouldn't have even known what was going on in your own home—what went on for years under your very nose.

What do you mean?

Want to know who Anya's real father is?

He looked at me suspiciously.

What do you mean? Who Anya's **real** father is.

Just that, I said.

Even then I knew by the frightened look on his face that he still had not guessed.

Who?

Me, I said. Me, me, me. Anya is **my** child. She's **my** daughter.

THREE

What does eternity matter to me? To lose the touch of flowers or a woman's hands is the supreme separation.

Camus

20

After I received Wolfi's package I heard nothing more from him. Nor was I able to contact him. All I knew of his address in Berlin was that he lived in a condemned tenement somewhere in Kreuzberg. I had no idea what Karl's theatre group was called or where they met. I didn't even know Wolfi's address in Klagenfurt. Through the Austrian Embassy I was able to get hold of a Klagenfurt telephone directory. There were half a dozen entries under Schönborn, T. I wrote letters to Wolfi at each of these addresses. Two of these were eventually returned unopened months later. I have no idea what happened to the others. I also wrote to Wolfi's father at Graz University, but again there was no reply.

It wasn't until June 1986, when I was invited by the Verein Deutscher Schriftsteller to attend a conference in Berlin, that I had the opportunity to try to relocate him. I would, I decided, stay on a couple of weeks to see what I could turn up.

Arriving in Berlin by air is a bizarre experience. The Wall runs through the city like a huge scar through a beautiful face. One side is expressive, vibrant, alive; the other is inert, pale and vacant. Or so it seems. West Berlin is an elegant city, self-conscious, chic and vital. There is a sense of energy, an energy that is fuelled by the manifest absurdity of its partitioning. People seem to be aware of living their lives at the very cutting-edge of the East–West conflict. It is a city where tomorrow doesn't exist, where the only moment is NOW.

So much for Berlin.

As the conference dragged on, I realized I had merely used it as a pretext to get myself back to Germany. Now that I was actually here I was more interested in the reality of finding Wolfi than in discussing endlessly subtle questions of narrative technique.

I had been sitting in the conference for two days, bored and fed up, when suddenly something in my brain locked instantly into the words of the speaker at the front of the auditorium. He was quoting from a sheet in front of him:

Sie erinnerte sich, wie die Strassenlaternen die platten Pflastersteine in schimmernde Lichtbögen verwandelten, Lichtbögen die, als sie sich ihnen näherte, wie Hunderte von winzigen, glänzenden Flügeln zu flattern schienen. Sie hatte den Eindruck, nicht mit dem Boden verbunden zu sein, sondern zu schweben.

I could not believe my ears. I flipped quickly through my conference programme until I found:

Kleist: Unveröffentlichte Fragmente.
A discussion of a recently discovered
unpublished manuscript by Heinrich von
Kleist.
Speaker: Dr T. Hatzenbühler

244

I could not have been mistaken. It was almost exactly the same image Wolfi had used five years earlier:

> She recalled how the street-lamps transformed the polished cobblestones ahead of her into shimmering arcs of light, arcs which seemed to flutter like hundreds of tiny radiant wings as she moved towards them. She had the impression that rather than walking, she was floating over them.

I listened stunned as I heard what was essentially a recapitulation of Wolfi's account of the Bessermann trial, except that this account had been written in 1810, just eighteen months before Kleist's death.

At the first opportunity I slipped out of the conference and took a taxi to the State Library. Here I went through the microfilmed back issues of the *Süddeutsche Zeitung* for the period March to May 1981. The only report I could find that in any way resembled the Bessermann story was the pathetic account of a man who had abducted his daughter as a result of a custody dispute. But the resemblance between what Wolfi had told me and the Kleist story was indisputable. All the major details were there: the parents, the fiancé, her disappearance, the baby, her grief, the subsequent calamitous recognition, everything. It was extraordinary.

When I walked back down the steps of the library, I was too agitated to go back to the conference. I decided to hire a car and drive around Kreuzberg. I spent the next four hours just driving round and round the crumbling old tenements. My intention was not so much to find the building in which Wolfi had lived—this had more than likely been demolished years ago—but to feel myself into part of what had been his world for a time. As I drove I kept saying to myself—perhaps he had walked down this street, waited at this bus stop, sheltered under the eaves of that shop one cold day in the rain, saw this section of skyline in the twilight. Perhaps the same faulty neon sign or cryptic piece of graffiti had caught his eye. 'Happy Birthday Dad, love Dave', I saw scrawled in English on the grey expanse of the wall near the Bellevuestrasse viewing platform. Maybe Karl had modelled himself on an old woman I glimpsed making her way down one of the side streets with an odd rocking motion, her plastic shopping bags held strangely away from her body.

The next afternoon I went to Maximilians. I tried to imagine which seat it had been that Karl had been sitting at when Wolfi saw him through the window. I imagined them arguing, watched as Karl stormed out, heard the coffee machine hiss. Ja, bitte?

That same afternoon I made my way down to the Kaiser Wilhelm Gedächtniskirche which overlooks the plaza where Wolfi and Karl had waited that fateful afternoon. I too sat in the sun watching people come and go. My eyes kept returning to the blue U-bahn sign above the stairs leading down to Zoo Station. It seemed to beckon me. I got up and began walking towards it. This was not a wholly conscious decision and as I neared the top step I became aware that for some completely irrational reason my heart was pounding. It was as though I had stepped into another dimension, as though Wolfi were there standing invisibly beside me. I had never experienced anything quite like this and, quite literally, the hairs on the back of my neck began to prickle. Down I walked.

On the underground platform, this powerful sense of unease seemed to intensify. I could see and hear what was going on about me perfectly, and yet I felt simultaneously cut off from it, as though by some invisible barrier. A train pulled into the station. People got anonymously off and others, equally anonymously, got on. I heard the loudspeaker overhead abruptly announce 'Zurückbleiben'. Everything **looked** absolutely normal and yet, as I watched people ascending the staircase down which I had just come, I had the overwhelming impression that the moment they had disappeared from view they disappeared altogether. I was sure that if I rushed back up onto the plaza I would find it completely deserted, ominously still, apart from a piece of white paper bounding mysteriously across the concrete. Worse, I would find myself teetering on the edge of a dark and infinite abyss.

I turned and began walking along the platform towards a corridor on my left the arched entrance of which grew larger as I neared it. Then I was standing in front of it. I looked down its long badly lit length.

Jesus! I said under my breath.

There in the flickering light, halfway along the corridor, someone was sitting slouched over, as if reading a train timetable. I glanced quickly up and down the platform, then began to make my way tentatively towards them. I could feel myself beginning to sweat as I tried to make out their features. As I got closer, however, I saw that what I had taken to be someone sitting there in the flickering light was not a person at all but a large plastic garbage bag squashed into the seat. Beside it an old coat spilled onto the floor. I laughed nervously to myself. This was ridiculous. But with this the spell had been broken and as I pushed open the washroom door and saw the graffiti-covered, cracked white tiles which Wolfi must have glimpsed as he ran through to where Karl was, I had completely regained my sense of calm. The feeling that I was being drawn along by some irrational force had gone. Objectively, calmly, I looked around. One of the washbasins had a large hole in it. Its taps had been removed. 'Fit mit Shit' had been sprayed in blue paint across one of the mirrors. I pushed open the other door. A row of half-opened cubicles confronted me. Out of curiosity I walked down to the end one. Suddenly something, someone, lunged out at me. Jesus, what the... Instinctively my hands went up to protect my face and I started to duck. I felt a body crash heavily against mine and then whirl around to face me. I stood ludicrously stooped for a moment. A short, dark man who was obviously not German stared suspiciously back at me. He was wearing overalls and carrying a mop.

Jesus, you gave me a fright, I said.

What you want? he said.

Nothing, I replied.

Then what are you doing here?

I shrugged my shoulders.

Nothing, nothing. I just had to see something.

He looked at me closely again, then turned and reached into the cubicle to retrieve a bucket.

You looking for boys? he asked.

No.

You a foreigner?

Yes, I said.

It's not safe here, he said. You want to shit, go shit some place else.

With this he brushed past me and went out. A few moments later, still a little shaky, I left myself.

I spent the next couple of days searching for other clues which might have helped me find Wolfi. I went back to the State Library and sifted through all the back issues of the local newspapers from June to September 1982 for any reference to a mugging at Zoo Station. I also went through the court reports. There was nothing. I went to Central Police Headquarters, a large and forbidding fortress-like building opposite the Tiergarten, to see if there was any record of Wolfi's arrest. Initially they refused to help me. The sort of information I wanted was confidential. I insisted on speaking to someone higher up. The young constable I spoke to was clearly unimpressed. He disappeared for a few minutes then returned.

You will please follow me, he said tersely in English.

He led me briskly to a door at the end of the corridor and we began rapidly ascending a long flight of stairs. He was taking them two and three at a time so that I was virtually forced to run to keep up with him. As it was I was barely able to keep his disappearing heels in sight, and to make matters worse the stairway was covered in a fine, choking dust which he kicked up as he went, making it almost impossible for me to breathe. I was on the verge of stopping, furious with his impudence, when I looked up to see him standing composed and utterly indifferent on the next landing. He was holding a door open with one arm and when I reached him he ushered me through with a sweeping, insolent gesture of his hand. I was then led through an unoccupied maze of partitions to a small office outside which we stood for a few moments before he knocked. When we entered I found myself standing opposite a sad looking, bald-headed man in his fifties who was sitting behind a large wooden desk which was absolutely clear except for a single sheet of white paper in front of him.

Entschuldigung, Herr Inspektor Schlossmann, das ist der Kerl der mit Ihnen sprechen will [this is the bloke who wants to talk to you].

I was about to protest his use of the term 'Kerl' when Herr Schlossmann interrupted me.

Ja, ja. Das weiss' ich schon! he said irritably. [Yes, I know that!]. Geh' jetzt [Now go].

The young constable did an about-face and left.

The Inspector turned to me and asked what my problem was. I began telling him my story. He sat there as I spoke, staring impassively up at me, merely swivelling from time to time in his chair. When I finished he remained silent for some minutes.

You like Handke? he said finally.

Well, I started to say, a little startled by his question, amongst the post-war genera...

Nein, nein, nein, he said angrily. Keinen solchen Mist! [No, no, no. None of that shit!]. Just tell me, do you like him or not?

Yes, I said shrugging my shoulders.

He looked away. He brought the fingertips of his hands which rested on the desk together.

Where are you staying? he said eventually.

I gave him the name of my hotel.

Someone will call you.

He got up, wordlessly shook my hand and showed me to the door.

The rest of the afternoon I spent finding out what I could about the experimental theatre groups that still existed in Berlin. I started at the Theater am Kurfürstendamm, then called by the tourist information office where I picked up a number of pamphlets on what was being performed at the time, and then finished by dropping into almost every performing arts café dotted along Kantstrasse and the neighbouring side-streets. By the time I finished I had quite a list.

I spent all the next day and most of the night driving from one renovated warehouse or tumbledown theatre to the next. Several of these were in Kreuzberg, but not one of the people I spoke to could remember anyone called Karl Richter or Karl Klebbermann, let alone someone called Wolfi Schönborn.

What about someone called Vladan or Vlad?

No, no one by that name either. Sorry.

I got back to the hotel late that night, tired and more than a little disappointed. I had just called down for some coffee to be brought up to my room when the phone rang. It was the police. They had been trying to get me all day. There was a pause. I could hear a muffled voice in the background. Then they came back on.

Yes, here we are. You were after some information on a Wolfgang Schönborn.

Yes, that's right.

I'm afraid that our Personal Assault files show no record of anyone by that name.

Nothing?

No, nothing at all. I'm sorry.

Another blank, I thought.

I thanked them and hung up.

I began to think that perhaps the world which Wolfi had created in his correspondence really didn't exist, and had never existed. I lay down on the bed to think over where I would go from here. The phone rang again. Distractedly I reached out and picked up the receiver.

Hello, I said. Hello...

The line was bad and I could barely make out a voice on the other end.

Kaiser Marine, Kaiser Marine, it kept saying.

I'm sorry, I yelled into the receiver. I can't hear you...

Then I heard a female voice say clearly: Karl Richter. Karl Richter. You were looking for Karl.

I sat up.

Yes, I yelled. Actually I'm looking for Wolfi. Wolfgang Schönborn.

Wolfi?

Yes, yes. Do you know him?

The phone crackled incomprehensibly. I cursed it.

What?

Do you know him?

Yes. Can you meet me?

When?

Now, in...

When? I can't hear you. God damn this bloody phone.

Half an hour. At Vivaldi's.

Vivaldi's?

Ask the hotel desk.

What's your name?...Your name?

Marianne. Marianne...Scheysermentsch. In half an hour, okay?

Marianne!...Hang on.

Too late. She rang off.

I stood looking at the phone in my hand.

I grabbed my coat. As I opened the door and hurried out I narrowly missed colliding with a young, uniformed boy with bad skin from room service carrying a tray with cups and a pot of coffee on it. He stood looking at me.

Just put it on the table, I said quickly. I pushed a ten-mark note into his hand and retreated down the corridor.

At the reception desk I asked the night-porter where I could find a place called Vivaldi's. He bent down and got out a map of the inner city area and spread it out on the counter before him, smoothing its creases.

This is us here...with the red circle, he said slowly. Well not exactly us if you get my drift. He looked up at me and smiled inanely.

I wasn't sure what he meant.

His finger meaningfully tapped a spot at the base of an arrow pointing to the red circle.

Sie sind hier, it read. [You are here.]

I began to get impatient.

Theater des Westens is here and Vivaldi's...Let me see, Vivaldi's...ah yes, Vivaldi's is here. It's about four blocks away. You can't miss it. So from here you go...

Yes, yes, I said. It's okay, I think I can find it. Thanks.

I turned and headed towards the door. Outside, the reflection of the lights glistened on the pavement. It was raining.

Damn!

I glanced back at the desk. The night-porter was already holding an umbrella towards me in his outstretched arm. He smiled.

Eile mit Weile, he said as he handed it to me.

He was right. More haste, less speed.

Danke. Danke schön, I said.

Bitte schön, he said, inclining his body towards me slightly. I could almost feel the imperceptible click of his heels.

I stepped out into the wet night, raised the umbrella and began walking quickly towards town. Finally, after the disappointment of the last couple of days, Wolfi's world was becoming a reality.

On Kurfürstendamm, despite the rain, which had begun to ease, the streets were already alive with people. The distorted, inverted shapes of traffic lights, flashing neon signs and illuminated interiors of passing cars shone back up at me, reflected in the glazed surface of the wet pavement. Mushroom-shaped silhouettes moved mysteriously about in twos or threes or congregated at the kerbside briefly before launching themselves collectively towards the other side. The Germans have a word for the sticky swish of tyres on

254

wet pavement—it is 'zischen'. Its 'z' is pronounced 'ts'. As I walked along I could hear the repeated tsisch-tsisch of the car tyres as they passed, interrupted from time to time by the blast from a car horn. In the brightly lit doorways of the numerous peepshows and strip joints located at this end of Kurfürstendamm sleazily suited men stood repeating a monotonous litany of sordid suggestion to any passer-by who strayed within earshot. A young woman stepped out of the shadows and said something to me. I walked on.

Don't you like me? I heard her call softly.

I felt as though I was walking on a precariously thin, transparent laminate between the mirror image of two separate worlds. Any minute, if I lost my rhythm and missed meeting the foot which rose to meet mine, I ran the risk of falling through. I began to feel giddy as I concentrated on keeping exactly in step with the unknown person walking beneath me.

About twenty minutes later I walked past the Theater des Westens and turned into the narrow side-street the night-porter had indicated on the map. A little ahead of me and on the opposite side I could see the name 'Vivaldi's' written in large Gothic letters across one of the shop-front windows.

I stood for a moment under its awning shaking the rain off my umbrella and then pushed the door open.

Inside, only half a dozen tables were occupied and all of these by groups. I ordered a drink from the bar and sat at one of the tables by the window and waited.

I had been there less than five minutes when I saw a tall attractive-looking woman in a dark, high-collared coat quickly cross the street. She came in, dropped her umbrella in the stand, unbuttoned her coat and hung it on the rack. She shook her head and ran her hand through her hair a number of times. Although they were completely different, for some reason I was reminded of my night with Andrea in Heidelberg years earlier. The thought passed fleetingly through my mind that perhaps at the end of the night we would end up in bed together. She turned.

Sorry I'm late, she said.

I went to get up.

That's okay, a male voice beside me answered, we've only been here a couple of minutes ourselves.

She smiled at me as she squeezed by to join a group of young people sitting at the next table. She kissed her friend lightly on the cheek. His hand rose to rest on her shoulder. I settled uncomfortably back into my chair.

God, what a night, I heard her say.

I sat looking across at her, wondering what opportunity had been missed, what loss incurred.

Once she even appeared to look across at me, as if suddenly she had become aware that I was thinking about her. I saw her hand rise as if to say to her companions: Just a second, I can hear something. Can you hear it? It's like someone talking. She looked down at the table, frowned and then looked back up at me. Perhaps I was imagining it but I am sure that in that instant something had passed between us. The moment was broken, however, by another group of people who came noisily through the door. Shortly after, she and her friends got up and left.

I waited until after eleven. Marianne had rung at ten and still she hadn't arrived. Finally I went across to the bar and asked the barman if he knew anyone called Marianne who may have been a regular. He didn't. I waited another fifteen minutes. I guess I already knew she wasn't going to turn up. I decided to leave a note at the bar asking her to phone me again and then left myself.

Outside it had begun to rain again. I walked slowly back to the hotel.

The next night I phoned to see if anyone had asked after me or if my note had been picked up. No one had. For the remainder of my stay in Berlin I was not to hear from her again.

The following week I caught a flight to Vienna and from there took the train to Klagenfurt. I booked into a little hotel a kilometre or two from the centre of town.

After dinner I went for a walk through some of the older, more romantic streets until I found myself high up on one of the slopes of the hills. In some ways it reminded me of Heidelberg. I sat there for a long time watching the dimming evening settle into the creviced network of streets below.

In the morning I was up early. I had decided that my first plan of action would be to go through the phone book once again and ring every T. Schönborn listed. So at about eight-thirty I began making calls. Of the half dozen or so I made, only two answered. Neither of them knew of any Wolfgang Schönborn. I would have to try again later. On the spur of the moment I decided to walk into town.

I am convinced there are times in everyone's life in which fate seems to intervene directly in the course of events. There is simply no other explanation that adequately explains why a particular thing happens or why a situation turns out as it does.

My route into town took me past the local cemetery. I had almost gone completely by and was making a mental note of how strange some of the headstones were when it suddenly occurred to me that had Wolfi's mother died she would probably have been buried right here, and that if she had been I would more than likely be able to find out Wolfi's address from the cemetery register. I hurried back.

The caretaker's cottage was located under two large elm trees just to the right of the main gates. I knocked on the door. It was some time before anybody answered, but eventually the door opened and an elderly man with a prominent stoop stood there looking up at me. He had large, watery eyes set in an incongruously cheerful face.

I was wondering, I said, if you could tell me if a Mrs Schönborn is buried here, a Mrs Eva Schönborn. She died in...

1982. Yes, yes. Eva Schönborn. Born 6 June 1939, died 4 September 1982, requiescat in pace. He crossed himself.

Yes, that sounds right, I said. Could you tell me where she's buried?

He pulled the door to.

Come, he said.

He led me down a number of rows of indescribably grotesque tombstones before stopping in front of a simple plaque in white marble.

I stood looking at it for a while, not knowing what to say.

A tragedy, the old man said finally.

I nodded.

A tragedy, he repeated. First the mother, then the son. The son!

Yes. A terrible business. Terrible, terrible. Shot himself. And then the father refusing to allow them to be buried together. Terrible.

He led me around to another row of graves and there before me was what I had never expected nor ever wanted to see:

Wolfgang Schönborn
3 March 1958 – 10 September 1982

I stood there numb.

Wolfgang Schönborn
3 March 1958 – 10 September 1982

Wolfgang Schönborn...I couldn't believe it, wouldn't believe it. I felt as though the ground had been swept out from under my feet. Utter stillness, invisibly solid seemed to begin to descend upon me, as though it were being poured around me, encasing my feet, my legs, my arms, until it began to suffocate me. I wanted to cry out. Far off in the distance I could see the retreating figure of the old care-taker. I felt myself choking. Shakily I stumbled over to a nearby bench and sat down.

I sat there for a long time just thinking about Wolfi, thinking about the things he had written, about conversations I had had with him. I remember thinking that discovering his death in this way seemed so malevolently capricious. Relocating Wolfi had been something I had been indulging myself in, innocently savouring its sense of mystery, of real-life adventure. Then—bang. Suddenly I had collided with something which seemed to send my life crashing wildly off course. A thousand questions clamoured for answers against the numbness in my head. Why had he done it? Nothing in what he had written had given the least indication that he had intended taking his own life. Had this been what he had meant by his note: 'Perhaps **you** can make something of this?'

I sat there thinking of all the life he had breathed into the recounting of his experiences. And now—nothing, absolutely nothing.

Eventually I got up and walked slowly back to the caretaker's cottage. He was sitting outside filling his pipe. I sat down near him.

You a friend of the family? he asked.

No. I knew Wolfi, the son, a couple of years ago. This has come as a great shock to me.

He nodded.

Do you know any more about what happened?

No. Just that. One week the mother died. The next week, the son. He had to be flown back from Berlin.

Berlin? So he didn't die here then?

Nope. They found his body by the river. Shot through the head like I said.

I winced.

Although, now I come to think of it, there **was** some

260

doubt about whether it was suicide or not. Something about the angle the bullet entered the brain…

He held a match to his pipe, sucked the flame into it, then expelled a couple of small bursts of smoke.

There was talk about some trouble with the police, about the son being mixed up with drugs, something like that…If you ask me, he was bumped off [abgemurkst]. Yep, he was bumped off alright if you ask me.

He sat looking out over the cemetery, his watery eyes squinting.

Look, I said, I'd like to get in contact with his father. Would you have his address by any chance?

Yep, but it won't help you none.

Why not?

Round the twist, that's why. Completely barmy [total bekloppt].

He tapped the side of his head. They've put him away. There's a daughter though who comes here every week to put flowers on the son's grave. Good-looker. I think I've got her address someplace.

He got up and went inside. A few minutes later he came back with a slip of paper.

Here we are, 40 Schröderstrasse. It's on the far side of town.

I thanked him. I stood there for a moment debating whether to go back to Wolfi's grave. When I turned back to him the old man had already disappeared inside.

Still a little dazed I decided to leave the cemetery and I wandered into town. I sat under one of the chestnut trees in the park. Had I been blind to some hidden message in what Wolfi had written? Had he foreshadowed his death in some subtle way that I had not perceived? And if I now went back over what he had written would I be able to read a single sentence of it without his death staring me in the face? Is this what Wolfi was talking about when he referred to the teleology of memory? Already I could feel an insidious sense of logic seeping up between the interstices of apparently arbitrary and unrelated events, morticing them together.

As I sat there, images of Wolfi kept floating up through my mind: watching him the first day through the doorway; me, standing on a chair, examining his head for imagined but non-existent baldness; watching him queue for food at the mensa. I saw him at the beach with Elena; saw him make his announcement 'Ich bin ein Mann' to his stunned family; watched him watching Karl flip things into his stomach; saw the look of horror on his face at the sight of the old guy slumped back against the toilet. My own experience of him through his writings had become amalgamated in my head. I could no longer distinguish between the two, so perfect the sense of continuity between them now appeared.

I walked back to the hotel and sat on the side of my bed going through the bound volume of Wolfi's material I had brought with me. I stood looking at the photo of Elena and Anya again. Anya, his child.

As I sat looking at the photograph I recalled what the old fellow at the cemetery had said: 'Now I come to think of it, there **was** some doubt about whether it was suicide or not. Something about the...' I imagined Wolfi confronting his father, telling him Anya was **his** daughter. I tried to envision in the moments that followed his father's reactions to the discovery that he and Elena had been lovers.

What, I wondered, had actually taken place in the time between that conversation and his death?

When I decided to go and see Elena I was not blind to the significance of a meeting with her. It would be the first time that the world which Wolfi had created in my mind and my own world would actually coalesce in fact.

The next day as I walked up the shaded path to 40 Schröderstrasse and knocked on the door I felt a strange mixture of nervous elation and residual depression.

The door opened and a young girl poked her head around from behind it. She had strikingly intense blue eyes which looked enquiringly up at me. I felt momentarily caught off-balance as I stared down at her. She would have been five or six years old. Her hair had grown darker and I watched as she brushed a lock of it back from her forehead.

Anya? I asked.

Yes, she said.

Is your mother home?

Without answering she turned back into the house and I heard her yell: Mummy, there's a man here to see you.

So, I had been right, I thought to myself.

I heard another set of footsteps approaching the door. This was really it.

The door opened fully to reveal a young woman in her twenties. Standing there she was even more remarkably attractive than the photographs of her had led me to believe. Her dark eyes looked at me almost expressionlessly at first, then she began to frown slightly. Her hand reached up in

263

the same gesture Anya had made to brush a loose strand of hair away from her face and then returned to rest on the door frame.

Yes? There was a slight edge to her voice, something anxious in her tone.

Are you Elena, Elena Schönborn?

Yes, she said again.

I'm a friend of Wolfi's. We were students together at Heidelberg. Look, I know this is probably difficult for you but could I come in for a minute? I won't keep you long.

She hesitated a moment and then opened the door and led me into a small sitting room.

Won't you sit down, she said. Would you like something to drink, tea or coffee or something else?

No, no thank you.

Anya came back into the room and stood by her mother's chair. Elena wrapped her arm around her waist. Apart from their eyes, the similarity was remarkable.

You see, the thing is, I said, I came looking for Wolfi. I had no idea that he was...Well, I had no idea what had happened. It was only by accident that I found out yesterday. It came as quite a shock to me...Quite a shock.

How do you mean, it was only by accident that you found out yesterday?

I told her what had happened, the phone calls, walking into town, the cemetery, seeing Wolfi's grave.

Yes, she said when I had finished, it was a terrible time, absolutely terrible. And now with my father's illness...

She got up, took a cigarette out of a packet on the mantelpiece, lit it and sat down again.

Do you know what happened? I said.

No. No one really knows. It was horrible really, not knowing. Anya darling, why don't you go out and play for a little while.

But I want to stay here with you.

Come on, sweetheart, it's just for five minutes. I won't be long, promise.

She pulled Anya to her and kissed her on the forehead. Okay?

Okay.

She watched as Anya left the room.

Where was I...Ah, yes. The thing is, we didn't know where Wolfi was. Oh I mean, we knew he was in Berlin; my father used to send money to an account there for him every month. Then in, it must have been May or early June, my mother suddenly became ill. A week later she was diagnosed as having cancer. They gave her a year, perhaps two.

She paused to take a puff of her cigarette. She waved the smoke away.

She died three months later, she said almost to herself. You know, my mother had never been sick a day in her life. Never. When she was young she had been quite extraordinarily beautiful...

She got up from the couch and went to the window. She pulled the curtain aside a little and looked out.

Yes, I said. Wolfi once showed me some photographs of her taken around the time she married your father.

Wolfi absolutely idolized her. She could have been a great pianist if it hadn't been for...She hesitated. Well, if things had been different.

265

If your parents had got on better?

She looked at me.

Wolfi told me your parents didn't get on.

Yes, she said. Although at first, they did. In an odd sort of way I'm sure my father also adored my mother. But in the end she came to represent everything he was not. She was alive, vibrant, passionate, while he saw himself as dead, sterile, passionless. He just closed off inside. Wolfi and he used to have the most awful fights. My father thought himself the great realist, the great rationalist. To him, Wolfi was just a dreamer, an escapee from reality. He saw my mother and Wolfi in an alliance against him. Eventually things became so bad Wolfi couldn't take it any longer. That's why he went to Heidelberg—to get away, and to complete his studies. But mainly to get away. Then the next thing we heard, he was in Berlin.

How did you manage to get in contact with him?

We didn't. About two weeks before my mother died there was a telephone call from the police in Berlin. Wolfi had been arrested for beating somebody up. My father was supposed to go and sort things out but that night my mother collapsed and she had to be taken to hospital. During the next couple of days she seemed to pick up and my father decided he would go to Berlin after all. She died the following Saturday. Wolfi was allowed to come back for the funeral on the condition he return to Berlin the next day.

At the funeral, things were terribly strained. Wolfi told me that on the night before they left Berlin he and my father had had a terrible argument, about my mother. When my father returned to Berlin Wolfi had disappeared. Two days later they found his body. He'd shot himself.

She paused for a moment.

The awful irony was that by this time all charges against him had been dropped.

Dropped?

Yes. I never was too sure about the exact details, but apparently the old guy whom he was supposed to have beaten up was involved with under-aged boys, sexually involved I mean. He's quite a prominent businessman in Berlin. So the charges against Wolfi were dropped. He knew that all of this would come out in court. Then he'd face criminal prosecution himself. The whole thing was just hushed up.

I see. At least that explains why the police in Berlin had no record of any charges against Wolfi.

She looked at me.

I went there you see...to Berlin.

Yes, but how did you know Wolfi was in trouble with the police?

He wrote to me. It's a long story really. You wouldn't believe what I've been through over the past ten days. Then again, perhaps you would. I paused for a moment. Is it possible that Wolfi didn't commit suicide?

What do you mean?

Well, that he was murdered.

Who'd want to murder Wolfi?

Well, from what I understand he was trying to get money for a friend to pay off a drug dealer. Or maybe the old guy had him killed to stop him talking. I don't know. But apparently at the coroner's inquest there was some doubt about whether he could have fired the shot or not, because of the angle the bullet entered the head.

267

Who told you that?

The old caretaker at the cemetery.

Himmelfarb?

I don't know. Probably.

I doubt it. They found the gun beside his body. It was one of my father's guns.

Your father's?

Yes, when my father was a young man he had been a military cadet. He was an excellent ma...

Her voice trailed off.

...an excellent marksman.

She looked across at me. I could see a moment of panic register on her face.

Wolfi had apparently taken one of the guns when he was here for the funeral, she said, half to herself. No. I don't believe it. He couldn't have. When my father arrived at the hotel Wolfi had already gone. He hadn't been there for days. My father had immediately phoned the police. That's when he found out the charges had been dropped.

How do you know all this?

My father told me...Look, you have no right to do this. It's taken me years to get over what's happened to my family. All I have left is Anya. You're saying that my father killed his own son. Why would he? He had no reason to. No, I won't believe it. It just isn't true.

She got up.

I think it might be better if you left, she said.

Look, I'm sorry. I'm not saying he did. In fact, until this very moment it never even crossed my mind that he had killed Wolfi. But...it's a possibility isn't it?

No, it's not! Why would he?

He didn't mention anything about having also argued about you and Anya that night in Berlin?

No, nothing. Why?

She looked at me suspiciously. Her hands were shaking.

Look, I don't know how to put this…but your father found out about you and Wolfi.

What do you mean he found out about Wolfi and me?

Her voice was trembling. She lifted her cigarette clumsily to her mouth.

Wolfi told him. He told him that **he** was Anya's father. That was what the real argument was about.

Oh God, oh God, she said.

She stood up and walked unsteadily to the mantelpiece. At that moment Anya came back into the room and ran to her. Elena bent down to embrace the child, tears streaming from her eyes.

It's okay, sweetheart, sweetheart.

She kept repeating the word as she bent to gather Anya into her arms.

Mummy, are you okay? Mummy?

I'm okay, sweetheart.

She stood up again. She looked at me, her face distraught.

I'm sorry, she said. I think you've said enough.

I went to say something else. She raised her hands.

Please, she said. No more, no more. Just go. **Please.**

She went to the door and stood by it without looking at me.

I stood by her for a moment on the threshold trying to think of something to say but nothing came. I wished

I could take back what I had said. I walked slowly down the steps and the door closed behind me.

What, I asked myself, did it really matter if Wolfi's father **had** killed him or if he had killed himself. He was dead, that was all that mattered. His father was now intractably insane. Elena and Anya were still together. All I had come to Germany for in the first place was to find out what had happened to him. In any other context I would have been determined to resolve the question one way or another. But to do this now would merely have been to cheapen the life of my friend, to turn it into a conundrum, a murder mystery in need of solution.

In recounting the story of my friend Wolfi, I have been guilty of the same sort of bad faith that I accused Camus of earlier. Or have I?

Of course I knew of Wolfi's death before I began writing his tale, indeed long before I had decided to put my recollections of him down on paper or to edit and assemble the material he sent me. It seemed to me that in the essentially three episodes of his life that he himself related he had created a self which was both separate from and an augmentation of the person I had known in Heidelberg. I could of course have done a number of things to expand and refine the picture I had of him. I could have gone back to his school to interview old friends or acquaintances. I could have tried to locate Andrea, if indeed she existed, or spoken with his grandmother. But, ultimately, what purpose would this have served? Wolfi had, in a sense, become displaced by a collection of memories, papers and photographs. I had become caught up in the 'fiction' of what he had written. Yet I could not help feeling that this was what was so cruel about his death—the sense of being left with a feeling of absolute loss, of irrevocable absence without appeal.

To return to Camus and narrative bad faith for a moment. In concluding Wolfi's story at this point I realize that in terms of its 'fictional' conception this is hardly satisfactory. As a 'story' it seems to have been wound up too quickly. The narrative momentum seemed to promise more. Too many questions remain unanswered. Unlike Camus, Wolfi's death does not seem to have been adequately prepared for. So be it. In some ways this mirrors the abruptness of my own discovery of the death of my friend. Suddenly everything just seemed to stop. Someone who had seemed so alive one minute, just ceased to exist the next. Instead of existence seeming meaningless and irrational, non-existence now appeared to me to be equally meaningless, equally irrational. Death is an arbitrary, not a necessary, condition of life. I must admit, however, that I do not fully understand this.

I might as well ask myself why Ingeborg Bachmann burnt herself to death one afternoon in her Rome apartment.

In her recollections she wrote how, often, she found it strange walking into a bookstore seeing her own books on the shelves. Strange how what she had spent hours and hours toiling over in her tiny room, what had become literally the transubstantiation of her self, had ended up being dispersed around the world in the form of complex patterns of ink printed onto sheets of bound paper.

What was she doing the day before her death? What were her thoughts as she lay in her petrol-soaked bed? What was going through her mind as she struck the match and sat propped up watching the small flame dancing around its bent black spine before, at last, she dropped it onto the bedclothes? As she lay back into the flaming pillows, had she caught one last glimpse of the outline of the fire before she finally lost control?

She was from Klagenfurt. Wolfi's father and she were contemporaries. They would have known each other. Perhaps Wolfi had even met her himself or had unknowingly seen her shopping in the local supermarket. Perhaps.

The more I reread Wolfi's material the more I am convinced that he took his own life. I do not know why I think this. I cannot see why he would have gone to the trouble of sending me what he sent me if he hadn't meant it to be read as some sort of long valedictory note. Then again, maybe he suspected his father would try to kill him. Maybe his account of their meeting that night is incomplete. Who knows? Who will ever know?

But the real impact for me of Wolfi's story ending here is the sense of a life wasted. I have no idea of how, had he lived, his life would have evolved, what ultimate destiny awaited him, or even what we would have said to each other had I eventually caught up with him.

I wrote Elena a short note expressing my regret at having come blundering into her life, re-opening old wounds. I left her my address in Australia to contact me in the event that she wanted me to send her any of Wolfi's material. I rang the airline in Frankfurt to see if I could get an earlier flight back home but was unable to. The remaining four days of my trip I would have to spend in Klagenfurt unless I wanted to move on to somewhere else. But by this stage I was overcome by such a strong sense of lethargy that I let my body have its way. Besides, I said to myself, if my mood improved I could still wander about the town that had produced Musil and Handke and Bachmann...and Wolfi.

But instead I spent the entire next day lying on my bed in my room, the curtains drawn, the overhead light on, my feet crossed, my hands behind my head, staring at the wood-panelled ceiling, inventing faces, weird animals and whole scenarios from its irregularly patterned grain. I watched a fly struggling in a small piece of cobweb beside the light fitting, half-expecting a spider to emerge at any moment to bundle it up for safekeeping. But none did. I worked out that the apparently randomly patterned wallpaper really consisted of regularly repeated motifs about forty centimetres square. In the end I could no longer look at it without instantly seeing how rigidly fixed this randomness was.

Two days before my departure I was again sitting in my room after the evening meal when there was a knock at the door. I opened it and to my surprise Elena was standing in the corridor.

Elena! I said.

May I come in?

Yes, please, I said gesturing to the only chair beside a small desk against the wall.

It's not very comfortable I'm afraid. Would you like me to have some coffee sent up?

No, no thanks.

Something else?

No. Nothing, really.

She sat down.

I went and sat on the side of the bed.

You said Wolfi had sent you a lot of material?

Yes. Quite a bundle.

Do you have it with you?

Yes. Well, not all of it. I've had most of it typed up, apart from 200 or so pages of philosophy notes, most of which I can't make head nor tail of. I don't know what I'll do with those. Wolfi's handwriting is not the easiest to read. And I don't have most of the photographs. There were a lot of photographs.

Could I see it?

Sure.

I went to my suitcase and retrieved a thick well-thumbed, paperbound volume and handed it to her.

God, he really had been busy, hadn't he.

Yes, from what I can gather, this is what he must have been working on in Berlin.

Could I borrow it?

I must have looked a bit taken aback.

I'll return it, she said immediately. I promise.

The only thing is, I leave Klagenfurt the day after tomorrow…

Please. Even if I don't finish it I'll return it tomorrow evening.

274

I suddenly felt quite mean. After all, it was her brother's. What right did I have to it at all?

No, look, I said. You keep it as long as you like. I had intended to use it to write a story about Wolfi, but if you'd like to hang on to it, you hang on to it.

She got up to go.

Will you be in tomorrow evening?

Yes, I should be. If not, you can leave it at the reception desk.

I knew already that I would be. I was delighted I would be seeing her again.

Till tomorrow then.

She took my hand and shook it.

Early the next morning the phone rang. It was Elena. She asked me if I would like to accompany her on a visit to her father, on the condition that I didn't try to interrogate him.

Why?

I thought you might like to meet him. I think you might change your mind about him.

Have you started reading Wolfi's stuff? I asked.

Yes, I've finished.

Finished?

Yes, I was up virtually all night. I need to see you. There are some things you should know.

What sort of things?

I can't explain over the phone. Can you be ready in half an hour?

Sure.

Okay, I'll pick you up outside the hotel.

275

She hung up.

Twenty-five minutes later she pulled up beside the kerb where I was standing, leant across and unlocked the door. I got in. She looked in the rear-view mirror and pulled away.

She was wearing sunglasses and her face was lightly made up. She had on a light blouse and a brightly coloured cotton skirt. I looked across at her and was reminded of Wolfi's description of Andrea. I wondered if for some reason Elena had deliberately dressed that way.

Where's Anya? I asked.

At my O...mi's, my grandmother's. But I guess you already know about her.

Yes, it's strange, I said. I feel like I've known her all my life and yet I've never even met her.

She smiled and shook her head. I looked through the windscreen.

She's still alive then?

She nodded.

She's eighty-five. Still bright as a pin. If Wolfi **did** get something right it was my grandmother.

She seemed relaxed now, calmer, as if finally something had been put in place.

I really am sorry about the other day, I said. It must have been awful for you to have someone suddenly resurrect the past.

Yes, yes it was, she said softly to herself.

We stopped at an intersection. She looked each way before swinging the car left and into the traffic.

You said there were some things that you wanted to tell me?

There are. But I want you to meet my father first.

We drove on in silence.

Half an hour later we pulled into a circular drive in front of a large red-brick building flanked by rows of ornamental conifers which had been trimmed to look like perfect green spheres balancing on short dark pedestals. Below the steps of the building was a large fountain, the centrepiece of which consisted of a writhing column of gleefully obscene potbellied putti pissing out into the water. It was wholly incongruous.

Elena parked the car and we made our way without comment past the fountain, up the stairs, through the doors and into a large open foyer.

As we approached the desk the nurse on duty looked up and said without being asked: He's in the garden. I watched as her eyes passed from Elena's to mine and behind the not unfriendly smile I could see a number of questions formulating themselves in her head, questions about who I might be and what the nature of my relationship with Elena was.

We turned and headed towards a pair of large plate-glass doors. Out in the garden we stood for a moment while Elena quickly scanned the other patients, most of whom were wandering about on their own or were being pushed along in wheelchairs by the hospital's orderlies.

Other visitors were sitting hopelessly by vacant-looking elderly relatives, forlorn, empty husks of people. At the far end of the garden a couple of children were playing badminton, either bored by or oblivious to the destiny which might one day be their own. Their laughter rose and fell in time with the pathetic trajectory of the shuttlecock.

I watched it shoot into the air, watched it catch the sunlight momentarily against the sombre backdrop of the firs and then saw it fall lazily to ground like a tiny toppled ballerina. A small boy scrambled after it.

There he is.

Her hand came away from her forehead and she started to walk across a narrow gravel path towards the shape of a man sitting with his back towards us on a bench about fifteen metres away. He was wearing one of the hospital gowns and as we approached I thought that except for his slightly unshaven face he looked more like one of the doctors than one of the patients. His legs were crossed and one arm rested along the back of the bench.

Even when we walked around in front of him and he looked up at both of us for an instant I thought that he was completely sane. But his expression quickly changed to one of slightly anxious confusion. Elena took off her glasses.

Papa, it's me, Elena.

Elena?

She kissed him on the forehead.

Elena, he said smiling. He appeared to recognize her.

Elena, he repeated.

She looked at me.

Papa, I want you to meet a friend of Wolfi's.

Her hand reached out and touched my coat sleeve. Her father looked at the ground and frowned.

Wolfi, he said to himself and looked up. He got stiffly to his feet. He took a step closer to me and took my hand without shaking it. He stared into my eyes as though searching for something, some memory which would not quite come into focus. I began to feel slightly uncomfortable.

You knew my son? he said clearly.

Yes, I said. We were students together at Heidelberg.

Heidegger? he said. You knew Heidegger? He released his grip, gave a dismissive wave of his arm and sat back down.

Elena crouched before him and took both his hands in hers.

Papa. Papa, are you listening?

He looked at her.

Papa, I want you to concentrate for a minute. Will you do that for me, just for a minute?

Concentrate, he said. Yes, concentrate.

What's my name, Papa?

Elena.

Do you remember Berlin, Papa?

Berlin? Yes, I remember Berlin.

Do you remember going to get Wolfi that night in Berlin?

Yes, I remember. Wolfi is in trouble. I have to go.

He looked around.

What happened, Papa? What happened that night?

He stared off into the distance. Then he looked back at her. His eyes had begun to water. He looked tired, defeated. He went to say something.

What happened Papa?

He looked away from her again. In the distance I could hear the children laughing. A small dark circle appeared on the cement beneath his feet as if magically it had floated up through the cement's solid mass to its surface. Then another. Elena ran her hand across his shoulders.

It's okay Papa. It's okay.

She stood up. She too had tears in her eyes.

You see. It's no use, it's no use.

She turned back to her father.

Papa, I've got to go now. I'll come back again tomorrow, okay?

She bent and kissed him on the forehead again.

Back at the reception desk she asked the nurse who had smiled at us if she would keep an eye on him. As we turned to go I caught one last glimpse of his slumped form through the window.

Out in the car park as we walked back to the car I turned to her.

You didn't have to do that you know.

I know. But I wanted you to see my father. The picture Wolfi painted of him wasn't very flattering. My father could be pompous and arrogant but that was only one side of him. I'm not saying as a father he was sweet and doting. He wasn't. But he wasn't all bad either. Besides, I wasn't sure you wouldn't have come here yourself. You can see what he's like. If you had started questioning him...This way it was easier.

She paused for a moment.

There's something else I want to show you. Hop in.

We got into the car.

Where are we going? I asked.

You'll see.

We headed back across town in silence. Now that my

curiosity had been re-aroused I kept thinking of questions I wanted to ask Elena. I could see, however, that she still seemed troubled by our visit to her father. She frowned as we drove. We sat isolated by our own thoughts, watching the city streets pass by. We were soon driving through the outskirts of town.

Have you ever been to Yugoslavia? Elena suddenly asked.

No. Is that where we're going?

She burst out laughing.

No, God no, she said.

Her mood began to change.

So you've never been to Dubrovnik, or the little town just to the south that Wolfi described?

No.

And, in that case, the Hotel Belvedere wouldn't mean anything to you either.

Obviously.

She paused for a moment, as if confirming something to herself.

Why do you ask?

Well, if you've never been there, how do you know they exist? How do you know that Wolfi didn't invent the lot?

I thought for a minute. Of course, what she was saying was a possibility. I already had proof that Wolfi had invented or, at least, falsified certain things, Bessermann for example.

What you're going to say is that Wolfi invented the whole scenario of the argument with your father and that none of what he said was true.

281

It's a possibility, isn't it?

It's a possibility, but hardly likely.

Hardly likely, I thought to myself. Why? Simply because there was too much external corroborating evidence. In the first place, I had **known** Wolfi, I hadn't invented him. And I certainly hadn't invented Elena, and if Wolfi had, he had had a pretty powerful imagination. Then there was Marianne's phone call. Wolfi **had** been in trouble with the police and Elena's father **had** gone to Berlin to find him. And, ultimately, there was Anya.

But you see, neither have I.

Neither have you what?

Been to Yugoslavia. I'm not even sure Wolfi had.

I looked at her, scrutinizing her face. She glanced at me.

You don't believe me, do you?

I shrugged my shoulders.

How do I know that you're not doing to me what you claim Wolfi did to us both? Why would he have invented having a holiday in Yugoslavia? What's the point?

That's what I'd like to know.

We drove on in silence again. The houses became fewer and further between. A couple of minutes later Elena stopped the car and we sat looking out over the township of Klagenfurt a couple of kilometres away.

This is a beautiful place, don't you think?

I looked out over the view below us and nodded.

Do you mind if we stretch our legs for a bit? she said.

Out of the car the air was crisp and still. We headed further up the hill.

You're a writer, aren't you?

282

Yes, I said.

And while you were in Heidelberg, you and Wolfi were good friends? You knew him pretty well?

Yes. At least, I thought I did. I'm beginning to wonder now.

Doesn't it strike you as odd then that in all that Wolfi wrote he didn't mention you once, and said virtually nothing about his time in Heidelberg.

Odd in what way?

Well simply because of the fact that you and he were friends.

I suppose. I don't know. I still don't get what you're driving at.

And, in Heidelberg, Wolfi knew you were a writer then, didn't he?

Yes, of course. We often talked about writing and what it meant to be a writer. He used to get quite excited about the parallels between the creation of a fictional world and how we perceive what we see as the real world. From what I understand he saw imagination as central to both.

Yes, but don't you get the impression that Wolfi was writing to you as a writer. That the reason he didn't include anything about Heidelberg was because he deliberately wanted to exclude your point of view. If he'd written about Heidelberg then you could always have said: No, that's not true, that's not the way it happened at all.

But why?

To, as you say, parallel the creation of a fictional world with the way we perceive the real world. What he invented you took for real. What I think Wolfi was saying was that

283

there is essentially **no** difference between a fictional world and the real world—that each world is particular to the mind that simultaneously perceives and creates it.

God, now **you're** beginning to sound like Wolfi.

Yes, well if you had lived with him for twenty years you'd end up sounding like him too.

But if what you're saying had been the case wouldn't he have been better off if, for example, he had exclusively dealt with our time together in Heidelberg. For me to have said as I read: No, I didn't say that, or if I did, that's not what I meant. He would then have had the paradox of the creation of two completely different worlds based on the same apparent facts. No, I don't think that's the reason. It's too complicated.

Then what **do** you think?

I honestly don't know.

She looked disappointed.

It's funny, she said. Somehow I thought you had all the answers.

I wish I did, I said. I wish I did.

She stopped for a moment and searched in her bag for something. She found what she was looking for and I went to move on. Elena, however, turned towards a heavy wooden gate set into a high stone wall beside which we were standing. I had been so engrossed in what we had been saying that I was totally unaware that we had been walking in its shadow for the last fifty metres. As she inserted the key into the lock I knew instantly where we were.

So this is what you wanted to show me, I said as she pushed the gate open.

284

Yes, I thought it might interest you.

The garden was overgrown and had obviously not been tended for some time. But as I stood just inside the gate under the canopy of trees looking up to the house I recognized it as being essentially the same image as the image in the photograph Wolfi had sent me years earlier.

So, I thought to myself, he had not invented everything.

I shivered involuntarily as I imagined that I was probably standing in exactly the spot where Wolfi had stood when he'd taken the photograph, and where he had stood that day listening to Debussy's music floating down through the leaves. I felt almost as though I had passed through him, as if he were there watching us.

We went and sat on an old stone garden seat under one of the trees. I began to realize how much Wolfi **had** written with me in mind. I imagined him at his desk writing the description of himself standing there, smiling to himself, knowing that one day I would be standing in exactly the same spot.

It's like he's here, isn't it, Elena said. Like he's part of the leaves, like this is the soil he turned, the garden he created, the house he built—in his imagination. And now, behind this wall, here it is. It's as though by isolating individual details he became part of them, as if everything he wrote had been projected here, and now he has become re-absorbed into its projection. Don't you get the weird feeling that in writing what he did he imagined us eventually reaching this point, that somewhere between the lines of what he wrote is the story of this instant? I can almost feel him smiling, rubbing his hands together in delight, saying: I did it, I did it.

Yes, I said. I was just thinking the same thing myself. Weird, isn't it.

I looked up towards the house.

But why kill himself?

I don't know. Wolfi always had this strange sense of fatalism. Fatalism's not the right word, of determinism, as though he were never really in control of his own life, as if he were just a part of somebody else's hidden scenario, just a minor character in somebody else's fiction. Remember, that's how he felt when my father first arrived in Berlin.

So you don't believe your father killed him?

No, I don't know. I doubt it. It's possible, but I don't think so.

Then what do you think happened?

I'm not sure, but to tell you the truth, I think Wolfi did shoot himself.

But why?

Remember I said I had something to tell you. Well, you know, Wolfi was pretty smart. I really do believe that he saw us meeting here one day, that he knew you would find out about Anya, that he wanted you to know. This was all part of the hidden content of what he wrote.

She looked away.

But I already knew about Anya. It was obvious from the start.

But that's just it. That's what Wolfi wanted you to think, at least initially. But what he wanted you to know, eventually, I'm sure was that Anya is not my child. She's not my daughter.

She looked back at me.

Then whose child is she?

My mother's...She's my sister. That's what Wolfi was telling you all along. That's what he told my father. He adored my mother and hated the way my father treated her. It all fits, don't you see? They must have been lovers for years.

I sat there thinking about what she had said. It would take time for it to sink in, to piece things together. Now, in a way, it no longer mattered.

I looked up to the balcony and Elena's room. I could swear I could hear music drifting down through the open door. In my mind I could see an image of Wolfi's face floating before me and through it, the image of the room in the Hotel Belvedere and Elena lying in bed. Her nightgown had fallen open and one breast lay exposed.

*

Watching my hand write these last words is like watching the last scene in a film. In close focus the camera shows my hand writing while the credits roll up. Most of the audience still sit and watch. A few get up to leave. Others are saying: Wait, it hasn't finished yet. Look, see it says: Wait, it hasn't finished yet. Finally the last credit disappears at the top of the screen and the camera pans slowly along my arm up to my face which smiles enigmatically out at you.

Wolfgang Schönborn
Klagenfurt
June–October 1986

Text Classics

Dancing on Coral
Glenda Adams
Introduced by Susan Wyndham

The Commandant
Jessica Anderson
Introduced by Carmen Callil

Homesickness
Murray Bail
Introduced by Peter Conrad

Sydney Bridge Upside Down
David Ballantyne
Introduced by Kate De Goldi

Bush Studies
Barbara Baynton
Introduced by Helen Garner

The Cardboard Crown
Martin Boyd
Introduced by Brenda Niall

A Difficult Young Man
Martin Boyd
Introduced by Sonya Hartnett

Outbreak of Love
Martin Boyd
Introduced by Chris Womersley

When Blackbirds Sing
Martin Boyd
Introduced by Chris Wallace-Crabbe

The Australian Ugliness
Robin Boyd
Introduced by Christos Tsiolkas

All the Green Year
Don Charlwood
Introduced by Michael McGirr

They Found a Cave
Nan Chauncy
Introduced by John Marsden

The Even More Complete
Book of Australian Verse
John Clarke

Diary of a Bad Year
J. M. Coetzee
Introduced by Peter Goldsworthy

Wake in Fright
Kenneth Cook
Introduced by Peter Temple

The Dying Trade
Peter Corris
Introduced by Charles Waterstreet

textclassics.com.au